HOW TO WIN AT PIT FIGHTING WITH A DRUNK SPACE NINJA

THE ADVENTURES OF DUKE LAGRANGE
BOOK II

JAY KEY

For Olive, the universe's best writing buddy.

Uncle Tofu's Adventure Land—It Won't "Meat" Your Expectations, It Will "Meat Substitute" Them!

UNCLE TOFU'S ADVENTURE LAND
BROADCAST COMMERCIAL

CHAPTER 1

REAL HERO STUFF

THE CATAPULT RELEASED WITH A swoosh and hurled a glowing rock at breakneck speed towards the enemy lines. Mid-flight, the boulder caught fire, an iridescent flame that formed a tail. It was a man-made comet—or, in this case, a Psitakki-made comet—and it was usually pretty effective. The projectile landed in a huddled mass of the attackers, which was, after all, the specific aim of the catapult operator. Unfortunately, the rock found a way to miss them all and collided with the ground instead. Grozzel couldn't help but think of all of the other places on Psitakki that he'd rather be than watching the loyal battalions of his home world hurl giant flame-covered rocks with the accuracy of a blind furgosi bird. The thunderous thump of projectile-meeting-earth reverberated all the way back to the Psitakki camp. The flames fizzled and the enemy marched forward, undeterred.

"Are they ghosts?" Grozzel asked his commander. "Who can avoid something like that? I don't think they even blinked. I don't think they even have eyes."

Commander Churzzel grunted back at the infantryman. It was hard to tell if his annoyance stemmed from the fact that he was being addressed informally by an inferior, or if he just didn't have a good answer. The commander about-faced and marched behind the front lines.

Typical, thought Grozzel.

"Infantry, prepare for the push," shouted Grozzel's battalion leader, an overly zealous, hardwired Psitakki named Serjarzzel. He stomped on the dirt with his bare feet, his posture remaining authoritative and almost statuesque.

The Psitakki were one of the few cephalopodan species in the known universe that had not only developed the ability to walk on land, but had became extremely adroit at it. They had evolved into a rather athletic bipedal race, equally at ease climbing trees as being submerged in their murky aquatic abodes.

"A bit enthusiastic to start your own death march, oh fearless leader of mine," whispered Grozzel to himself.

"What was that?" yelled Serjarzzel, looking around to identify a culprit. "Who said that? If you have a problem with my orders, you have a problem with Commander Churzzel. And if you've got a problem with him—you have a problem with High Command."

Grozzel mouthed the last of these comments silently in sync with Serjarzzel. It was a statement that he had heard numerous times.

"Got it?" Serjarzzel roared.

The battalion grumbled half-hearted affirmatives.

"What was that?"

The collective "Yes, sir" had a bit more volume and body, but it still lacked complete conviction.

Serjarzzel stroked the tentacles that extended from above his upper lip. He appeared satisfied enough with the level of pep amongst his troops.

"Prepare to march!"

The foot soldiers began to mobilize. A large homogenous chunk of Psitakki warriors slowly began a path toward the mysterious invaders. Grozzel estimated that there were at least a few hundred in his battalion—and probably a few hundred battalions on the front line. The indestructible enemy force was only a fraction of their size—but they were *indestructible*, so the size of their army wasn't relevant.

"This is idiotic," Grozzel said to a soldier next to him as they paraded towards the enemy.

"Shut up, Grozzel. What are we supposed to do? Tell High Command to go suck a finback jorquoia egg?" responded Zorzzel. Zorzzel had been Grozzel's best friend since primary school, when they merged the district lines so that some of the residents of the swampland would comingle, scholastically speaking, with the residents of a few of the towns in the much dryer plains. Due to the places of their rearing, they were of slightly differing skin tones—Grozzel being a muted grayish-green, Zorzzel somewhere between heavy cream and sunburned grass.

"I mean, it would probably be the most productive thing they've done in a few cycles."

"You can't honestly blame them for this invasion? These creatures, these things came out of nowhere. It's not like High Command provoked them."

"I don't blame them for the invasion, of course not. I *do* blame them for having every able-bodied Psitakki march blindly into the teeth of a monster that we don't understand. And can't seem to hurt. Not even a 'boo-boo on the knee' hurt."

"What would you do then, General Grozzel?" Zorzzel said sarcastically.

"Run away," Grozzel replied assuredly.

Zorzzel's eye ridges raised. "Run away?"

"Yes."

"Dare I ask—where to?"

"Yes, you may dare," Grozzel snickered. "To the swamps."

"To the swamps?"

"Yes. Any of them. All of them. And hide."

Zorzzel rolled his eyes as another rock, destined to fail, whizzed over their heads. "You're made of real 'hero' stuff, you know."

"When they first came to our planet a few days back, they didn't hurt anyone. They crept around. Floated here and there. Sure, they spooked a few kids. I mean, who wouldn't be scared by a creepy floating demon thing that's taller than three male Psitakki and doesn't have a face or feet?"

"And can't be hurt in any way," reminded Zorzzel.

"Yes, and can't be hurt in any way that we've discovered," continued Grozzel. "Then High Command, in their infinite wisdom, said, 'Hey, let's lob some rocks at 'em.' I'm not even sure they're made of solid matter. They look like a cloud of smoke with arms. So, even if we ever managed to hit one with our catapults, it'll probably just go straight through 'em. And that's how we ended up where we're at now."

"But what good would hiding do?"

"First off, we won't die. Or we're less likely to die. I give you and I a—I don't know—two percent chance to survive this direct attack on these guys."

Zorzzel nodded several times, perhaps processing the odds himself.

"If we hide, let them do their thing, whatever that thing might be, then they might leave. We live. The race goes on."

"You're missing the obvious 'what if,' Grozzel. What if they just stay? Or what if they're looking to drain our resources and leave us to die on a dried-up planet?"

"I still like the odds."

"It's not too late to go present your well-crafted plan to High Command. If you run back now and Serjarzzel doesn't execute you as a deserter, I'm sure Churzzel will be an eager audience."

"I think I've quickly come to grips with my destiny—complaining about High Command while I get ripped to shreds by one of these shadow demons."

"I'll be ripped to shreds right by your side, old friend."

"Thanks."

Another comet flew overhead and deposited itself onto the ground harmlessly. The gaseous ghouls barely seemed to notice.

"Hey now, that was too close for comfort!" shouted Zorzzel. He gestured wildly. "The bad guys are *that* way."

"Do you think it would hurt more to be friendly-fire catapult fodder, or lunch for those bodiless monstrosities?"

"You're insane, Grozzel. Can we just march ahead and try and not die?"

"We can try."

The sky above the shadow demons' encampment began to rumble. The clouds turned from their usual deep green to a smoky metallic gray. Moments later, they were charcoal black. The sky seemed to pulse like the heart of a celestial deity that was going into cardiac arrest. Rain came crashing down irregularly; Grozzel even thought he saw it flow into the clouds from the ground. But he just chalked that up to exhaustion and his state of rapidly coming to terms with his mortality.

The Psitakki infantry instinctually halted.

We're sitting furgosi birds, thought Grozzel.

The shadowy invaders began to emit bolts of obsidian lightning from their faceless, feetless floating bodies. It struck the Psitakki ranks and killed instantly any soldier within a radius the size of a small farm. The bolts came from every angle and at erratic intervals. The armor that the Psitakki wore provided no defense to the salvo. The line broke and they began to flee.

"Okay, you got your wish, Grozzel," screamed Zorzzel as he sprinted away from the chaos. "We can run *and* hide."

"Hiding from curious terror-beasts was what I had in mind, not hiding from lightning bolts conjured out of nowhere."

"Beggars can't be choosers," Zorzzel replied.

The pair leapt over their deceased comrades and plunged into a grove of ancient tarzantia, brawny and impenetrable trees that will only grow near the edge of a swamp.

"This way," barked Grozzel. "This isn't far from my home. I know a good place to hide."

"I'm right behind you."

A piercing crack echoed through the grove of tarzantia trees. Grozzel stopped and turned back. Zorzzel was on the ground, face down. Smoke rose from his back. Grozzel could smell the charred skin. Zorzzel looked up—his eyes glassed over—blood dripped from the corners of his mouth, along his tentacles.

"Hide," he mouthed as his head hit the ground, his life force extinguished.

Floating above his lifeless body was one of the invaders.

They're bigger than I thought, concluded Grozzel. *Maybe he didn't see me?*

The shadow demon whipped its substanceless arm towards the Psitakki. A stream of black electricity zipped by him and struck down an entire tree.

Grozzel fled deeper into the swamp. He wasn't as fleet of foot as Zorzzel—or any land-born Psitakki, for that matter —but once they entered the thick liquid of the swamp he was as adept as any in his race. But he wasn't really sure how fast these shadow creatures could float, or if they would even want to chase a single soldier deep into an unfamiliar landscape. Then again, Psitakki with titles far more prestigious than his had been wrong about everything to do with these beasts. Grozzel assumed that his pursuer was hard-wired to massacre him at all costs.

He finally approached the edge of the swamp. He leapt in. The lukewarm water hit his skin and his body instantly relaxed. He was at home. A grimy home, but home none-theless. His feet kicked, propelling his streamlined body deeper into the water. The sediment and debris floating about made the water too opaque for most life forms, but the Psitakki's vision was specially adapted to navigate these depths. It was an evolutionary trait that helped his race become the alpha species. Even though other animals evolved keen smell or the means to echolocate, being able to see trumped everything. Grozzel pivoted underwater, turning his body to face the faint glow penetrating the surface of the swamp.

Damnit, he's following me, concluded Grozzel.

The Psitakki stayed submerged for as long as he could withstand. Though their ancestors could breathe under-water indefinitely, the Psitakki lost that benefit eons ago. Grozzel couldn't help but think that his ancestors would point and laugh at him for needing boring old air to survive.

Grozzel hoped that the shadow monster would eventu-ally give up and leave. No such luck. Hours passed. The greater battle on the surface was probably over, with the peculiar intruders likely claiming another easy victory. More would likely join his pursuer in his chase, and soon.

However, Grozzel had to resurface. Knowing he only had a few more moments before he would pass out under-water, he shot himself as far as possible from the beast's location. His propulsion landed him near the opposite bank of the swamp and, he hoped, out of sight of the enemy. But Grozzel couldn't help but think that his guesswork about the monster's range of sight wasn't likely to yield useful results since he had never known another life form that had no face. *Nothing really to compare it to; no point of reference. He might be able to see into outer space for all I know,* he thought to himself.

He gulped air as he emerged from the murky water. He scanned the area. Sure enough, the shadow demon remained hovering over the swamp. Its faceless torso angled downward until it was nearly touching the surface. *How could something with no eyes see?* Regardless, Grozzel came to the conclusion that it was definitely contemplating what it was going to do next. It then raised an arm and sent another bolt into the water. It pierced the surface and cut through the water as if it was air. Grozzel could see and hear the crash as the bolt struck the swamp floor. Fish and swamp worms and water womblers scurried in every direction. *That's not good.*

The shadow beast loosed another strike, with the same result. It seemed pleased with the outcome; it was shrugging what could be best described as shoulders up and down rapidly as if it were in a state of uncontrollable hysteria. Grozzel, on the other hand, was frozen at the realization of this physics-defying weapon. He now knew his cover would provide no safety from the beast. Unfortunately, his catatonic state lasted a few moments too long. The shadow demon ceased its movement. Its body shifted; it didn't need a face for Grozzel to realize that it was facing him. It darted to intercept the Psitakki soldier.

Grozzel didn't know which gave him a better chance at survival: diving to the bottom and hoping that the beast's aim was predicated on having a clear view of its target; or making a break for it on land and hoping to locate a hiding place before he was fried with one of those lightning beams.

If I'm going to meet the Colossal Calamari in the sky, I'm going to do it on my own terms... in my swamp, decided Grozzel. He quickly dunked his head, turned effortlessly in the water, and darted to the other side of the swamp.

The electric bolts entered the water at a frantic pace. Grozzel bobbed and weaved to avoid a fatal strike. They came with such rapidity that they appeared to form a sort of underwater latticework. Grozzel didn't stop to admire them; he swam as far away as possible from the onslaught.

The demon paused, presumably waiting to see a limp corpse float to the top. After a brief moment, he moved on to another area. And Grozzel did as well. This game continued for what seemed like hours. Outside of brief moments of surfacing for air, the Psitakki stayed one step ahead of the tenebrous predator.

Regrettably for Grozzel, the invader had friends. They showed up in droves and surrounded the body of water. Grozzel surfaced near the far bank under the exposed roots of a tarzantia; the shadows and mud made him invisible to the naked eye of most biological entities. He wasn't so sure with these guys.

Grozzel noticed that the beast was communicating with his comrades. He must have been telling them that the ammunition that they flung from their bodies pene-trated the water, because they all started to test it out. In short order, the real estate within which Grozzel could hide shrunk dramatically. The demons unleashed a coor-dinated pelting; the strikes stirring the swamp into an ocean of sludgy waves. If Grozzel re-entered the swamp, it would only be a matter of time before he was struck down by the same kind of bolt that had killed his best friend.

This is it, he thought to himself. *At least I get to die in the place that birthed me.* He liked the symmetry of it.

He took one last deep breath and submerged himself in the comfort of his swampy home, waiting for the bolts to appear. He wasn't sure how long he could dart about and avoid their sting, but he would try until he took his last breath.

As soon as a charge snaked past his head, he pushed off from the submerged bank and headed in the opposite direction to a portion of the swamp that he hadn't yet used as a hiding spot. He dove deeper and deeper. *This is new*, he realized. He continued his descent towards a nook that was easily four times deeper than most of the swamps in the area. He hoped that the added depth would provide added cover. The frequency of the bolts decreased. *Maybe this will work*, he hoped. *Until I have to resurface for air, that is.* The latter thought deflated his newfound optimism rather quickly.

The velocity of the bolt that zipped by was so great, even underwater, that it spun Grozzel around completely. It struck something solid; the crash sent him into another aquatic tumble. He felt more crashes in rapid succession but saw no additional bolts. It was as if the strikes had triggered the eruption of an underwater volcano. But Grozzel knew that swamps typically didn't have volcanoes. The shaking stopped.

Maybe it scared away the shadow beasts?

The Psitakki swam through the newly-created debris, searching for cover from any subsequent attacks. As he navigated through the murky water, he noted that the swamp kept going and going. *I should've hit the bank by now*, he thought to himself. It was clear that the strike had opened up the mouth of a hidden cave. Some of the larger swamps in this area had submerged caves, but Grozzel was familiar with this particular body of water and had been relatively sure it didn't possess one. He was very happy to be proven wrong.

Maybe this is my lucky break... or my future tomb.

The passage narrowed. A tunnel. He pursued the trail and swam for some time until he surfaced in a cavern. He had never seen or heard about this place, though Psitakki had traversed all of the swamps and waterways on their home world.

He took in a deep breath of stagnant cave air, enough to fuel him for another prolonged retreat. He treaded water as he tried to collect his thoughts. His meditation was interrupted by an unusual glow coming from behind a cluster of stalagmites. It was bright white—blindingly bright. Even though a large portion appeared to be blocked by the rocky formations, Grozzel didn't look at it directly as he feared it might burn out his pupils.

Oddly, as he approached it, the intensity of the glow lessened. He wasn't even sure why he approached it. As a young squidling he had been taught to avoid bright and shiny objects stashed away in hidden caves. But investigating just felt right.

He peeked around the stalagmites. The glow was now faint and subtle. It was coming from a mound of circular disks. The pile extended farther than Grozzel had realized.

Shields? Why is there a heap of glowing shields in a secret cave on Psitakki? His mind began to race. *Clearly not made by the Psitakki smiths. Alien? Could this be what those demons are looking for?*

He knelt down and picked one up. It wasn't heavy at all; in fact, it was extremely light—too light. The material was foreign to Grozzel and he concluded that it wasn't likely to be able to withstand much impact. That wasn't a good trait in a shield. He slid his arm into the strap and the shield rested on his forearm. *Kinda useless*, he concluded.

A dozen or so explosions rocked the cavern and pushed Grozzel onto his posterior. The strikes ripped off the ceiling of the cavern, exposing Grozzel and his mound of alien shields to the night air. Five shadow beasts peered down at the trapped Psitakki soldier. But they didn't pursue.

All five slowly entered the dwelling. Grozzel hadn't previously seen them act in any manner that would be described as cautious. After the initial five beasts entered, one after the other, more flowed in. The sky was obscured by the mass of shadow demons. It was impossible to tell where one stopped and the other started. Grozzel's game of hide-and-seek was finally at an end. He cowered and covered his face with a forearm, though he knew it would provide little defense against one of the demons' obsidian death bolts.

The shield on his arm pulsated and vibrated, then shrieked and whined, then swished and whooshed. It let out a reverberating bellow and shot out fiery flares from its perimeter. The bellow turned into a wheezing sound as if the shield was inhaling. Then out shot a ray of light that permeated every crevice of the roofless cave. The explosion of light from the shield caused a massive recoil. However, the force didn't knock Grozzel off his feet. It pushed against his forearm but the pressure was manageable. The light continued to blast through the cave into the night sky. The banshees wailed and screamed in pain. The blast stopped and then the beam seemed to be sucked back into the middle of the round shield.

Grozzel opened his eyes and looked upward. Nothing. Not a single shadow beast remained. The shield had obliterated them all. Every one of them.

This is exactly what they came for, he concluded.

The Psitakki was too shocked to move the shield—or to move at all. He stood petrified near the stalagmites, the shield still strapped to his forearm. He lost all track of time.

"Is that you, Grozzel?"

The gruff voice belonged to Commander Churzzel. He unfastened himself from his rappelling harness and approached Grozzel. Other Psitakki soldiers were also careening down the cave wall from the newly formed roof entrance.

"Yes," Grozzel replied meekly.

"We saw a light shoot out from the trees and hurried over here. What's left of us, that is. What happened?"

Grozzel did not respond right away. He collected himself and glanced at the mound of shields. Churzzel also seemed to notice the pile. Grozzel straightened his posture.

"Commander, tell High Command that I have a much better plan."

CHAPTER 2

SOL'S BAIL BONDS-O-RAMA

SOL WAS NOT THE MOST hygienically sound being in the universe. In fact, he flat-out stunk. But he ran one of the most lucrative bail bond outfits in his sector of the galaxy. So a bounty hunter looking for a payday could turn a blind eye—or nose—to Sol's unsavory fragrance. That was exactly why Duke LaGrange and Ishiro'shea were on Tardasio 7 in the waiting room of Sol's Bail Bonds-O-Rama. It had been a month or so since the bounty-hunting duo had returned from their adventure on Neprius. They had been canvassing the sector but hadn't picked up a single gig in that time span. It was a record low. It was even crazier that they hadn't heard of any sub-space chatter from any other bounty hunters. The only thing bounty hunters love more than bounty hunting is bragging about how good they are at bounty hunting. Maybe Duke wasn't the only one suffering from a dry spell.

The lobby of Sol's was as unkempt as the owner. If the furniture wasn't broken, it was dirty. If it wasn't broken or dirty, it was uncomfortable. Pictures of Sol shaking hands with the who's who of bounty hunters adorned the walls. Some of the frames had pieces of glass missing or noticeable cracks. All of them hung crookedly. It annoyed Duke to no end, especially the ornate frame made of faux jewels hung above the receptionist's desk that housed a warped photo of Sol raising the hands of Duke and Ishiro'shea as if to announce that they had both won a prize fight. Duke was one of Sol's top clients.

What was unusual, however, was that Sol's waiting room was empty.

"Sol will see you now, gentlemen," whined the overweight receptionist. Women on Tardasio 7 were typically bigger boned than most humanoids in the sector, so they tended to carry a bit more girth, but she was especially flabby. And sweaty. *She might be related to Sol*, thought Duke.

The Nova Texan tipped his hat and smiled. The receptionist swooned and giggled. As one of the most recognizable bounty hunter-playboys over the last fifteen cycles, Duke LaGrange knew that behind every unattractive lady could be a more attractive best friend. His Irish-Japanese ninja sidekick bowed slightly.

Other than his sloped forehead and narrow cylindrical nose that came to a sharp point—both typical traits of Tardasian males—Sol could have blended in with the humans on Earth or Nova Texas. At least, the grotesquely obese ones. Even though he was a disgusting man in a disgusting office, he was good at his job. From its outward appearance you couldn't tell it, but Sol's Bail Bonds-O-Rama was a well-oiled machine. Duke and Ishiro'shea had brought in bounties for Sol on hundreds of occasions. He was a fair businessman and easy to work with, if you could stand the stench.

He waddled towards Duke frantically.

"Close the door, LaGrange. Close it now," he said in between grunts. He had to hike up the waist of his pants with every step to prevent them from falling to his ankles. *Probably don't make belts in his size,* thought Duke.

"Sol, my good buddy," Duke began. "How goes it? Any more sightings of three-headed ice wombats?"

"No time for chitchat, LaGrange," growled the bondsman. "We gotta hurry."

"What are you talking about? Why do we have to hurry? What's going on, Sol?"

"Those damn toughs from that government thingy, they're trying to shut me down."

"What toughs? What government thingy?"

"You know, those hard military bastards. With the guns and the warships and whatnot."

Duke looked blankly at the overweight Tardasian.

"Come on, LaGrange! The organization that's trying to take over the frickin' universe, man!" Sol yelled, throwing his hands in the air in frustration.

"I got nothing."

"Where have you been lately?"

"Actually—"

"Never mind, I don't care. Anyways, out of nowhere, this organization starts claiming to be the one true government in the known universe. All I know is that they're big. Real big. They sent squads to every corner, every planet of any consequence, and started to... well... govern."

"Come on, Sol," Duke protested. "And all of the planets and races just went along with it?"

"Of course not, meathead. Some resisted and were shut down—but not as many resisted as you'd think."

"Did they come over from some alternate reality? Have they seen how successful governments are in *this* universe?"

"This one seems different, LaGrange. In one month, they've done more than any of the previous outfits. More than the Cosmic Council, or the Planetary Senate, or that one weird tyrant guy with the eyepatch, or..."

"I get it, I get it," Duke interrupted. "So why are you freaked out? You said they've only gone to planets of consequence. Seems like Tardasio 7 is pretty safe, then."

"Funny, LaGrange. They're on their way."

"Why are you so worried? It's just some government pencil pushers with submachine guns. You've seen worse. It'll probably be just a few more minutes of paperwork a cycle—maybe a tax hike or two. Nothing you can't survive."

"You don't know, do you?"

"Know what?"

Sol paused for the first time since Duke and Ishiro'shea had entered. He took in a deep breath.

"They're outlawing bounty hunting."

Duke and Ishiro'shea looked at each other.

"They're outlawing bounty hunting?"

"Yes, what are you, deaf? No offense, Ishiro'shea."

"He's mute, not deaf," Duke said. "And it's by choice. But why?"

"I don't know, ask him. He's your friend."

The bounty hunter pinched the bridge of his nose with his fingers and sighed. "No, Sol, why are they outlawing bounty hunting? It's not exactly a bad thing. I mean, we bring bad guys in. For the most part."

"Yeah, LaGrange, but you see... it's not regulated."

"So?"

"So, these guys don't like what they can't control."

"Tough," scoffed Duke. "Not my problem."

"Oh yeah," Sol snickered. "How's business? The last month in particular?"

Duke looked at Ishiro'shea again. Then he pulled up a chair and sat down. "That's why no one has been returning my calls, huh?"

"Yep. They shut down Big Rudy yesterday. Warthog Phil went down last week. Mama Fong fought back—no one has heard from her since."

"Mama Fong, the three-eyed Zylantian? The one that used to be a bounty hunter?"

"Yes, *that* Mama Fong," smirked Sol.

"It doesn't make sense. In the whole scheme of taking over the universe—"

"Not taking over the universe, LaGrange. Controlling it. They don't seem to care for power like a mad dictator would, they just want to control it. Have everything be neat and tidy. A single set of laws. In my opinion, it's worse. At least a crazed power-hungry megalomaniac is relatable to most of us. Order, structure—who needs that nonsense?"

Sol mimed spitting on the floor.

"But outlawing bounty hunting and upstanding bondsmen like yourself seems pretty petty and insignificant at the onset of a universal takeover," said Duke. "Right? Even if what you've said is correct and they've accomplished a ton in the last month, more than others that have sought to organize the infinite number of planets and races, are they that efficient that they can also enact bylaws to eliminate harmless little sub-industries like bounty hunting?"

"Honest answer?"

"Yes."

"Yes," said Sol. "They are. And they're coming for me next."

He rushed behind his desk and started organizing items and miscellaneous decor. He tossed them into a duffel bag.

"Why are you running?" asked Duke. "Can't you just say, 'Fine, I'll shut down'?"

"I've heard that they've been burning the places down

to the ground and taking every valuable on the premises. Right down to the clothes you're wearing."

"I don't think they have any interest in seeing you without clothes," joked the bounty hunter.

"Laugh now, LaGrange, but what are you going to do without any benefactors, huh? Not sure the playboy racket pays enough. I know and you know that bounty hunting pays the bills. Keeps your freaky ship in the air. Keeps your bar tab at Joe's paid off."

Duke couldn't disagree. The playboy part of his title—bounty-hunter-slash-playboy—was the part that typically got him in trouble. Bounty hunting was the steady gig and he knew he couldn't let it slip away.

After watching Sol load up his getaway bag, Duke asked, "So what about the other bounty hunters in this sector? Surely they're trying to fight this?"

"Bounty hunters trying to unite against this?" Sol snorted. "Are you mad, LaGrange, or just stupid? Once the word went out and a few bondsmen disappeared or were kicked to the curb, the hunters scattered. They hid. Did you see my lobby? Not a damn soul. I was shocked when I saw the *Deus* arrive. I thought you'd skedaddled with the rest of 'em."

"You know there's a Bounty Hunters Union, right? It's on Brenatto in the Gordget system. Or maybe it's Torlanus in the Protitroxx Limpor system. I'm not sure, but I get the mailers."

"You're kidding, right?"

"What?"

"It's a myth, LaGrange. There's no union for bounty hunters. It's a scam to swipe a few coins from your purses."

"Shut up, Sol."

"Seriously. I think they busted the guys that made it up.

They made a fortune before they were caught. Don't tell me that you paid dues to that thing."

Duke looked at Ishiro'shea. The ninja provided no help.

"Oh man, Duke."

"It's real, Sol," pleaded Duke.

"Gotta give 'em credit. Always best to exploit folks that are rich and dumb. If they kept their mouths shut, they probably would be in some Oscavian cave right now, living the life."

The Tardasian zipped his bag shut and hurried past the bounty hunters. He opened the door and motioned for them to follow him. "You guys leaving? Or are you gonna wait around for these feds to show up? I don't think they are the talkative type."

Duke and Ishiro'shea entered the lobby.

"Come on, Wanda!" shouted Sol. The pudgy receptionist left her post to stand next to the bondsman. She carried a duffel bag equally as robust as Sol's.

"Duke, Ishiro'shea—this is Wanda. Wanda, these are—"

"I know who they are, silly," she interjected in a wheezy tone. She batted her eyelashes and blushed. Sol looked a bit peeved at her reaction.

"Well, these two morons didn't even know that these new government types outlawed bounty hunting. They came looking for work," Sol said with a bitter laugh.

"You didn't know about the decree making bounty hunting illegal?"

"Nope."

"What about the one on brothels?" she asked.

Duke threw up his hands up. "My day just got a little worse."

"And portals," she said.

Duke and Ishiro'shea turned as one to stare at Sol. He cowered.

"Wanda, we gotta get out of here," Sol said. "Let's go. See ya', guys."

He trudged to the door, pulling Wanda with him. A few items fell out of his duffel bag.

Duke fired his laser revolver above their heads. The pulse hit the wall above the entrance, knocking down a photo of Sol hugging the noted bounty hunter, Maxx Gemstarr. Duke hated Maxx Gemstarr; the placement of the blast wasn't entirely unintentional.

"Sol," he said. "Why didn't you tell us about the portals?"

"Whoa, whoa, whoa," the rotund Tardasian said, his arms in the air. "It slipped my mind, it slipped my mind. Okay? Yes, they've announced that unregulated portal manipulation is illegal." He gulped in air and continued, "Extreme force will be used to prevent the breaking of this law."

"There's only one place with portal manipulation, regulated or otherwise. And that place doesn't respond nicely to extreme force."

"Yep," Sol groaned.

He tugged Wanda's arm firmly. She winced but didn't say anything. The two plump Tardasians fled through the door.

Duke and Ishiro'shea were left standing in the deserted reception room of Sol's Bail Bonds-O-Rama on Tardasio 7, a shattered photo of Maxx Gemstarr and a stray pair of Sol's socks on the floor next to them, and instead of a new gig, all they had been able to secure was a basketful of confusion and unanswered questions.

"Let's go see the Queen," said Duke after a moment's thought. "She might be having a worse month than us."

CHAPTER 3

ASSISTANT DEPUTY
ASSOCIATE DIRECTOR

THE *DEUS EX MACHINA* WASN'T a quiet ship, nor did it have a smooth ride—not like certain newer, sleeker, sexier craft. But it was reliable when it needed to be reliable and, more importantly, unpredictable when it needed to be unpredictable. It always managed to pull Duke and Ishiro'shea out of jams when there was no hope. Surviving massive offensive attacks from disgruntled Jungafallowian princes even when its shields weren't operational—done. Teaching primitive alien races to access and fire its weapons system accurately, ignoring a good thousand generations of evolution in the process—sure, why not. And this was only in the last few months. There was no doubt that the two bounty hunters that called this ship home would have been cosmic roadkill countless times over had it not been for the *Deus*.

Currently, the *Deus* was on a trajectory to the planet Kelt and, more specifically, Cyborg Joe's Grill N' Go & The Why Not Saloon, having left Tardasio 7 a few hours prior. Duke and Ishiro'shea had some questions that needed to be answered, and they wanted to warn Queen Joe about the new sanctions that were being levied against her by this new bureaucratic upstart.

"How many times have we made this trip, Ish? Sol's to Joe's. Sol pays us. We give that hard-earned cash to Joe. We need more money. We go to Sol. Lather. Rinse. Repeat. An unhealthy cycle, if you ask me."

The ninja nodded in agreement.

"But a fun one."

Ishiro'shea concurred again.

"I still don't get why Sol was so squirmy. I mean, I get it. He doesn't want to be the next 'missing' bondsman or have his stuff taken away, but why didn't he tell us about the portals? Joe has to be pissed, if she knows. Or at least a bit annoyed."

The ship trembled.

"Inertial stabilizers operational?"

Ishiro'shea gave Duke a thumbs-up, then quickly tapped a few buttons on the control panel. The ship ceased its convulsions and steadied.

"Thanks, little—"

Duke was interrupted by a more violent jerk. And another. The ninja threw up his hands in confusion.

"Screens up."

Nothing appeared on the front view screen.

"That's odd. No visible culprits," Duke observed.

The *Deus* began to slow, but the rocking continued.

"Did you check the back scanners?"

Ishiro'shea projected the rear view to the main screen.

"What's going on? This doesn't make any sense. And it's nothing with our equipment? Is she malfunctioning?"

The ninja shook his head and flashed up the diagnostics report to the main viewer.

"She should be purring like a kitten," Duke concluded.

The ship dipped precipitously and Duke fell out of his captain's chair.

"Hey, wait a minute," he said from the floor, squinting intently at the screen. "Look there. On the back of the *Deus*, connected to us. Zoom in."

The projection focused in on the back of the *Deus Ex Machina*. Four metal suction cups were affixed to the outer shell. They were massive but barely visible due to their being camouflaged.

"Those aren't part of our ship. At least not normally. Do you think it's another one of the *Deus*' 'improvements'?"

The ninja did not respond.

"Me neither. I have a feeling that we might have company, little buddy. I don't like uninvited guests."

Duke stood up, vaulted over the rail that separated his captain's chair from the rest of the bridge, and landed gracefully next to his companion.

"Let's try this," Duke said, punching sequences into the panel.

A symphony of lasers lashed out from the posterior of the *Deus* in all directions. The beams rotated and fanned out to cover as large a footprint as possible. Tiny explosions appeared in what seemed to be open space.

"Extend the phasers out. I know they won't be as strong, but this is more exploratory in nature."

Ishiro'shea followed the order and increased the range of the lasers.

The tiny explosions remained but, farther out, they grew in size. The lasers were hitting something. Something invisible.

"Let's ratchet up the intensity. Let's make 'em feel it!"

The *Deus* roared and unleashed a more persuasive wave of firepower.

Four long towing cables appeared where the explosions

were sprouting up. Three snapped immediately due to the intense fire. At the ends of the cables, four towing ships uncloaked.

"Recognize these guys? They obviously have some cool tech. Not even the *Deus* can cloak. But what do they want with us?"

The ninja shrugged his shoulders.

"Can you hail 'em?"

Ishiro'shea opened up a communication line. Within seconds, an image appeared on the screen. It was a humanoid male dressed in tactical gear. He looked like he could be from Earth or Nova Texas, on the whole, generic and unremarkable. Duke did, however, remember seeing a similar uniform during one of his recent visits to Cyborg Joe's.

"Greetings, my sneaky little friends," began Duke. "I'm Duke LaGrange. Adventurer. Poet—"

"Mr. LaGrange, I'm the Assistant Deputy Associate Director of this ship."

"Wow, they really threw the big guns at us, huh?" Duke snickered to Ishiro'shea.

"And you have been deemed a criminal by the new galactic government," the deputy continued. "You are to halt and be boarded by our team. You will await trial at the star system of our choosing. Please do not resist. Intergalactic Infrastructure—"

Duke cut off communication.

"He was boring me, little buddy. So since we are so close to Joe's, I think we head that way. See if we can outrun 'em. I don't really want to fight off four of these guys, especially since we don't know what type of firepower they're packing. If they can cloak, they probably have some pretty good gear."

Even as Duke was finishing his thought, Ishiro'shea had

initiated a course to Joe's at top speed. The immediate acceleration jarred the bounty hunter enough to send him backwards into the railing around his chair.

"Holy hedgehogs, one's still attached to us," shouted Duke. "Hey, I have an idea. Try this."

Duke hopped in front of Ishiro'shea to sit at the manual controls. The *Deus Ex Machina* dove and wiggled, spasmed and spun, all at max power. The tow ship chose not to release the cable. Bad decision.

"Watch this!"

The fourth tow ship, still clinging to the cable, struck the neighboring vessel. The explosion was much larger than Duke had imagined. The cable fell limp as it released from the demolished tow ship. The two operable ships swiftly exited the immediate space as the other two continued to disintegrate into a pile of space junk. But they didn't flee.

"Now, wasn't that easy? Two down, two to go. Poor Deputy Assistant... whatever he was. Anyways, let's step on it and outrun these bastards to Joe's."

The bounty hunters sped towards Kelt with two government tow ships on their tail. Duke was once again a wanted man—but he wasn't exactly sure why they were so keen on flushing him out.

Duke looked at Ishiro'shea.

"You don't think that Sol set us up, do you?"

"Sol totally set us up. That fat son of a bitch."

The federal blockade surrounded the entirety of the planet Kelt. There were at least a dozen battle cruisers, a ton of single-seat fighter scouts, and one behemoth Armada Titan, one of the largest makes of warship in the known universe. Duke had never seen a force of this size so close to Kelt. Joe had to be really pissed now.

"That bulbous bastard. He told us that portal crap because he knew we would beeline it directly to Cyborg Joe's to talk to the Queen. Those four ships were waiting on us. Even if we escaped, they'd drive us directly into an entire flippin' fleet. They even have an Armada Titan, for crying out loud. Who has a godforsaken Armada Titan?"

A pulsing light flashed on the screen.

"They want to talk again," Duke sighed. "Might as well hear what they have to say, right? Maybe it will buy us some time to figure out how to get outta this jam, because right now I'm out of ideas. Barren. Empty. I got nothin'.'"

Ishiro'shea pressed the button to open the hail.

"What do you want now?" barked Duke.

"Mr. LaGrange, it is now time for you to surrender. There is no hope for you as you are now facing our entire 42nd legion. Did you see the Armada Titan? If you attempt to escape again, we will render your ship inoperable."

"You think I'm scared of that oversized tin can?" Duke asked. "The *Deus* has taken out badder ships than that more times than I can count."

"Please stop your advance," responded the officer, ignoring Duke's question. "We will board you. It will be painless and swift. You will be taken to the Armada Titan to await—"

Duke cut the communication off again. "Nope. He's still boring me." He stood, arms crossed, and tapped his foot. "What to do, what to do? Any ideas?"

Ishiro'shea was also deep in thought. A moment later, his eyes expanded, bugging out of his head.

"What?"

The ninja pointed to the captain's chair.

"Not again."

In the middle of the left armrest was a plastic dome the size of a big-boned hamster. Inside it was a clownish red button. Duke remembered what the manual said: *Always push the red button.*

He looked up at the ceiling of the *Deus*. "Hey girl, you know I love you, right? I'm sure I'm going to really appreciate whatever that button does—but I also know it probably means that any second we're going to be in a pretty dire situation. I'm not overly thrilled with that part. But thank you. I think."

He sauntered to the chair and opened the dome. He gave Ishiro'shea a timid thumbs-up. He pushed the button.

A buzzing sound consumed the *Deus*. Duke closed his eyes and clenched his teeth, bracing for something dramatic... and painful.

Nothing.

The buzzing stopped and all was as it was before.

"You're losing your touch, old girl," he said to the *Deus*.

The communication light pulsed again.

"I really hate this guy," he sighed. "Let's see what he has to say this time. I'm sure it's exhilarating."

The enemy ship's representative reappeared. His face was bright red.

Why's he so mad? thought Duke.

"Mr. LaGrange, whatever you're trying to do, whatever your game is, it's futile. You can't just disappear and escape our entire fleet. We will find you in due time."

Duke didn't respond. He cut the communication immediately. He turned to his masked co-conspirator.

"You don't think..." He paused. "No way. Do something for me, Ish. Let's head directly toward that ship—the battle cruiser directly in front of us."

Ishiro'shea shot back a confused look.

"Trust me. Do it. I have a hunch."

The ninja hit the thrusters and the *Deus* darted directly towards a well-armed battle cruiser.

"Check the back scanners."

Ishiro'shea pulled the rear view on the screen. The tow ships hadn't moved. They weren't chasing them. Ahead of them, the battle cruiser remained equally motionless. Their weapons systems were very much idle.

"Holy hedgehogs," Duke proclaimed as he hugged the rail around his captain's chair. "Thank you, old girl. Thank you."

Ishiro'shea still looked perplexed.

"Ish, we're cloaked. They can't see us. That damn button gave us cloaking tech. It probably saw that those puny tow ships had cloaks and decided it wanted the same. She was probably a tad jealous. This ship, man." He shook his head in disbelief.

"So, if we know anything about the *Deus*, it's that these upgrades don't last forever. I say we try and navigate this minefield and get to Joe's before it wears off and we become sitting ducks again."

Ishiro'shea jabbed his finger in the opposite direction.

"You're right, we *could* run and get out of this mess. However, if they got to Sol, who's to say that they haven't gotten to our other friends? I'd feel better talking to the Queen. You know they didn't get to her. They're trying to make her illegal. There's no place safer than Joe's. From an invasion, at least."

Duke could make out a smile through Ishiro'shea's mask.

Yep, he agrees, thought Duke.

"But let's stay as far away as possible from that Titan."

CHAPTER 4

FOUR I'S

"THANKS, EARL," SAID DUKE. "DRIVING through an entire armada can really make a man thirsty."

Duke downed his purple liquid. His face puckered.

"Is it not to your liking, Mr. LaGrange?" asked the mannerly Glyptodian barkeep.

"Is Ootrelian oyster juice to anyone's liking? I can't believe y'all are out of Erontian saké. And Glyptodian ale."

"And most of our whisky selection," chimed in the enigmatic Queen Joe. She was an attractive female and most believed she was one of the most powerful beings in the universe. Duke tended to align himself with that hypothesis. She also controlled the portals that made Cyborg Joe's Grill N' Go & The Why Not Saloon one of the most popular destinations in the universe.

"Hey, Queen. Yeah, I guess if I was a supplier, I probably wouldn't want to try and traverse that blockade, either."

"It's unfortunate. Earl said that you wanted to see me."

"Well, yes. There's an entire fleet of battle cruisers in orbit around Kelt. And you're violating their new mandate."

"The one about my portals?"

"Yeah."

Queen Joe rolled her eyes and helped Earl clean some glassware.

"Aren't you worried?" asked Duke.

"Not at all. How many times have we seen these pop-up governments?"

"Queen, no offense, but they always ignored you before now. These guys are on your front doorstep."

"You should be more worried about their ban on bounty hunting."

"And brothels," slurred a familiar voice from the table behind them.

"Oh hey, Po'l. How ya' doing?"

"Amazing," said the intoxicated Neprian. "I love this place. Best thing that I ever did was leave that boring rock that I was on. Right, Queenie?"

She turned to Duke and leaned in.

"He's been portaling more than any other patron that we've ever had. Hits up a pleasure planet one day, goes on some 'epic quest'—as he calls them—the next. I'm worried about him."

"How does he afford it?"

"He's been working here. Earl hired him."

"Hey, how 'bout some more of this purple stuff? It's my new favorite drink, Queenie!"

She ignored him. Earl picked up on the clues and brought another round of Ootrelian oyster juice to Po'l.

"Last round, Mr. Po'l," bellowed the Glyptodian. "Your shift starts in a few hours."

"Alright, you big hairy..." Po'l trailed off, but then perked up and refocused his attention. "Good seein' you, Duke. Ishiro'shea," he said between belches. He pounded his drink and headed to the back of the bar.

Duke flashed a bewildered look at Queen Joe.

"We threw a hammock up in one of the back closets. He likes it."

"He's always been an odd one," replied Duke. "But back to the question at hand, what are you going to do about these guys?"

"Duke, I told you. Nothing. They'll go away."

"I don't think they will, Queen. These guys seem different. They got to Sol. He set us up. They've already taken over a few not-so-insignificant planets in a few weeks. No one has ever done that before, not this quickly. This just seems *different*."

"We're fine, Duke."

"They said they're going to use 'extreme force' on you."

"They haven't yet. I can take care of myself and this bar. I'm not concerned."

The bounty hunter knew that he was fighting a losing battle. He had to trust the Queen—because why wouldn't he? She was the Queen.

"Earl, get Duke and Ishiro'shea a drink. On me. See if we have a shot of whisky left. Guys, it might be Erontian. I know it's not the best. But, hey, free is free."

"Sounds good to me."

"You know, Duke, I'm more worried about what I'm hearing from some of my customers about the goings-on at the other side of the sector."

"What's that?" asked the bounty hunter, puzzled.

"I've been hearing some whispers that Admiral LePaco is back and causing trouble."

"LePaco?"

"Didn't you try and track him down before?"

"I'd rather not talk about it," snapped Duke.

"I'm just telling you that his name's been popping up here and there. Seems like he's out of hiding again. He's insane enough to actually do something dangerous. These uptight middle-management types with battleships, they don't worry me; a sociopathic murderer that's escaped *your* clutches—that makes me nervous."

"Not interested. At all. He's probably just trying to scheme on folks while everyone else is so focused on this new group of misfits. Not worth my time."

"Okay, what *is* worth your time?"

"This," said Duke as he plucked a glass full of whisky from a tray balanced on Earl's oversized, furry paw. "This is worth my time. At no point in my existence, no matter how gruelling the situation or how tranquil and beautiful the moment, would *this* not be worth my time."

He stared longingly into the glass before he downed the booze in one fluid motion.

"What about Mazilda Cloax?"

Immediately, Duke choked on the remaining splashes of whisky still working its way down his throat. A cough slipped out. And another.

"Thought so," Queen Joe smirked. "You know that she came through here not too long ago."

"You mentioned that a month ago. If I recall, you dropped that on me right when we returned from Neprius after dealing with a maniac and his magic rock. Thanks for that, by the way."

"You're welcome."

"How is my favorite magic rock?" asked Duke.

"It's safe," replied the Queen soberly. "I promise you, it's safe."

"That's good to hear. The only thing so far that has been. I mean, since I've showed up, it's been LePaco, Mazilda, and a giant Armada Titan floating above Kelt. Are you trying to get me to leave?"

"And Prince Korzo-Tapor."

"I almost forgot about that two-headed whackjob."

"He came through a bit before Mazilda. They both went through the same portal to the same destination. I forget which one. Not even sure of the planet. Something about getting ready for a tournament of some sort. Maybe a combat tournament? I think I recall something along those lines."

"I doubt Mazilda would enter into a combat tournament," replied Duke smugly.

"No, she never struck me as someone that would get dressed up and fight for the amusement of others."

She paused and a smile crept onto her face.

"But her new boyfriend did."

"What new boy—" Duke began, but caught himself. "Don't care. None of my business. Don't care one bit."

He tried to stop his teeth from gritting but failed. He tightened his grip on his empty glass.

"Okay," the Queen said, shooting a glance towards Ishiro'shea. Duke interpreted it as a not-so-subtle 'yeah right.'

"You don't care about Mazilda and her new boyfriend?" began Queen Joe.

"Nope."

"Or Prince Korzo-Tapor?"

"Couldn't care less."

"Or that Admiral LePaco's name is popping up again?"

"Who?" Duke feigned.

"Okay then," responded Queen Joe.

"But I do care about that armada outside of your bar."

"Like I said before, I'm not," the Queen replied. "They're harmless. If we ignore them, they'll go away."

"You can't ignore a flippin' Armada Titan!" Duke shouted.

The Queen appeared to be caught a bit off guard. It

wasn't every day that someone raised their voice to Queen Joe. *I hope she doesn't kill me,* thought Duke.

After a brief pause, she went back to cleaning more glasses. She looked up momentarily, locking eyes with Duke. "If you're so worried about them, why don't you ask them to leave?"

"What?"

"One's coming over, right now."

Duke pivoted on the barstool.

Standing in the entryway of Cyborg Joe's was a humanoid wearing the same attire as the two tow-ship officers that they had engaged with on the *Deus*; he was clearly a representative of the enterprise that was currently surrounding the planet Kelt. He looked important, or at least he appeared to possess a high rank, as he wasn't in traditional tactical gear. The officer wore glasses and medals adorned his left breast. He looked as if he was after something—and Duke didn't like that.

"Prepare to be bored to death by this Four I's paper-pusher," said Queen Joe.

"That's a bit beneath you, Queen," gasped Duke. "Heck, that's beneath most primary schoolers. I thought you were all about tolerance, blah, blah."

The proprietor looked genuinely confused, which, for a nearly all-powerful being, wasn't a common look. Then she appeared to come to some sort of realization. "No, Duke. Not 'four eyes.' Four I's. Acronym. The organization that's surrounding us—the one that you are so freaked out by. They are Intergalactic Infrastructure Improvement, Incorporated. Their mission is to improve the order of the universe with a sound infrastructure—or something like that. I. I. I. I. Four I's."

Duke looked embarrassed.

"They have a jingle, I think, if it helps you remember," the Queen added.

The bespectacled man was still standing at the entrance of Joe's. He stood perfectly erect with his arms folded behind his back and his chest puffed out.

He cleared his throat. "Patrons of this establishment," he boomed.

The amplification of the man's address reminded Duke of a behemoth monster named Toby he had once encountered on Neprius. The bounty hunter was impressed by the volume that this average-sized humanoid was able to unleash.

The officer continued, "I'm looking for a criminal that is likely seeking refuge amongst you."

"What did I tell you guys? I'm not going to go peacefully. If you bug me again, I'm going to get really angry," shouted the Queen from the bar. "There's really no point in you trying. You're just going to waste time, resources—all the things that you guys preach about maximizing with your —what do you call them?—'pillars of efficiency.'"

The Four I representative remained stone-faced.

"Queen Joe, we've received your warnings and are taking them into consideration. Our decision on how to move forward with you and your alleged crimes of portal manipulation are still under discussion. As are our plans to turn this lackluster, low-output planet into an effective member of the universal community. This visit, however, is about something else. *Someone* else, to be precise. The outlaw bounty hunter Duke LaGrange and his accomplice, Ishiro'shea of Earth, are to report to Four I's Disciplinary Committee immediately."

Duke stood up and faced the representative.

"Hey, we haven't bounty hunted since the law was enacted. Ask anyone. Look at my bank account."

"Bounty hunting is the least of your offenses, Mr. LaGrange. The destruction of two Four I tow ships is the reason I am here to collect you both this evening."

"Oh yeah, that. We *did* do that. You are one hundred percent right."

"Please come with me."

"I don't think that's going to happen."

Duke unholstered his laser revolver and spun it on his right index finger.

The representative did not fail to notice the firearm. "It might be worth noting, Mr. LaGrange, that we've confiscated your ship."

Duke immediately pointed the gun at the representative. "Not a smart move, man. Not at all."

As if on cue, a squad of armed Four I soldiers burst through the door and surrounded the representative. They were heavily armed and armored.

The Queen whispered in Duke's ear. "You and Ishiro'shea go. Now. I'll handle this."

"To the portals?"

"Yes."

"Just any? Where do they go?"

"Not sure where I had them programmed to. Probably a pleasure planet—thanks to Po'l."

"Not a bad hiding place," responded Duke. "What about the Bounty Hunters Union headquarters? We could rally some support there and come back and fight."

"Duke, I don't think that's a real place."

"It's a real place! Why doesn't anyone believe me?"

"Just go."

Queen Joe stepped from behind the bar and parted with Duke and Ishiro'shea. She headed towards the Four I squadron.

"I said go," she yelled without turning around.

The bounty hunters vaulted over the bar and headed towards the portals.

"You better not harm my ship!" Duke shouted as they stepped through one of the ornate portal doors. He heard what sounded like a firefight breaking out behind him. It became fainter and fainter as his body deconstructed and was sent through the portal.

CHAPTER 5

CEPHALO-GOD

SHAMAN OF THE HIGH COMMAND Klorzzel IV ordered Grozzel to the edge of the overlook. Commander Churzzel flanked him and Serjarzeel followed a few paces behind. Grozzel looked down on the thousands of Psitakki that filled in the grasslands below the cliffs. They roared and cheered as he stepped to the ledge. Shaman Klorzzel and Churzzel both raised Grozzel's hands. The gathering erupted with even greater fervor.

The Shaman hushed the crowd. He leaned into his voice amplifier and spoke. "Psitakki, you've come from all corners of our home to celebrate our continued freedom. We, as a people, together and undeterred, have driven the shadowy interlopers from our world."

The Psitakki whooped and shouted. Flags waved and trumpets made celebratory honks.

"But, as you may have heard, and I can confirm it this very moment as gospel, we would not have made it to this day without a great discovery by the fearless Grozzel."

The Shaman motioned to Grozzel, who waved timidly. Churzzel draped his arm around Grozzel, sharing in the boisterous applause from the spectators. *Of course he is,* thought Grozzel.

The Shaman repositioned himself at the vanguard and the crowd silenced immediately.

"It has been determined, following much debate and counsel, that the trove of magic shields that were discovered on the final day of battle by our dear Grozzel here were, in fact, sent to us by the Colossal Calamari in the sky."

Murmurs of discussion rippled through the droves of Psitakki in attendance. *Not sure they're buying the Cephalo-god angle,* thought Grozzel. *Typical High Command brainwashing.*

The Shaman slammed his staff on the ground and the muddled debate halted.

"I repeat, my Psitakki brethren, it has been decided that the almighty and all-knowing Colossal Calamari sent us these tools to defeat our demonic foes. If anyone thinks differently, please speak up. Don't be shy. The elders of this world and I would love to discuss this with you."

The catapults rumbled to the edge of the cliff, in plain view of the audience.

Chants of "Ca-la-mar-i" broke out. The Shaman smiled. *Figures.*

"Excellent," began the Shaman, the leader of High Command, still grinning wryly. "Now that we know where they came from, it's time to decree how we will celebrate our great fortune that they were given to us and, of course, discovered by our beloved Grozzel."

The Psitakki cheered at the idea of a celebration.

"We will hold a tournament. The Tournament of the Shield..."

They erupted. The Shaman motioned for silence.

"...of the Colossal Calamari!"

They clapped less enthusiastically. A chuckle escaped Grozzel. Churzzel sneered at him.

"It will be a tournament of combat. Being versus being. Sixteen of the bravest, strongest, and most honorable combatants will battle. The winner will be awarded one of the very shields that saved our species!"

The valley below the cliff was jolted into excitement.

"All one hundred shields will be awarded over time, in order to honor our triumph and signify our perseverance."

Shaman Klorzzel IV held aloft his staff in dramatic fashion as the Psitakki below fell silent.

"And the first tournament begins in a fortnight!"

He slammed the staff down. A thunderous roar filled the Psitakki countryside.

Grozzel sighed dejectedly.

<hr>

After surviving his first three opponents by outsmarting them—more or less—Grozzel found himself in the finals of the first Tournament of the Shield of the Colossal Calamari. He thought that since he was the symbolic hero of the war, the tournament planners may have given him some easier competition to avoid upsetting the adoring masses. Grozzel wasn't even sure how they chose the tournament entrants, since thousands had applied. He wasn't complaining.

Staring at him from across the arena floor, however, was a different opponent to the ones he had faced so far. This one was bigger. Meaner. There was a good chance that he represented Grozzel's imminent death. Even though death wasn't required to win your tournament bout—the rules specified submission to your opponent or the physical inability to continue as the official outcomes—no one was going to get too upset if someone was mortally wounded, especially to honor the Colossal Calamari. For some reason, the Shaman and High Command thought death and mortal sacrifice were the best ways to become buds with the celestial cephalopod. Most of the regular folks on Psitakki didn't have time to worry about what a squid in the sky was thinking.

Of all the possible opponents, it had to be Churzzel.

Grozzel could hear the grizzled commander's growl from across the arena. Churzzel pounded his chest; his eyes filled with primal rage.

Grozzel looked up at the sea of spectators. The arena was packed. A temporary third deck had been built in the last week to accommodate the anticipated crowds. He turned to look at the decorated seats in the center of the primary grandstands. The Shaman sat there, his staff in one hand, a drink in the other. He tapped his staff and the crowd cheered.

This is going to hurt, thought Grozzel.

Since no projectile weapons were allowed, Grozzel didn't have his sling with him. It was his favorite toy. He used to practice on the tarzantia trees near his house. He could knock a rogue twig off a branch from the other side of the swamp. For this fight, he had opted for a wooden club. It wasn't particularly ominous, but Grozzel felt that he could swing it with some authority. Churzzel toted around an iron mace the size of a Psitakki female, making Grozzel feel wholly inadequate. The commander twirled it around to the crowd's delight. Even across the arena floor, Grozzel could feel the breeze that the humongous weapon generated.

This is going to hurt a lot.

The first part of the bout didn't go so well for Grozzel. It mostly involved Churzzel picking him up over his head and tossing him to the ground, to the accompanying sound of admiration from the crowd. Churzzel would then turn and soak in their praise. With each toss, they cheered louder. Grozzel had lost his club after just one swing—Churzzel had blocked it with his mace and then pushed Grozzel to the ground, forcing him to release it. He had tossed it away from the action.

Grozzel was bleeding from the mouth. The urge to submit began to overtake him. For some reason, however, he pressed on. *So many of these folks here think I'm a hero,* he thought. *I must continue.* But he wasn't a hero—just some guy who had found some shields in a cave when he was running away. He decided he would give it one more go before admitting defeat. One more last-ditch effort. He owed himself that much.

He charged Churzzel. The commander turned around as Grozzel was leaping for an attack, and swatted him down in midair.

That was anticlimactic.

The attendees clapped. Churzzel picked up Grozzel and flung him to the other side of the arena. Grozzel skidded to a stop, his face resting a few paces from his club.

He gathered himself and gripped the baton.

What to do? What to do?

His hand hovered over a stone. It wasn't an insignificant rock—but it wasn't large by any stretch of the imagination. It could be categorized as being between pebble and mountain range.

Grozzel didn't know what came over him or why he thought of it—he tossed the rock in the air and struck it with the club. It arched across the arena floor and hit the commander square in the back. Churzzel stumbled forward a few steps, then turned around slowly to see Grozzel standing with his club in hand.

Churzzel charged. Dust kicked up behind him and

formed an arch of spray as he raced towards Grozzel. He waved his iron mace erratically.

Grozzel picked up another rock and struck it. Wide right. Churzzel was closing in. Another rock. It hit the commander in the knee. Churzzel stumbled momentarily, then collected himself and continued his approach. Grozzel had one rock left.

"This is for Zorzzel."

He threw the rock in the air. It connected with his club with a loud crack.

The rock struck the commander with such force that it burrowed into the area between his eyes upon impact.

Churzzel collapsed. He was unconscious.

The Shaman smashed his staff against the stone floor. The sound echoed throughout the arena. The fight was over.

What just happened? Grozzel thought to himself in disbelief.

"The winner of the first Tournament of the Shield of the Colossal Calamari—our own war hero, Grozzel!"

Grozzel fell to his knees in exhaustion. All went black.

He was suddenly awakened by a splash of cold water. The Psitakki opened his eyes to see the Shaman looking down at him. Two guards lifted him to his feet. Grozzel wasn't sure if the crowd was cheering or if the sound was the ringing in his ears. Either way, it was loud.

"Friends, I present to you our champion, Grozzel," boomed Shaman Klorzzel IV's voice through the amplifier.

He handed one of the shields to Grozzel. It radiated with a glow that seemed to fill the arena. The crowd seemed mesmerized by its beauty. Grozzel couldn't tell if it was the actual shield that he used to obliterate the shadow demons in the hidden cave, but he wanted to believe it was.

The dazed victor tapped the Shaman on the shoulder. Klorzzel looked back with an expression of disgust.

"You're really going to give away all of these shields? Is that smart? I mean, you know best and all, but it seems—"

Klorzzel's sneer stopped him in mid-sentence. The Shaman leaned in and whispered, "Don't question what I do, peasant. Shut up, take your shield, and did I mention shut up?"

The guards released Grozzel and he fell to the arena floor still clutching his shield.

"And friends," the Shaman began, "to honor the ten thousand Psitakki that lost their life forces at the hands of these ruthless marauders, we will hold the tournament again in ten thousand cycles. And every ten thousand cycles after that."

The entire arena went silent. The Shaman looked back at Grozzel and rolled his eyes.

Of course it's every ten thousand cycles. The Shaman would never let something so powerful out of his sight until he has milked it for all its worth.

"I really hate High Command," Grozzel said under his breath.

<hr>

Grozzel didn't feel like a champion anymore. It had been many cycles since he had won the Tournament of the Shield of the Colossal Calamari. The shield sat on his table, serving no purpose other than acting as a window into his past. A window covered in the fingerprints of time, rendered opaque with the smudges of irrelevance. There were no more promotional appearances, no more autograph signings or store openings. He shook no more hands and kissed no more babies. He was a relic, just like his magical shield.

The aged Psitakki sat down with a bowl of hashed jiarfu as a late breakfast. His body ached. The shield pulsed softly as he ate. It had seen better days as well.

One more daily entry in the boring book of my life, he thought.

The jiarfu slid down his throat. He was delighted that it was so mushy. Chewing hurt.

Only those clinging to the last cycles of life would find happiness in soggy breakfast food.

The shield started to pulse at an increased rate.

"What's wrong with you?" Grozzel asked the shield. "You haven't blinked like that in ages, old friend."

The speed of the shield's pulsing picked up exponentially. The light grew brighter. It illuminated Grozzel's entire home.

"Hey now, stop that," he screamed at the inanimate object.

Why am I talking to a shield? I've really gone crazy.

The shield started to buzz and whirl.

Then it exploded.

Grozzel, his house, and the tarzantia trees that lined his swamp were wiped from the face of Psitakki in the blink of an eye.

CHAPTER 6

CRASHING THE PARTY

"I THINK I HAVE A fork in my armpit," grimaced Duke. "No wait a minute, that's a... is that a spork?"

They had successfully materialized upon exiting their hastily-chosen portal; it just so happened to be about five feet above a banquet table. Covered in plates. And silverware. And a spork. The impact of the two bounty hunters hadn't even dented the monolithic slab; the only tabletop casualties were a fruit platter and some congealed pudding substance. Duke and Ishiro'shea were the clear losers in the collision.

They both sat up, sending a few more plates crashing to the floor. The hall was jam-packed with beings from all corners of the universe. Duke didn't even recognize some of the species. The room was elaborately decorated; it was a full-on gala.

Within moments the bounty hunters were surrounded by Psitakki from all angles. Those seated at the table they had crashed into quickly made room for the armed cephalopodan guards. The barrels of their rifles were mere inches from Duke's and Ishiro'shea's faces.

"Who interrupts this celebratory evening?" boomed an

artificially projected voice, coming from the direction of a stage at one end of the hall. The speaker was an elderly Psitakki cloaked in a dazzling lavender robe. His upper lip tentacles hung down to his chest.

He has to be really old, thought Duke.

"My apologies," began Duke, finding and donning his Stetson. "I'm Duke LaGrange. Adventurer. Poet. True man of the universe. And this is my faithful partner, Ishiro'shea. Salutatorian of the College of Cohorts—"

"Why have you chosen to crash our party?" the Psitakki interjected. "And when I say 'crash our party,' I quite literally mean crash our party."

"Again, apologies. It seems our portal did not calibrate properly. This was not our intended destination."

"What was your intended destination, Duke LaGrange?"

"I don't know, man. A pleasure planet, probably. That was what I was hoping for."

"I'm not surprised by that," chimed a familiar voice from somewhere behind the guards.

A curvaceous female stepped out in the light. Her skin was a subtle yellow hue whereas her eyes, hair, and lips were electric purple, the color of Ootrelian oyster juice.

"Oh hey, Mazilda," Duke said nonchalantly, without making eye contact.

Duke turned to Ishiro'shea and mouthed, "Of all the portals..."

The ninja shrugged.

"State your business," shouted the Psitakki elder.

Duke looked at Mazilda. She gave him nothing. He looked at Ishiro'shea for some guidance but the ninja provided no aid either.

"We just want to get outta here."

"I think that could be arranged."

"Great. Wonderful. Apologies again," said the bounty hunter. He brushed some unknown culinary substance from his pants.

"However, before we let you leave our planet," said the Psitakki, "we do want to take you in for some questioning. It's standard procedure."

"Smart thinking, Grand Shaman," shouted a muscular human adorned in bright spandex.

Not him, Duke pleaded internally. *Please don't let that be him.*

"It's what I would do," the beefy partygoer continued. His hands were on his hips, his elbows fanned out. His chest jutted out and his chin pointed to the ceiling. His striking pose was positively camera-ready. "That's exactly what Maxx Gemstarr would do."

"I'm glad you agree, contestant Gemstarr," replied the luxuriously-clothed Shaman.

"You're a tool, you know that?" Duke said to Maxx.

Gemstarr did not respond. Instead, he pulled Mazilda Cloax closer to his side. He planted a kiss on her cheek, then winked at the Nova Texan.

Duke's intestines constricted as if he had just been kicked by a Quibbian erecto-varmint.

"Take them away," said the Grand Shaman.

The guards yanked Duke and Ishiro'shea off the table and led them to the back of the hall.

"Easy, tiger," Duke snickered at one of the guards, "I thought this was just some standard questioning."

The guard ignored him. Four rifles were trained upon the two party crashers at all times.

They were ushered to the back of the hall and forced to sit against the wall. The guards did not take their weapons, but Duke did not consider fighting back. A little interrogation never hurt anyone—nor were he and Ishiro'shea likely to take out an entire dining hall worth of guests. With any luck, they would be off of Psitakki by the morning.

One of the guards returned to the main stage and whispered something in the Grand Shaman's ear. He nodded and sent the guard back.

"Friends, as we wait for our Chief Interrogator General to arrive and take away our uninvited guests, I feel we should continue."

The crowd clapped politely.

"I am Grand Shaman Klorzzel XVMMMDCCXXIII, the direct descendant of Klorzzel IV, the first Shaman of the Tournament of the Shield of the Colossal Calamari."

More applause.

"I wonder how you get promoted from Shaman to Grand Shaman?" Duke whispered to Ishiro'shea. The ninja did not respond. His eyes remained focused on Klorzzel.

"It is my honor to announce the one hundredth and final tournament honoring the unique magic shields sent by our always-present deity, which saved our people from invasion so many eons ago, when time was young and our planet was a mere infant. The winner of this tournament will not only win the final shield, the last link between the present day and that fateful event that saved our race, but they will also bookend the million-year history of this contest with the inaugural champion, our legendary hero and finder of the shields, Grozzel the Great."

The applause picked up a notch. It was still classy and dignified applause, only much louder.

"Your participation honors the Colossal Calamari in the sky. I know that you have all been busy for the last month training, meeting locals, conducting interviews and other assorted pre-event tasks. We appreciate the focus. It honors our planet and our ancestors. It shows that you respect our customs and our history. Truly, it honors us all. I wish you all luck and a good battle."

The Shaman bowed and exited the stage.

Another Psitakki took the stage. He sported no robe and generally looked less prestigious.

"Honorable combatants and guests, as by ancient law, I shall read the rules of the tournament. Many originate from the first tournament; others have been modified over the course of time."

"I thought this tournament was a joke," Duke said to Ishiro'shea. "It doesn't seem up Maxx's alley, though. Unless he plans to blow so much smoke up their asses that they all explode. It's a pretty good superpower if you ask me."

The Psitakki on the stage unrolled a scroll and began to read aloud.

"As you know, the Tournament of the Shield of the Colossal Calamari will pit sixteen of the most honorable beings against each other in fair and regulated combat. Fifteen, from as far as the mystic Silver Mountains of Mrelock to the turbulent tides of Zylantia, have been selected by the Grand Shaman and awarded invitations. All fifteen have accepted and no alternates were required."

"Ladies and gentlemen," Duke muttered to Ishiro'shea, "I have discovered the fifteen dumbest individuals in the universe and they're all in the same room."

The Shaman continued, "The sixteenth spot will be determined tomorrow, on the eve of the tournament, by means of a voluntary melee battle in the arena."

"Okay, *they* might be the dumbest individuals in the universe," Duke said, correcting himself. "A melee battle to get into a tournament of death? So dumb."

"The rules of combat," the Psitakki continued, "are simple but final. No contestant can be robotic, mechanized, cybertronic, or artificially manufactured. If you have some upgrades here or there, we're cool with that."

A few hoots and hollers came from pockets of the great hall. Duke and Ishiro'shea looked at each other quizzically.

"I hope one of those cyborgs beats Maxx's face in."

"There will be no projectile weapons allowed. No guns or lasers or arrows—unless it's part of your natural biology. If you spew a toxic muck from your belly button, we'll allow it."

Duke could hear some hissing from the front.

"Weapons are fine but need to be preapproved. We have all of the submissions from the combatants. All are approved!"

Boisterous applause filled the room.

"Magic is strictly prohibited."

"Hear, hear!" shouted Maxx Gemstarr.

Duke rolled his eyes. *What an ass. He probably still believes in magic.*

Duke had always believed that magic was just undiscovered science—but then he remembered the mysterious Orb on Neprius, which was now under the Queen's watchful surveillance. On reflection, he decided that he was firmly *undecided* on the topic. Anyway, Maxx had other quirks to mock and snicker at; no need to waste time on such a gray-area issue.

"In order to advance in the tournament, you will need to defeat your opponent," said the orator.

That's the usual requirement in a tournament, Duke smirked to himself.

"This can occur by your opponent giving up and submitting to your dominance. Or if the Shaman considers them unable to continue. Or if they die. We will do our best to prevent victory by death but, hey, stuff happens."

"It would take a *complete* idiot to fight in this thing," said Duke. Ishiro'shea nodded in agreement.

"Good luck and good battle. For the Colossal Calamari!"

"For the Colossal Calamari," the crowd responded in unison.

"What a bunch of—"

"Morons?"

The speaker of the voice that interrupted Duke appeared from the shadows. He had a reptilian head on top of a long, cylindrical stalk of a neck. It was next to an exact duplicate neck and head.

Jungafallowian.

"Nice to meet you in person, Duke LaGrange," the newcomer said in a slithery voice.

"And you are?"

"Surprised to see that you survived my attack."

"Prince Korzo-Tapor, I presume?" Duke said despondently.

"Yes, the pleasure is mine." Both of his heads bowed to the bounty hunters.

"Come to finish the job, with us handily tied up and surrounded by gun-toting squids? You are extremely brave, Princey."

"Oh, not in the least. I have no need. I've lost interest in avenging your misdeeds against the Trampling Death Robots. Water under the bridge, my friends."

"Right."

"In fact, I agree with you. It would take an idiot to fight in this tournament."

"Why are *you* here then? Seems like a perfect weekend activity for a Jungafallowian."

"It is. But not for *this* Jungafallowian. I have more, let's say, refined interests. However, I am here supporting my own entrant. He's not here at this particular moment. In fact, I don't take him out in public that much. He tends to —" The prince paused. "—cause a scene."

"Not a black-tie sort of hombre?" quipped Duke.

"That's an understatement, I'm afraid."

"Well, good luck with all of this. I hope he bashes in Gemstarr's head."

"As do I. He's quite annoying," Korzo-Tapor remarked.

"Not that we don't love your company and all," Duke said sarcastically, "but why are you over here talking to us? Don't you need to go strategize, or something, for this dumb tournament?"

"You know that Psitakki interrogation is actually a euphemism for torture, right?" said the prince, changing tack.

"What?"

"Yes, you two are scheduled to be tortured for ruining— or almost ruining—the Shaman's gala."

"Shut up."

"I'm being serious," the other head hissed. "This Shaman really likes burning people alive. Or is it flaying them in public? I can't remember. He's a being of many unorthodox desires."

"If you're telling the truth, why? Why would you, of all people—peoples? Is it peoples? Anyways, why should we believe you?"

"I think it would be interesting to see you in this tournament. This tournament of morons."

"No chance, Princey."

"It might behoove you to know that if you put your name in the proverbial hat for that final spot in the melee bout tomorrow, you will be spared the inquisition. The toasty inquisition. Or the skinless inquisition. You get the point. It will be bad."

"I'll take my chances. I have two guns and a ninja. It could be worse."

"True. That disappoints me, it truly does. But good luck to you, Duke LaGrange. It was nice meeting you before you die a ridiculously agonizing and stomach-turning death."

Duke grimaced. *Why do I believe this guy? I shouldn't believe him, I really shouldn't. He tried to kill us, after all. But I kinda believe him. I hate myself a bit more now.*

"And the author of your grizzly demise approaches," said Korzo-Tapor. "I present to you the Chief Interrogator General. I hear he's a lovely man."

Korzo-Tapor slid away, back into the shadows from whence he came.

A hulking Psitakki lumbered towards Duke and Ishiro'shea. He walked with a limp and had a crude hooklike instrument in place of his right hand.

Wonderful. Just wonderful.

CHAPTER 7

CHIEF INTERROGATOR
GENERAL

"THIS JAIL ISN'T THAT BAD, is it little buddy?"

Ishiro'shea did not respond. Duke knew what his answer would have been.

"Okay, fine, it's not the *best* jail we've ever been in," Duke admitted, "but it's not the worst."

The ninja turned his back to the Nova Texan and walked to the bars that separated the duo from freedom. He gripped them and examined them intently. He rattled them. And then some more. The usually stoic martial artist allowed an inkling of frustration to creep through; his shaking grew more violent.

"Hey, Ish. Calm down. We'll figure it out. That interrogator guy didn't seem too bad, ya' know."

Ishiro'shea's eyes shot lasers at Duke. At that moment, Duke would have preferred actual lasers.

"Fine, the hook hand wasn't super inviting. But we've had it worse. Remember—"

Duke was cut off by loud shouting from another room. The muddled grumbling of the Chief Interrogator General was apparent—but the other voice was distinctly female.

Mazilda?

"Are you going to tell me that just because two morons are dropped onto a table by some obviously unhinged portal, you have to tear their eyes out and burn them alive?" Mazilda said.

"Miss Cloax," began the interrogator, "I assure you that I won't be tearing anyone's eyes out. Not today."

"Or burning alive?"

"Well, I do like that part. But, sadly, no. It's not on the schedule."

"That's better, I guess," Mazilda's tone became slightly more relaxed.

"For their crime against the Shaman, I'm going to slice off their feet," the Psitakki added.

Even though Duke couldn't see him, he had a feeling that the interrogator flashed a creepy smile at the thought of them writhing in footless agony. Shivers racked Duke's body.

"You've got to be kidding, Interrogator," Mazilda said, her voice back to a scream. "These two buffoons aren't to be blamed. If anyone, it's whomever is operating the portal. They sabotaged the Shaman's gathering. Not these two."

"Do you consider a gun without any ammunition a weapon?" asked the interrogator calmly.

"What? What are you talking about?"

"Do you, Miss Cloax?"

"Yeah, sure. I guess."

"And the ammunition?"

"Yeah, of course. The ammunition is what does the damage to the target."

"And it only works with a gun."

"Uh, yep. That's the usual arrangement."

"So, both are guilty of causing the damage?"

"I guess. What does this have to do with anything?"

Mazilda was clearly angered at the interrogator's byzantine questioning; her voice doubled in volume. "What are you talking about?"

Duke and Ishiro'shea could hear footsteps as the interrogator and Mazilda approached the cell. The thick-bodied Psitakki stepped from around the corner, followed by Mazilda, her pewter robes flowing behind her. The interrogator pointed at the bounty hunters with his hooked appendage.

"Miss Cloax," he bellowed, "these two are the ammo. The portal is the gun—or rather, the portal operator. And we know who that is. Both are to blame—but, unfortunately, at the moment I can only interrogate these two. And I don't think I would try and interrogate the Queen of Cyborg Joe's."

"You know, Mazilda," Duke began calmly, "this one here has more layers than I gave him credit for. You aren't as dumb as you look, are you, Chief?"

The Chief Interrogator General didn't pay any attention to Duke's remark. He produced a rectangular metal box seemingly from out of nowhere and placed it on a knee-high table in the corner of the room. Under the table were an old Sonic Widowmaker shotgun, a laser revolver, and a katana. The latches of the box opened with a dull clank and the top of the box swung back to reveal a plethora of metallic instruments. Duke had a good idea as to the purpose of these instruments. He did not like it.

He also didn't like the expression on Mazilda's face, a ferocious glare aimed directly at him. She could be quite scary. This was one of those moments.

The majority of the time, Duke just thought of Mazilda as cunning. Really, really cunning. The most painful part was that she was a whole lot better at bounty hunting than he was. She was also extremely beautiful. Even now, with a look of pure disgust upon her face. Duke always thought of her attractiveness as singular and distinct—in a universe filled with infinite complexities, she was unique. Her skin had a yellowy tint; a healthy sort of jaundice that gave her a splendid luminosity. Typically, one could only achieve this unique tan with increased levels of bilirubin in one's extra-cellular fluid, or a really painful tattoo—but Mazilda Cloax had no time for liver disease or body art. All of her visible hair—which sprouted in the same places as an Earth or Nova Texan woman—was a deep blue violet. She possessed penetrating pupils and full lips that perfectly matched the radiant color of her locks, painted by the same biological paintbrush. Her build was athletic yet voluptuous. She always knocked Duke's socks off—when she wasn't knocking other people's heads off.

"You're going to make jokes now? I'm here trying to plead your case and you think it's a good time to be funny? I knew you were an idiot—"

"I believe you called them 'morons,' Miss Cloax," chimed in the interrogator as he sharpened a nasty-looking utensil that sported four razor-sharp prongs.

"Shut up!" she screamed back at the Psitakki.

He paid the retort no attention and went back to preparing his equipment.

Mazilda approached the cell. Duke wasn't sure what material the bars were fashioned out of, but the visible pulse marks led him to believe that his laser revolver wouldn't have done much damage even if he still had it. Ol' Betsy would, no doubt, have turned the bars into a smoldering pile of ash, but, at the moment, she wasn't in her leathery home across Duke's back. Mazilda glanced at the bars. She seemed impressed at their construction.

"Nice to see you, Ishiro," she said in a voice barely above a whisper. "I'm working on getting you both out of here."

"And how's that going?" quipped Duke.

Mazilda's gaze did not leave Ishiro'shea. "I'm not talking to you. I'm talking to Ishiro."

"And you know how much of a conversationalist he is. Why are you helping us, Mazilda? I mean, it's been a long time since we..." Duke searched for the proper terminology.

"Were friends?" Mazilda said, finishing his thought. "Since we were friends."

"Sure, since we were friends. Why are you helping us?"

"You know, Duke, most people would be content having someone trying to free them from a round of torture with that psycho." She pointed at the interrogator.

"Thanks," the Psitakki added, genuinely appreciative of Mazilda's acknowledgement.

"But I'm not 'most people.' That's why I—" Duke paused again. "—intrigued you so much. That was our thing, Mazilda. There was no one like you, no one like me. It worked."

"Did it? If I recall, it did lots of things... Working wasn't one of them."

"So, why are you helping us then? If I was such a pain in your ass."

Mazilda went silent for a second. She glanced at Ishiro'shea, then back at Duke. She looked back at the interrogator. He was polishing a blunt pipe covered in tiny metallic teeth. It looked painful. She refocused her attention on Duke.

A voice broke the silence. "There you are! That Jungafallowian goon told me that you were in here. I thought he was joking; I'm glad that I am such a thorough investigator."

"Hey Maxx," said Mazilda with a half-smile.

"Hello, my fair love," Maxx replied in his naturally booming voice.

Maxx sported his trademark polished yellow helmet with its color-changing fins and placed it in the crook of his arm. Duke thought the helmet made him look like a radioactive dolphin.

"And hello, friends. It is an honor to be here tonight. I know that you must be saying—what in the cosmos is Maxx Gemstarr doing here in a prison?"

Is this guy for real?

"Nope. No one's saying that," said Duke.

Maxx ignored the bounty hunter and turned his attention to the Chief Interrogator General.

"My good man, I'm honored to be here in your quaint prison. As a public servant, I am sure that you are well aware of the Shaman's upcoming Tournament of the Shield of the Crispy Calamari."

"*Colossal* Calamari," Mazilda whispered to Maxx, but his self-centered theatrical trance rendered him oblivious to Mazilda's attempt at correcting his faux pas.

"I, Maxx Gemstarr, the universe's most beloved crime fighter and bounty hunter, a man that has saved countless lives, civilizations, and planets, has embarked on yet another grave and perilous challenge. One that, you know, I will meet head on and overcome in the name of all that is good and right in the universe."

Maxx's pectorals were puffed out so far that Duke expected his internal organs to burst through his chest cavity.

"Let me guess, you're in the tournament," the interrogator said blandly. "Good luck with that. Try not to die."

"Ha, my good man! Maxx Gemstarr needs no luck. For I have honor on my side. And a good woman."

He squeezed Mazilda. She smiled.

I think I'm going to be sick, thought Duke.

The Chief Interrogator General rolled his eyes.

At least the guy that's going to gut me with extremely sharp tools also thinks Maxx is a fool. There's that.

Maxx turned his attention to his girlfriend. "My sweet love, why are you here talking to these criminals?"

Duke sneered. "We asked her the same thing. I guess she needed a real man again."

Gemstarr's face turned an intense shade of red. His muscles—which were plentiful and covered the entirety of his body—flexed and almost tore his baby-blue spandex jumpsuit. He snarled and took a step towards the cell.

Mazilda grabbed him by the arm and spun him around. She pulled his face down to hers and planted an aggressive yet sensual kiss on his lips.

"I have a real man, Duke," she said when she re-emerged. "Maybe I was wrong to try and help out an old friend."

"I still can't believe that you used to date this guy," Gemstarr said. His face had returned to its amber hue.

"We all make mistakes."

"You're lucky that I am so forgiving. Duke LaGrange is a pretty big blunder to look past," said Maxx.

He slapped Mazilda on the backside. She leapt up in the air a few inches.

Duke clenched his teeth. He felt like he was going to be sick.

The interrogator butted in. "It's time for a few questions," he said with a smile. In his good hand he held a cartoonishly oversized needle. Duke recognized the pink slime oozing from its tip as an immobility solution. One prick and they would wake up strapped into the interrogator's favorite chair.

"Let's go, Mazilda," said Maxx. "I need to rest before the tournament. I fight in two days, remember?"

"Yes, I remember," Mazilda said. She turned her attention back to Duke. "Why do you have to be such an ass?"

Duke knew that she wasn't picking a fight—she was truly curious. Maybe she was right. Maybe this was the one step too far that would send Ishiro'shea and him over the cliff and into the torture chair of a sadistic squid man with a hook hand. Events were certainly trending in that direction.

"Wait a second," he screamed as the interrogator reached the cell. Mazilda and Maxx paused and turned to face Duke. "In this tournament, Maxx, will I get to fight you?"

Maxx looked Duke up and down. He smiled.

How are his teeth that perfect?

"If you survive the melee tomorrow and earn a spot—which is highly unlikely knowing your..." Maxx coughed. "...skills, then yes, you could potentially meet me in the arena. However, the chances are—"

"I'm in."

"Duke," Mazilda began, "this tournament isn't—"

"I'm in. You hear that, you gross bastard? Put the needle away. I'm in."

The interrogator appeared genuinely sad. Upon his droopy face was an even droopier frown. Then he turned to Ishiro'shea and smiled.

"Nope," said Duke. "He's my trainer. He's free, too. You can go away now. Tell the Shaman guy that Duke LaGrange—adventurer, trailblazer, poet, true man of the universe—will take part in that melee fight tomorrow."

Mazilda stormed out. Maxx followed suit.

"Bye Maxxy," Duke called. "See you soon."

"Good luck, Mr. LaGrange," said the Chief Interrogator General, "I think that you will find that a day or two in my company would have proven to be a lot less painful than what you are about to endure."

He inserted a key into the lock, turned it, and the door opened.

"But don't expect me to say 'adventurer, trailblazer, and whatever' to the Shaman. That's below me. And I stick objects into folks for a living."

Duke and Ishiro'shea grabbed their weapons from under the table and left the jail.

"What does Mazilda see in Maxx, Ish?"

CHAPTER 8

THE PONDSCUM TAVERN

THE PONDSCUM TAVERN WASN'T CYBORG Joe's and Duke wasn't sure if that was a compliment or not. It was what one might call "traditional" in its styling.

"So this is the only bar on Psitakki?" Duke asked the young Psitakki bartender.

"Yes sir. It's a sacred place."

"Most bars are, my young friend, most bars are," replied the bounty hunter philosophically.

"No, sir, it's *actually* a sacred place."

It just seems like an old dingy cavern with a sunroof, thought Duke. *Not exactly awe-inspiring.*

"And what, pray tell, makes it so sacred? If you don't mind me asking, that is," he queried.

"Not at all. The legend is that the Pondscum Tavern was built in the very place that Grozzel found the magic shields—the very ones that repelled the shadow demons and saved Psitakki. Are you familiar with that story?"

"Increasingly so."

"This is the very place where that seminal moment in our history occurred."

"And you built a bar over it?"

The Psitakki froze, his eyes unblinking. It was clear that he did not know how to respond to his patron's inquisition.

Duke sipped his drink and smiled. "Maybe Psitakki is my kinda place after all."

He downed the rest of the liquid and asked for another.

The Psitakki barkeep, seemingly oblivious to the most recent exchange, launched back into his train of thought. "Over the course of a millennia, bars would come and go, except for this one. After a while, we just gave up trying and the Pondscum Tavern became the only bar. It didn't seem right to have other bars take away potential patrons from this holiest of holy places."

"Well, it's a lively little dive, that's for sure," commented Duke.

The bartender nodded and handed Duke and Ishiro'shea another drink.

"It's not typically this crowded, but it's been ten thousand years since the last Tournament of the Shield of the Colossal Calamari—so folks are making sure they pregame appropriately. And I think the locals are hoping to see a fighter or two before they... you know?"

"Before they what?" asked Duke cautiously.

"Before they fight."

"Ah yes, before they fight." Duke exhaled.

"And, most likely, die," the bartender added.

"Wait a second, I thought that fighters died only on the rarest of occasions."

"Yes, but our Shaman is a bit—well, a bit of a sadistic blood-hungry maniac."

"Great," Duke replied. "Just great."

"Just be glad you aren't fighting in it, sir."

Duke nodded and tossed the bartender a tip.

"I think we're going to go grab a seat over there. Thanks

for the history lesson, kid. Maybe I can score an autograph from one of the combatants tonight."

"Good luck, sir. If they're in the melee..."

"Yes?" Duke eagerly asked.

"You better hurry up. It's likely your last chance."

"Dumb kid," said Duke under his breath.

He and Ishiro'shea sat at a long wooden table against the back wall of the bar. The Pondscum Tavern was buzzing; combatants, locals, and media personalities from all over the sector were mulling about, imbibing alcohol, conducting interviews, and generally having a pretty okay time.

Duke was drinking, but he definitely wasn't having a good time. His entry in the tournament had been made official, much to the chagrin of the Shaman and Maxx Gemstarr; now he just needed to find out what in the cosmos this melee match was all about.

"We meet again, Duke LaGrange and Ishiro'shea," said Prince Korzo-Tapor quite formally.

"You know, Prince, you tried to kill us not too long ago. I'm not sure I'm over that," Duke replied, drawing his laser revolver and spinning it around his finger. "I'm not really looking to become best buds and strike up a lively conversation with you. Bygones aren't quite bygones yet."

The prince did not flinch. "Fair point. In fact, when I left you, I thought you *were* dead. The ship was wrecked."

"Duke LaGrange always has a few tricks up his sleeve," the Nova Texan proclaimed.

He didn't look back, but he knew Ishiro'shea was either rolling his eyes or shaking his head.

"That was the case then. However, Duke, this is now.

And I hear that you've entered the tournament. How exciting. I for one am interested to see how you fare in this unique event."

"Yeah, thanks again for that bit of information. It actually was quite helpful." *Why am I thanking this guy?* Duke asked himself.

"I guess we're even now?"

"You tried to blow me up! We aren't even. Not even close."

"Fair point again," replied the prince. Up to this point, only one of the heads had been talking. The other head had been constantly surveying the room, either trying to find someone or make sure someone didn't find him. "Now I must say, I do wish you the best but if you do happen to fight my entrant, you will meet a quick yet painful defeat."

"Oh yes, I forgot about your mysterious, invisible 'sure thing.' Where is he? Or she?"

"He is preparing for the battle in two days. We aren't sure of his first opponent, but we were told it won't be the sixteenth participant."

"The melee winner?"

"Yes."

"He's just going to have to wait for me to kick his ass."

"The melee winner has never won the tournament before—not in the previous ninety-nine attempts. Not good odds, I'm afraid, Duke."

"I'm not one for odds. I just hope it's paired with Gemstarr. I owe that punk a few."

"Yes, he is quite—" the talkative head began, but it was the other that finished the thought, "—annoying. Full of himself. Impossible. Awful."

"I like this head much better," smirked Duke.

"Yes, Gemstarr is not our particular cup of tea," the

alpha-head began again. "But he has one thing going for him."

"And what's that?"

"He doesn't have to fight in the melee tomorrow. And you do."

"So what's this melee all about?"

The prince cleared his throats. Once again, it was the more formal head that addressed the bounty hunter's question.

Why did both of them have to clear their throats?

"The night before the tournament begins, the sixteenth entrant is determined by a battle royale in the arena. The same rules apply, but instead of one-on-one, it's every man for himself. You could be in the process of knocking someone out and then get a club to the back of the head. It's less about skill and more about survival."

"Like a barroom brawl?"

"On an epic scale, yes."

"So like a barroom brawl at Cyborg Joe's," Duke added.

"I've heard that there are thirty fighters registered for it —that's the most ever. It's just not the sort of thing that someone volunteers for. Mortal combat has its romantic element, no doubt, but this is so—primitive."

"And no one who's qualified via the melee has ever won the entire tournament?"

"I'm not sure if anyone has ever made it past the opening round. It does take quite a toll."

The bounty hunter was quiet, deep in thought. Beside him Ishiro'shea continued drinking his Psitakki booze.

"And Prince, do you know anyone else in the melee tomorrow?"

"Let me think," the prince said rubbing both of his chins. "I know a few Psitakki toughs joined up. They have a champion in the main tournament—apparently a descendant of Grozzel the Great—but these other guys are just some local loudmouths, likely out to impress a mate."

"Idiots," Duke murmured. Ishiro kicked him under the table. He turned to his masked sidekick.

"What? You think I joined up to impress—" Duke didn't finish his sentence. "I saved us from getting prodded by the old kook with a trunk of very sharp toys. That's it. Drop it."

The ninja turned away and finished off his drink, then rose to his feet and headed back to the bar.

"I'm surprised that your companion didn't enter his name. I hear that he's quite the master. His attack on our great Sprinkles has been frequently referenced throughout the Jungafallowian system."

"He probably would fight in my place had I asked him. Probably has a better shot at winning, too."

"Then why don't you?"

"I caused this mess. I cause most of our messes. Don't tell him I said that. It just wouldn't be fair. I don't know, call me honorable."

"Not a word that I have typically heard associated with your name."

Duke grinned, tipped his hat at the prince, and walked over to join his companion at the bar.

"Are you friends with that Jungafallowian?"

The Psitakki asking the question was muscular and had a youthful exuberance to him.

"That guy?"

"Yes, the one that you were talking with at the table. And the other night at the gala. Are you friends?"

"Kid," Duke sneered, "that guy tried to blow us up a

month ago. No, we aren't friends. In fact, there are few things that I hate more than Jungafallowians."

The Psitakki glared intensely at the bounty hunter. *Some sort of Psitakki lie detector test,* thought Duke. The Psitakki did not break his eye contact.

"I believe you," he said, relaxing and shifting his eyes off of the bounty hunter.

"Thanks?" replied a confused Duke.

"My name is Gjrazzel. I'm a descendent of Grozzel."

"Who?"

"Grozzel. The one that made this tournament possible. It's first champion. Our species' savior."

"Right. Grozzel. Of course. He's the reason why we're here, good ol' Grozzel."

The Psitakki male seemed perplexed.

"Would you like a drink?" asked the bounty hunter charitably. "My treat. And you can tell me why you care if I'm buds with the prince."

"I will pass on the offer of a drink, stranger. I am actually a participant in the tournament—the grand champion of Psitakki—and my training does not allow me to consume alcohol."

"You don't say? I'm in the tournament as well."

Now the Psitakki looked totally perplexed. "*You* are in the tournament? I know all of the contestants; I've seen many of them fight. Except for one."

"You haven't seen me fight."

"Are you the Jungafallowian's secret entrant?"

Duke took a deep gulp of his strange beer. He could sense that Ishiro'shea was giggling inside. "No, I'm in this melee tomorrow."

"I see," Gjrazzel said after a slight hesitation. "Good luck."

"Thanks."

"Should you prevail, stranger, it appears that I will be your first opponent."

"You don't say. Well, cheers to that!"

Duke hoisted his drink in the air. Gjrazzel's expression remained unchanged. Never one to leave a toast unclinked, Ishiro'shea stealthily sneaked to their side and pounded his mug against Duke's.

"Thanks, little buddy. Meet Gjrazzel. I'm going to fight him, apparently."

Ishiro'shea bowed.

"Pleasure to meet you," said Gjrazzel.

"Don't worry, kid. Ish here doesn't talk. He's not being rude."

"I see."

"So what's your beef with the prince? Not a fan of the Trampling Death Robots? Ish almost single-handedly ended their music careers, ya' know."

"I'm not familiar with the Trampling Death Robots but I am familiar with the prince. At least, I'm familiar with what he represents."

"Bad musical preferences?"

"Have you seen his arm?" asked Gjrazzel. "Right below his elbow?"

"No, I hadn't looked."

"He has a tattoo."

"So do a bazillion other folks. Probably half the people here at this bar sport some sort of ink."

"The tattoo is that of a fish."

Duke paused and placed his drink on the bar. Ishiro'shea did the same.

"Let me guess," began the bounty hunter, "a fish with a mustache."

"Yes. You are familiar with what that insignia means, then?"

"Unfortunately, yes. Admiral Lothario LePaco."

"I'm afraid that Prince Korzo-Tapor has something planned on behalf of the admiral. I don't know what or why, but I have a hunch that his mysterious combatant might have some role in this."

"How did an unknown fighter get an invite?"

"The Jungafallowians are known for their fighting prowess. Their government was awarded the right to send their system's champion—this was their selection."

"No name?"

"He's listed as 'Combatant 2.' No one has seen him."

"You know, Gjrazzel, I think I'm on your side on this one. Something isn't right. But I'm sorry, I don't have any insight."

The Psitakki looked dejected. "Thanks for your time, and I hope to meet you in the arena."

"Sure thing, kid."

"Good luck tomorrow."

"Cheers to my luck."

BLOPS, DURPHS, AND SABROMMS, OH MY!

THE VENUE ITSELF WAS NOTHING more than an underground cavern with a circular pit within which the combatants could wage martial war. The seating consisted of simple benches carved from the cave wall, but from the arena floor it was impossible to see where the seating stopped. Duke assumed there were at least two hundred rows encircling the pit. Maybe more. Even from the holding cell under the floor, the bounty hunter could hear and feel the rumble of the crowd that had gathered to view the spectacle of the melee fight.

When he stepped out, the roar generated a sound wave that almost knocked him over. Upon the announcement of "Duke LaGrange, human from Nova Texas," from the loudspeaker, he tipped his hat to the crowd. He quickly realized that all of the contestants received similar greetings. This bruised his ego slightly.

As he waited for the other participants to be introduced, he surveyed the landscape. In the middle of the circular pit was a mound of assorted weapons—mostly clubs and other bludgeoning instruments. Each contestant emerged from a tunnel at the perimeter of the pit, all equidistant from the pile of weapons. Since Duke didn't own a tournament-approved weapon, he grabbed a standard-issue spear from a tournament official. It was sturdy enough to do some damage, but its metallic makeup made it far too heavy to be a potent projectile.

I thought I was done with spears in Neprius, Duke thought to himself.

As he looked around, he noticed that many of the combatants were Psitakki—the "local toughs" that Prince Korzo-Tapor warned him about. He also noticed a particularly menacing-looking Jungafallowian opposite him. The sight of the two-headed reptilian behemoth instantly reminded Duke of a really bad day he had had at Cyborg Joe's recently. In addition to the Jungafallowian, Duke also made note of two Sabromms. If he avoided their massive skulls that they slung around violently on elasticized necks like powerful hammer whips, he felt confident that they wouldn't knock him out of the competition.

There was also a Durph. Duke hadn't dealt with Durphs too frequently, but he knew they had a reputation for being really ill-tempered. This particular Durph stood as tall as Duke, which was impressive for a quadruped. Its four red eyes were barely visible in a sea of thick matted fur that covered every part of its body. Though it was powerful —probably the strongest in the arena—it wasn't likely to sneak up on anyone; and Duke knew a club to the face could render its power moot.

The bounty hunter was shocked to see a warrior from Hausen-Ra. Their race lived in a remote system protected by an asteroid belt; their space travel was rudimentary and their piloting skills novice, so they rarely left. The Hausen-Ra were enigmatic from an evolutionary standpoint; they appeared like basic humanoids, but with no skin, no eyes, and no hair. Except for the fact that they could walk, talk, and fight, they could have been sold to any middle school science class learning human anatomy. In one of the universe's many quirks, the organs and overall life-supporting functions of the Hausen-Ra developed *inside* their skeletal frames. Despite their inside-out evolution, they were renowned fighters as they had no soft spots to attack—but a broken bone could be fatal.

The rest of the field was made up of some species not particularly known for their combat prowess, like the bird-like Dysortimom, and the sickle-armed Sicythian, and some species that Duke had never seen before.

He wasn't particularly concerned with any of them—however, he was intrigued by the smallest combatant. The top of his head wouldn't have reached Duke's waist and his hunched posture was so pronounced that he required a cane to stand upright. The diminutive being was almost formless, as if a naked mole rat infant had mated with a glob of used chewing gum. He was announced as Blop, a Blop from Blop.

He didn't have a very inspired mom, thought Duke.

As the introductions concluded, five Psitakki entered through a tunnel and surrounded the pile of weapons in the center of the arena. They each wore full bodysuits that glowed bright red. Duke surmised that these were the referees, the beings that would make the ultimate call about whether the participant could continue or if he was eliminated. They all faced the combatants, standing like statues with their backs to the mound of armaments.

The voice over the loudspeaker echoed throughout the arena. "Combatants, ready. Those in attendance, ready. Referees, ready. You've been waiting ten thousand years—well, *you* specifically haven't been waiting that long. Unless you're ten thousand years old—and if you are—kudos to you, because that's pretty sweet. I've never met anyone that's ten thousand—"

The voice suddenly stopped. A moment passed. The crowd seemed confused. Duke looked up and saw Ishiro'shea in the first row. They exchanged thumbs-up.

"Fight!" screamed a new voice over the PA system.

The crowd erupted, as did Duke's sweat glands.

The bounty hunter hung back along the perimeter wall, hoping to prevent sneak attacks. Some of these entrants were so amped up that he hoped they would take each other out and leave him with a clearer path to victory. For the most part, that was the case. The Psitakki attacked each other. They attacked the Dysortimom and Sicythian. The more ambitious locals tried to take out the Jungafallowian and the Durph, but proved little more than an annoyance. Many were racing to the pile of weapons to see if they could upgrade their own gear. It proved to be an unsuccessful strategy—typically, they were struck down from behind as they dug for better arms. The two Sabromms were fighting each other. Each cranium smash was louder than the previous one. Within a few moments, the referees had already carted out a handful of combatants. Duke looked over and saw that Blop, the Blop from Blop, was standing alone by himself.

I guess they don't consider him much of a threat. Duke felt a bit sorry for him.

An ax struck just to the right of Duke's head, taking out a piece of the wall behind him. It was one of the local Psitakki fighters. He reared back again but Duke struck his face with the shaft of his spear. The Psitakki staggered back but regained his composure and charged again. Duke sidestepped and swept the Psitakki's legs out from under him with the spear. As the Psitakki's body hit the arena floor, the ax flew from his hand and landed out of his reach. The Psitakki slowly sat up. His eyes narrowed.

"Come on, squid face," shouted Duke.

The Psitakki snarled.

The rock came from a few rows into the audience, and landed squarely on the head of the Psitakki.

He was out cold. Duke looked up and the crowd cheered.

The referee ran over and signaled that the Psitakki was eliminated.

"Hey," Duke said, grabbing the referee's arm, "the fans can throw stuff?"

"Yes, the Shaman encourages crowd participation. Especially when fighters aren't entertaining them."

"Great."

Then Duke noticed the Blop, who was still standing motionless. The fans near to him were starting to grow restless.

Out of the corner of his eye, Duke saw that the Jungafallowian, the Durph, and the Hausen-Ra combatants were each disposing of lesser fighters. The Hausen-Ra warrior engaged with the Jungafallowian and had the upper hand. The Jungafallowian was bigger and stronger but the skeletal soldier's trident kept the two-headed behemoth at bay. However, the Hausen-Ra likely didn't count on the Jungafallowian's alliance with the beastly Durph. The monster leapt and landed on the skeleton's back. If he had skin and squishy parts, there would have been a splat. Instead, there was the sound of cracking bones. The referee checked and there was no response. The Hausen-Ra was out.

Duke did not want to think about the two nastiest combatants joining forces to set up a mutually agreed one-on-one battle. He didn't like his odds of surviving that situation. But before his worry transitioned to unmitigated despair, he noticed that a group of Psitakki were surrounding poor Blop. Duke hustled over and stood next to the mushy alien.

"What are you doing?" said Blop in a plodding and melancholy voice.

"I know this is an 'every thing for himself' ordeal," Duke replied, "but five-on-one hardly seems fair."

Blop did not immediately respond. He appeared deep in thought, even as the Psitakki prepared to charge. "That is very kind of you, human."

"You can thank me later. Let's fight off these meatheads."

"Agreed."

"What's your skill? What do you do?" asked Duke frantically.

"What do you mean?" answered Blop, seemingly in no hurry.

"Can you punch? Kick? Breathe fire?"

"You are funny, my new friend."

"Okay. Get ready to do whatever it is that you do."

The Blop remained silent. He lifted his cane in front of Duke, signaling for him to stay put. He walked forward a few steps, now within striking distance of the bloodthirsty Psitakki. The Durph and Jungafallowian also approached a few paces behind the Psitakki. Duke wasn't sure if they were going to ambush the Psitakki or join in the beatdown that was likely to ensue. He was hoping for the former.

The Psitakki raised their weapons and charged.

This isn't going to be pretty.

Blop dropped his cane and extended his arms as if he was going to give the entire group a great big, affectionate hug.

The flames momentarily blinded Duke and knocked

him back against the arena wall. Through squinted eyes he saw a wall of fire emerge from where Blop was standing. It rose above the arena floor and crashed down like a wave of lava. Blop turned to Duke and smiled.

"Thank you for your help, human."

"*My* help? You're doing everything."

"My pleasure," said the Blop, still grinning.

"Why are you helping me?" asked the bounty hunter.

"Why were *you* helping *me?*"

Duke thought about it. "It seemed like the right thing to do," he said, unsure if that was the "right" response.

"*This* seems like the right thing to do," Blop replied.

"What do you mean?"

"I don't mean anything. Have fun, human. Good luck."

As the flames continued to set everything ablaze and the screams of the other combatants rang throughout the arena, Blop vanished in a puff of smoke. The fiery rain ceased and self-extinguished. The victims of Blop's attack were sprawled out, but all remnants of the fire were gone, as if nothing happened.

The referees ran over and counted the Durph, the Jungafallowian, and the Psitakki out. The crowd roared in approval. They had seen amazing martial theater this evening.

Despite the attack, Duke wasn't alone. On the far side of the arena and out of reach of Blop's spontaneous combustion, the Sabromms continued to fight each other, ignoring the goings-on that had consumed the rest of the arena floor.

They must really hate each other, thought Duke.

Duke slowly stepped over the unconscious bodies and made his way to the Sabromms. They didn't acknowledge his presence.

Their heads were cracked and caving in due to the

constant attacks on each other. They were formidable combatants.

Duke was only a few paces away when they both stopped their battle and looked at him, their chests heaving at an alarming pace.

Oh great. I have to fight both of 'em.

They pivoted to face the bounty hunter. Then both Sabromms crumpled to the floor.

Huh. Well, I'll be damned.

The referee sprinted over to Duke and raised his hand.

The loudspeaker voice shouted, "Your winner and final participant in the Tournament of the Shield of the Colossal Calamari—Duke LaGrange, human from Nova Texas."

Duke looked up and Ishiro'shea exchanged thumbs-ups. Just above the ninja sat Mazilda Cloax. She locked eyes with the Nova Texan, the corners of her mouth turned up. Duke blinked and she was gone.

CHAPTER 10

LIGHT OF GOD

"I HOPE THIS PLACE IS still open," Duke said to Ishiro'shea as he opened the back door of the Pondscum Tavern.

Inside he could hear a lively round of congratulations. "I guess they don't really have many options, do they? One bar, remember."

The ninja nodded.

Roars and chants rang throughout the bar. Duke wanted to believe that they were chanting his name but the sheer number of voices and the varying tonalities, decibel levels, and accents made it sound more or less like the groans of a chipmunk giving birth to a full-grown panda. It goes without saying that it wasn't very melodious.

Duke tipped his hat and gave the customers a wave. They continued to chant as he sat down at the bar.

"The drinks are on the house, Mr. LaGrange," said the young bartender. "And, about earlier..."

"No worries. Why would you have thought that I was competing in the tournament? Not your fault."

"Regardless, drinks for you and your friend are on us. Enjoy."

"That's mighty kind, and I do believe that we'll take you up on that offer. Two of your best... whatever you got."

"Coming right up."

The Psitakki barkeep made his way to the far end of the bar, unlocked a small cabinet, and poured a clear liquid into two cylindrical tubes. The liquid was transparent but glowed brightly; Duke wasn't able to tell if it was the actual drink or the container that caused the effect.

"Sirs, here's our finest imported alcohol. It's from the neighboring planet, Psitakki Minor. They call it the Light of God."

"So, the Colossal Calamari?"

"Oh, no. The Minors don't believe in the Colossal Calamari. They have their own god. It's some wandering commoner that ascended into the night sky with a special magic that he found in a mountain or something. I think there's something about snakes or maybe it's lightning. Not sure. Some real off-the-wall stuff, if you ask me."

"Not as logical as a massive mollusk watching over all of us and tossing shields down to save his people," smirked Duke.

"Exactly."

The bounty hunter's sarcasm was totally lost on the bartender. Duke turned his attention to the glass and cautiously sipped the illuminated liquor.

Divine.

"Holy hedgehogs, kid! This is spectacular."

He gulped the remainder of his drink; Ishiro'shea followed suit.

"I'm glad you like it, Mr. LaGrange. Needless to say, it's truly an honor to serve someone that has actually won a match in the tournament. It's a dream that I never thought would be a reality. Thank you."

"I'll have another, please," Duke said, ignoring the Psitakki's praise.

"I'm sorry but I have to limit you both to a single glass."

"Wait, what? You're cutting us off after one drink?"

"I'm sorry, Mr. LaGrange. It's—"

"I just fought in a brawl with thirty other nutjobs and you're cutting me off after one glass?" Duke asked, with bite.

"I'm not cutting you off because I think you're intoxicated. It's just that it's really bad luck to drink more than one glass in a lifetime." The bartender slunk backwards in fear.

"One in a lifetime? So you're pretty confident that I'm not going to be around to partake in the drink after today, huh?"

"That's not what I meant," said the barkeep in a pleading tone.

"What did you mean? Please enlighten me."

The cowering Psitakki shrank even further, almost into a fetal position behind the bar. He said something inaudibly.

"What's that?"

The Psitakki once again whispered something that even a four-eared trondylpip would have difficulty deciphering.

"Come again?" The agitated bounty hunter's voice grew louder.

"I'm sorry, Mr. LaGrange. I was just trying to do something nice. I want you to have a seamless ascension to the Colossal Calamari in the Sky—and the Light of God, despite its heathen origins, is said to provide its drinkers a beacon to follow in the afterlife."

Duke sat back down on his barstool and looked at Ishiro'shea. The ninja was still sipping on his drink and appeared amused by the goings-on. Duke folded his arms and sighed. "This place," he huffed.

The bartender made his way back onto his feet but leaned against the back cabinets, maximizing his distance from the enraged Nova Texan.

"So, what you're telling me, kid, is that I'm as good as dead tomorrow. I just won this melee, I'm pretty much unscathed outside of a few singe marks from Blop's fireworks, yet you think this is my last night alive."

"It's just that," the Psitakki stuttered, "no one has ever—"

"I know, I know," said Duke, cutting him off, "no one who has won the melee match has ever won the tournament."

"No. No one has ever—"

Duke cut him off again. "I know, no one has ever won their first-round bout."

"No one has ever *survived* their first-round bout," the Psitakki corrected him, speaking more quickly so that Duke wouldn't cut him off a third time.

Duke stared at the bartender. "Is that right? Wonderful. I guess that just means that I'm gonna have to win the whole damn thing."

He placed his foot on the barstool and vaulted himself to the bar top itself.

"Attention, attention," Duke shouted. "It seems that no one in my esteemed position has ever won—has ever survived—their first round fight after winning the melee. In fact, this guy here gave me a free glass of magical potion that is supposed to ease my transition into the great beyond because he's so sure that I'm as good as dead. Well, people, quasi-people, media, and local tramps and degenerates here in attendance, Duke LaGrange—adventurer, trailblazer, poet, true man of the universe—doesn't plan on continuing that trend. In fact, I plan on not only not dying, I plan on winning the entire tournament."

Some of the crowd cheered but it was obvious to Duke that most sided with the bartender's prognostication. He felt he did have the support of the local drunkards.

"And if I win tomorrow night, everyone in this bar will drink entirely on the house!"

The Pondscum Tavern erupted in raucous admiration. The chant that Duke wanted to believe was his name filled every crevice of the cavern. He leapt to the floor and was immediately embraced by the patrons nearest to him. He felt hands and tentacles and talons pat him on the back. He looked back at the bartender, whose jaw hung open.

"You better hope that I lose tomorrow."

"But I didn't promise that—"

"Kid, I'll let *you* tell them that."

"But I can't, they'll—"

"That stuff wasn't that good anyway."

CHAPTER 11

POTATO LIPS

EVEN IN THE BACK CORNER of the Pondscum Tavern, Duke was being hounded by locals and journalists. He enjoyed the praise and attention—and the free alcohol—but it was getting a bit repetitive.

"How do you plan on beating Gjrazzel?" one reporter asked. She was a Dysortimom.

"That's *my* secret. But I'm not scared of a squid-face. Bring 'em on."

Duke knew that most journalists, regardless of species, just wanted digestible soundbites with a hint of controversy. It helped them sell whatever they were hawking and Duke could give them what they needed. And the tastiness of the soundbites only improved as the drinks continued to flow.

He turned to face another gaggle of media types. "This punk has no chance!"

He turned to another group. "The Shield is mine! Gjrazzel won't know what hit him!"

And again. "Better get that squid a shot of Light of God because he's got a date with the Colossal Calamari!"

And again. "Maxx Gemstarr is a pansy and has really poor hygiene!"

The reporters frantically wrote down, recorded, or tele-pathically communicated Duke's many quotations back to their respective publications and forums.

Duke felt confident that his rapid-fire commentary would give them what they needed, but they continued to try and extract even more nuggets from the bounty hunter.

Suddenly, the sea of reporters parted and then scattered.

"Go away, Mr. LaGrange is done for the evening." The voice was booming but had feminine undertones.

Emerging from the mass of reporters was a hulking frame of fur topped by a set of boney horns that covered the skull like a cap and curved out just in front of the ears. She resembled the Gartoshian musk ox that Duke and Ishi-ro'shea had met a month back at Cyborg Joe's Grill N' Go & The Why Not Saloon, but she was even broader in stature and her fur was a sandier shade of brown.

The Gartoshian about-faced and snorted at the few reporters that had ignored her demand. They scattered immediately. She sat down at the table.

"Mr. LaGrange. Nice to meet you. Your speech earlier was interesting."

Duke tipped his cap and Ishiro'shea bowed.

"Thanks, and a real big thanks for pushing out those reporters. I know I probably deserved it for giving them some red meat to sink their teeth into, but it was getting annoying. Can we buy you a drink?"

"Thank you for the offer," the musk ox snorted, "but, like you, I have a match tomorrow. Unlike you, I'm choosing to stay away from the drink until I have finished the competition."

"No way! Well good luck to you. You know, I'm not surprised. We know a Gartoshian and we've seen her duke it out. She almost killed two Jungafallowians without even breaking a sweat. If you're half as tough as Lilly, you'll be a tough in this odd little dance, that's for sure."

"Lilly, you say? Lilly Arnaq of Moon Colony #3?"

Duke looked at Ishiro'shea for an answer. The ninja returned a blank stare and then shrugged his shoulders.

"Maybe," Duke replied. "She looks like you—maybe a bit darker—and can throw down like nobody's business. We met her at Cyborg Joe's on Kelt."

"Ah yes," the Gartoshian began, "that's Lilly. She's a great fighter. She was my toughest opponent back home on Gartosh."

"You fought her?"

"I have."

"And?"

"We only fought once, when she was just getting back into the game. I think that was the only reason that I prevailed. She demonstrated true grit. But, alas, with my victory, I became the Gartoshian champion and received an invite to this tournament. You see, we are known to excel at the combat arts and the annual winner of the Miss Bovine Boxing contest is held in high esteem throughout our system."

"You beat Lilly to win Miss Bovine Boxer of Gartosh? That's impressive," Duke said. "You have to be the odds-on favorite to win this whole shebang. I'm sorry, I didn't get your name."

"Yvonne. Yvonne Angerdlarnek. I'm from Gartosh Moon Colony #1. And no, Mr. LaGrange, I'm not considered a favorite to win this tournament. The other fighters here are much more accomplished. It's a pretty remarkable field."

"Oh."

"Do you know anything about the other fighters, Mr. LaGrange?"

She knows the answer to that.

"Please call me Duke. And no, not really. I mean, I know *you* now. And I know I'm fighting Gjrazzel. I met him yesterday and he seemed like an alright guy. Not too worried. And I know that there's some mystery fighter from Jungafallow III."

"Yes, we are all curious as to what the Jungafallowians are doing. They are not my favorite race."

"Join the club. Oh, and speaking of the universe's worst slime, I know Maxx Gemstarr."

"He's quite handsome though," said Yvonne.

"If you like pompous, arrogant, no-talent hacks. Anyways, this isn't a beauty contest."

"I've heard he's quite a skilled warrior too," added the musk ox.

"Not even in the top twenty toughest bounty hunters, if you ask me," Duke answered.

From the corner of his eyes, Duke noticed Ishiro'shea trying to convey to Yvonne that Maxx might not be as worthless as his compatriot was making him out to be. It was clear that she was having trouble understanding the ninja's non-verbal communication.

"What? You think he's a tough guy? So *you* like Gemstarr too. First Mazilda and now my best friend," Duke said gruffly. "Maxx is really pushing the limits of my hatred."

Ishiro'shea simply rolled his eyes and went back to his beer.

"There are others in the tournament besides the contestants that you mentioned," said Yvonne, redirecting the conversation.

"I guess some advanced scouting can't hurt, right?" said Duke, while still sneering at Ishiro'shea.

"Most people are concerned about the Jungafallowian

entry because it's an unknown. No records. No name. Just listed as Combatant 2."

"So I've heard. His handler tried to blow us up once. I would expect the worst."

"And the Psitakki champion that you mentioned is a skilled fighter. He will have a decided home field advantage; not only is he a Psitakki but he's the descendent of Grozzel himself. It's going to be loud."

"Anything that I should be aware of?"

"He will try and finish you off with a Psitakki staff made from a tarzantia tree. I've seen him practice; he strikes quickly and effectively."

"Great."

"The field is quite diverse. There is a Hiritai warrior. She is considered a favorite by many."

"I'm intimately familiar with Hiritai. And I mean intimately. Know what I mean?"

"I think I do," replied Yvonne.

"Aggressive in every way that you can imagine," added Duke.

"Right," Yvonne replied, "and a Gurlfian Goother Rat."

"A Goother? Those critters are insane."

"And tenacious fighters," Yvonne added. "Their size is their greatest strength because most underestimate them because of it."

"I've seen one tear up a Zylantian pirate in a bar once. It was pretty ugly."

"There's a Zylantian here as well."

"They let one of those four-armed sleazebuckets in this thing?"

"Have you ever been to Planet F?" asked Yvonne.

"No but I'm aware of it. A bunch of flying bugs, right?"

"Yes. One of the Queen's Royal Guard has been

entered in and, well, he can fly. That's makes him a tricky opponent."

"Great."

Yvonne looked as if she was about to launch into more detailed biographies of each combatant when the trio was interrupted. The visitor slid into her seat without a sound and removed her hood. Duke saw deep blue-violet hair and matching eyes.

"I'm sorry to interrupt," said Mazilda, bowing slightly to Yvonne. She extended a hand. "It's a pleasure to meet you, Yvonne. I've heard many tales of your pugilistic prowess and renowned fighting spirit."

Yvonne countered with a bow of her own and gripped Mazilda's hand. Duke noticed that Mazilda was trying to hide a wince. *That musk ox is strong.*

"I see why they call you the Furry Mountain of Moon Colony #1," complimented Mazilda.

"Cool nickname," added Duke. "Do I get one for this tournament?"

"You are officially registered as Duke LaGrange—" began Mazilda.

"Adventurer. Trailblazer. Poet."

Mazilda cut him off. "No. You're officially registered as Duke LaGrange—a bounty hunter."

"Are you serious?" Duke sighed dejectedly.

Mazilda turned her attention back to the anthropomorphic musk ox from Gartosh.

"Good luck tomorrow with Reginald. I hear he's a bit of a scrapper."

"Thank you..." the musk ox paused.

"Mazilda. Mazilda Cloax. I'm an old friend of these two."

"And a *friend* of Maxx Gemstarr," Duke announced with disgust.

Mazilda scrunched her face and glared at Duke.

"It seems that you have some catching up to do," began Yvonne. "It was nice to meet you, Duke LaGrange. And your friend. I will tell Lilly that I ran into you if I see her again."

"We'll do the same," replied Duke. "And thanks for the insight about the other fighters. Much appreciated."

"See you tomorrow at the Grand Entrance. And, Mazilda, it was nice meeting you. You must be quite the woman to catch the eye of Maxx Gemstarr."

Duke mimed being sick.

Yvonne "The Furry Mountain of Moon Colony #1" Angerdlarnek stood up and exited the Pondscum Tavern. The reporters that had hounded Duke earlier avoided the musk ox as she made her way out. Duke chuckled at the dread and fear on their faces.

"I saw you tonight," Duke said with a smirk.

"So?"

"Just saying."

"I wanted to make sure you didn't get yourself killed. I had two daggers at the ready just in case one of those Psitakki bastards got a bit too aggressive."

"That's sweet," Duke said, batting his eyelashes. "You still care about me."

"I don't know why that's such a shock to you. Yes, we were awful together. But I still care about you. And Ishiro'shea."

Ishiro'shea was on his twelfth or thirteenth beer. He acknowledged Mazilda with a groggy thumbs-up.

"I haven't seen you in a long time," said Duke.

"I know. I've been busy. You've been busy. In fact, where *have* you been? My sources said something about you getting eaten by one of Joe's portals."

"Something like that. I'll fill you in later. It's a long, long story."

"Let me guess, it includes some blue-skinned, big-breasted beauties—"

"Hey, don't go making fun of my choices in that arena. Do I need to remind you that you're here with Maxx Gemstarr? The galaxy's biggest ass. What do you see in that guy?"

"I will fill *you* in later on that."

"No thank you. The less I have to hear about Gemstarr, the better. I'm just surprised. I know we were a disaster but I thought I knew you better than that. I guess I don't."

"We weren't always a disaster," Mazilda said with a smile. "Some parts were great."

Duke pondered that thought for a moment. He wasn't sure if Mazilda was flirting, but he didn't want to chance it and get one of her daggers in his eye.

"Some were great. Key word being 'were,' unfortunately," replied Duke. "So why are you here *now*? What's so important?"

"Potato Lips."

Duke lifted his glass in the air and examined the liquid. Confusion consumed his expression.

"How much have I had? I could have sworn you said 'potato lips.'"

"You never were a good listener," Mazilda jabbed. "Yes, Seamus 'Potato Lips' O'Hoolihan. Ring a bell?"

"Nope. Should it?"

"He's from Earth."

"So are twenty billion other life forms."

"He's from New Tokyo. Ireland."

Duke slapped Ishiro'shea on the back of the head. The ninja sprang up and drew his katana.

"Simmer down, Ish. Mazilda has something that we need to hear."

Ishiro'shea returned to his seat sluggishly and stared cross-eyed at Mazilda.

"I've seen you in better shape," she said.

The ninja tried to focus his eyes but the booze was making an impact.

"You know that it takes Ish a night for his body to acclimate to new types of booze. He'll be drinking everyone under the table by the time we leave this rock."

"I have no doubt about that," said Mazilda.

"So who is this Potato Lips?"

"O'Hoolihan is a decorated soldier who worked for the Irish gangs back in New Tokyo. But he's no ordinary soldier, he's a mutant. His mutation gives him unmatched strength and skin as thick as a brick wall; he's so valuable that they've sent him on the most important mission of all."

"To win the Tournament of the Shield of the Colossal Calamari?" asked Duke quizzically.

"No, Duke. To track down Ishiro'shea's parents."

Instantly, every bit of intoxication drained from Ishiro's face, like a popped water balloon. He was sober. He inched closer to Mazilda.

"So why is he *here?*" asked Duke.

"I don't know. But someone here must know something. Why else would O'Hoolihan join the tournament while the wars rage on?"

"I have no idea."

"And you two haven't made any headway on finding Ishiro's parents?"

"None, unfortunately. We've been a bit busy of late."

"Oh yes, the portal thing."

"Yes, the portal thing," Duke replied with no shortage of sass.

"I want to do whatever I can to help."

"Why now?"

"What do you mean 'why now'? How many missions have I gone on with you two searching for Ishiro's parents? More than I can count. I was happy to do it."

"Yes, but we haven't seen you in a long time, Mazilda. Why help us now? You weren't seeking us out or anything. We kinda dropped in on the festivities, if you don't remember."

"Yes, I remember. And when it happened, it..." She paused. "...it reminded me of some good memories. I'm not one to get nostalgic, but I feel that this is something that I left unfinished. It's always haunted me. I was given a second chance to help you guys out. You two falling onto that table during the Shaman's gala was the universe's way of telling me something. I won't mess this up. And one more thing."

She reached into her robe and removed a communication device. It was an older model, mostly used for short range, which made it very difficult to intercept or decode. It was a popular design for thieves and other positions of ill repute. Mazilda pressed a few buttons and turned the screen towards Ishiro'shea and Duke.

It was a grainy image of two humans. The male was gray-haired and mature in years but broad-shouldered, and looked to be in prime physical condition. The woman looked around the same age but she was petite. She also had grayed but her beauty wasn't tarnished by her advanced age; if anything, it was enhanced.

The ninja's eyes widened. Duke noticed a twitch in his partner's upper cheek. It was as if joy and disbelief were dueling to see what emotion would win out on the ninja's face.

Ishiro'shea's parents.

"I was able to acquire this image from Potato Lips

without him knowing," Mazilda said in a hushed tone. "I'm not sure where it was taken. I don't recognize the buildings in the background or any of the reference points. But—"

"They're alive," Duke said finishing Mazilda's sentence.

"Maxx is here," she said with a sense of urgency. "I have to go. Here you go."

She pressed a few more buttons on the device and a printout of the image was produced. She handed it to Ishiro'shea.

"Do you have to go?"

"Yes, but we can talk again. Good luck tomorrow against Gjrazzel. I have faith in you."

Mazilda placed her hand on Ishiro'shea's shoulder and smiled at Duke. Then, in a blink of an eye, she was gone. Duke turned around to see her arm in arm with Maxx Gemstarr, exiting the Pondscum Tavern.

Man, I hate Maxx Gemstarr.

The bounty hunter turned to Ishiro'shea, who was still motionless from the shock.

"Little buddy, regardless of how this tournament turns out, it's been a worthwhile detour if you ask me. We finally have a lead on your folks."

Ishiro'shea did not budge.

"Let's go get some sleep. Tomorrow, we can try and find Mr. Potato Lips and ask him a few questions." Duke twirled his laser revolver. "Okay, maybe one more round."

CHAPTER 12

RATINGS KILLER

DUKE WAS HUNGOVER, WHICH WAS surprising considering it was midday. In fact, he and Ishiro'shea both would have still been asleep had it not been for a tournament official beating incessantly on their hotel door. Since most of the local accommodation had been booked up years in advance in anticipation for the Tournament of the Shield of the Colossal Calamari, and Duke and Ishiro'shea just happened to drop in at the last minute, their room wasn't exactly topflight. It wasn't even bottom flight. It was next-to-the-ice-machine bad. But it was near the bar, so it had that going for it. The official's rapid-fire hammering caved the door in. It swung open on a single hinge and hung limp.

"I'm not paying for that," Duke mumbled.

"Mr. LaGrange, you need to hurry up. You can't be late to the tournament's Grand Entrance."

"I'll catch the next one," said the bounty hunter. He repositioned his pillow to block the light.

The Psitakki official stepped over a sleeping Ishiro'shea and hoisted Duke up by his arm. "Mr. LaGrange, we have to go. Now."

"I thought the fight wasn't until tonight," Duke moaned.

"The Grand Entrance starts in..." The Psitakki looked at a communication device. "...it starts very soon. If you aren't there, the Shaman is going to be irate. He'll probably blame me."

"Who are you anyways?"

"I was assigned to make sure that you don't escape before the tournament."

"The Shaman thinks I'm going to run away, does he?"

The Psitakki sighed, clearly not wanting to begin a debate with the half-drunk Nova Texan. "Let's just say that we were concerned with the amount of alcohol that you had last night at the Pondscum. We just wanted to make sure that you actually made it to the arena. By the looks of it, our concerns were justified."

Duke reached for his hat and placed in on his head. It slid down over his eyes. "Can I rest for a few more minutes? I promise I'll meet you at the arena."

The Psitakki official jerked Duke harder, but lost his balance. He stepped on the snoozing martial artist. Ishiro'shea leapt to his feet and connected with a *shotei* strike to the official's chest. His eyes were still closed. *He's on autopilot*, thought Duke.

Ishiro'shea shook his head and came to his senses. He glanced at the door, then at the unconscious Psitakki at his feet, then at Duke.

"You just knocked out our ride to the arena, Ish."

The ninja knelt down to make sure that the Psitakki was still breathing.

"He's fine, he's fine," said Duke. "Apparently we have to go to some big ceremony at the arena. You know how to get there?"

Ishiro'shea shook his head.

"Do they have taxis on Psitakki?"

Ishiro'shea responded with a glance that seemed to convey his lack of hope for a suitable Psitakki public transportation system.

"If we get to the arena, maybe we have time to chat with Potato Lips before the show."

The ninja seemed to perk up at this suggestion.

"Mr. LaGrange! Mr. LaGrange, we are about to start. Get in your place. Hurry! Hurry!"

The Psitakki yelling at Duke was easy to identify as a member of the production team responsible for broadcasting the event across the universe. His headset was oversized to the point of being comical; it screamed, 'Hey, look at me! I'm important!'"

"Not there; *here*," he said, pointing to a compact metallic room.

Glad I'm not claustrophobic.

Duke recognized that they were near the holding area that led to the arena floor. His memory was a bit hazy, but the thunderous booms of thousands of spectators cheering, mere paces away, made it quite obvious as to where they were.

"Who are you, peanut?" asked the production supervisor in a pugnacious tone.

Ishiro is not going to like that.

"Only the combatants and their corner men are allowed here. Get out. Get out. Get out."

Ishiro'shea's eyes focused on the Psitakki and he grabbed the hilt of his sword. Duke gently took the ninja's wrist to make him halt.

"*He's* my corner man," said Duke.

"I was told that you didn't have one," snapped the producer. "He wasn't at the melee."

"I didn't know that I could have someone in my corner. Now I do. And he's it. Deal with it."

The producer flashed a scowl that could have bent steel. He screamed into his headset and stormed off.

"I guess this means that you're my corner man," said Duke. "Now sober up and look alive."

Ishiro'shea shot him a glance almost as menacing as the producer's.

"Fine, I'll try and sober up too. Apparently, I'm going to die today."

The roars of the crowd were accompanied by equally deafening trumpets. And then by ear-smashing drums. It was like being serenaded by the Trampling Death Robots while locked in a midsized sports utility vehicle. Duke grimaced; his headache had spread all the way down to his spleen.

"Maybe that room has a door," Duke said, his hands clamped over his ears.

He and Ishiro'shea entered the chamber. It wasn't as cramped as it appeared and, most importantly, it had a door. Ishiro'shea slid the door shut and the noise abated.

"Holy hedgehogs, that was loud," Duke proclaimed. He sat down on a smooth white bench that jutted out from the wall.

"Are you in your places?"

Duke and Ishiro'shea looked around confused.

"Who said that?" asked Duke.

"Look up, Mr. LaGrange," the voice said, sounding annoyed at the question. "See that tiny black box? That's called a speaker. I'm not some scary invisible god that is talking to you, right? I'm just a production manager that wants this event to be broadcast without any major screwups. Got that?"

Duke contemplated leaving the room and tracking down the producer. He wondered how the Psitakki would react to looking down the barrel of Ol' Betsy.

But, uncharacteristically, the Nova Texan took the high road. "We didn't see the speaker. We see it now."

"Good. First, remove your guns and give them to your corner man. It is strictly forbidden to have them on your person when you walk out for the Grand Entrance."

"Done," replied Duke, handing his revolver and Betsy to Ishiro'shea.

"When the door in front of you opens—not the one that you just closed—"

"Let's tone down the condescension a notch, huh?"

"Fine," the producer barked. "When the door opens, follow the path to the empty pedestal. Stand on it. Wave. Bow. Do whatever you want. When everyone is done, you will exit in reverse order and return to this room. Stay on the path."

"Sounds easy enough."

"It does, doesn't it?" replied the producer in a snarky tone. "In the meantime, you can watch the live broadcast from this screen."

The wall next to Ishiro'shea opened up and a monitor extended on a metallic arm. It turned on to reveal a still shot of the arena overlaid with text in a grandiose and gaudy font. It read: *The 100th Annual Tournament of the Shield of the Colossal Calamari—The Grand Entrance. Sponsored by Uncle Tofu's Adventure Land, home of the Screamin' Vegan, the universe's first roller coaster made exclusively from a fungal-derived meat alternative. Fun with less fat.*

"Wow, looks like the Cosmic Superstation is picking this up."

"Yes, and the Universal Superstation," chimed in the producer's voice from the speaker. "And the Galactic Superstation. Everyone is carrying this. It's the biggest event in the last ten thousand years."

"When do I go on?"

"You're second to last. Gjrazzel is last, for obvious reasons."

"Hometown boy?"

"Yes. A Psitakki hasn't won this tournament since his ancestor, Grozzel. That was ninety-nine tournaments ago. The world—no, the universe—wants him to win."

"So, I guess that you aren't rooting for me?"

"You, Mr. LaGrange, would be a ratings killer."

"Thanks. If it's all the same to you, I think my buddy and I would like to watch some of the broadcast and relax. You know, before I kill the ratings and all."

"I'm not worried about you killing the ratings."

"Because you don't think I can win."

There was a long pause. "Don't screw this up. When the door opens, follow the path..."

"I got it."

The broadcast cut to two announcers sitting in a booth suspended above the arena floor. One of the announcers was a well-dressed Trevlon. The Trevlon were about as nondescript a bipedal race as you could find, but they had deep and soothing voices. Most Trevlons left their home planet to seek employment as voice actors, lounge singers, and, if they were lucky, broadcasters. Next to the Trevlon was a brightly-colored robot wearing a top hat.

"Hey, Ish, we're famous. Look who's calling the action. I love these guys."

CHAPTER 13

RANDY AND ZEL

[INTRODUCTION MUSIC ENDS AND TITLE SCREEN DISSOLVES. BROADCAST OPENS WITH SHOT OF THE ANNOUNCERS.]

Zelarious Zan Alon: Hello, everyone in the universe! And welcome to the one hundredth annual Tournament of the Shield of the Colossal Calamari, live here on Psitakki. I'm Zelarious Zan Alon and, man, I tell you, I am honored to be here calling this exciting tournament. You are in for a treat, my friends. You won't see anything like it again, I can promise that. And to help me call the action is the best color commentator in the business. He's a veteran of over forty-two thousand broadcasts that span everything from the Slinky Racing Nationals to the Extreme Armadillo Juggling Grand Prix to Paint Drying Watching Battles on Gorma Gorma Zed. Yes, you know him, you love him—it's everyone's favorite spunky little android, Randy!

Randy: Thank you for that kind introduction, Zel. *Beep*. I'm ready to see some pain and suffering. And I don't just mean from your play-by-play call. *Boop. Beep.*

Zelarious Zan Alon: Oh wow, starting out strong, Randy.

Randy: That's what Mrs. Zan Alon said last night. *Beep.*

Zelarious Zan Alon: Let's leave that monster out of this, because we have sixteen other monsters that we need to talk about today. In a few moments, the final Grand Entrance will happen and we—along with the thousands in attendance—will lay eyes on the combatants that are fighting for that unbelievable prize, a shield of Grozzel. It's a million years old and is the last of the artifacts that helped Grozzel save the people of Psitakki from those mysterious shadow demon invaders. The previous ninety-nine have been lost to time, along with their owners, but we get to see the final one handed out. Pretty special, huh, Randy?

Randy: Sure. *Beep.*

Zelarious Zan Alon: Before the introductions start, here's a word from our sponsor. Uncle Tofu's Adventure Land—It Won't "Meat" Your Expectations, It Will "Meat Substitute" Them!

Randy: Speaking of meat, Zel... *Beep.* Your wife called me, asking about a pork. *Boop.*

Zelarious Zan Alon: Now that word from our sponsors.

[UNCLE TOFU'S ADVENTURE LAND COMMERCIAL PLAYS.]

Zelarious Zan Alon: Welcome back, fans, to the Tournament of the Shield of the Colossal Calamari. You can hear the music and the crowd cheering and that means it's time for the entrances. Sixteen of the fiercest, most distinguished warriors in the entire galaxy will do battle in a single elimination, no-holds-barred tournament. There can be only one winner. It's not for the faint of heart or the weak of stomach. It's going to be brutal, nasty, painful, and destructive, but oh so glorious. And all to honor that big squid in the sky. Do you have any favorites in the field, Randy?

RANDY: *Beep. Boop.* Yes, I do, Zel. The Grand Champion of Psitakki, Gjrazzel, is quite a specimen, especially with that weapon of his.

ZELARIOUS ZAN ALON: Yes, his tarzantia tree staff is deadly.

Randy: Oh, yeah, that too. *Beep.*

ZELARIOUS ZAN ALON: What are you talking about, Randy?

RANDY: Ask your wife. *Boop.*

ZELARIOUS ZAN ALON: Anyone else catch your eye?

RANDY: I really like the combatant from Hiritai. *Beep.* What's her name?

ZELARIOUS ZAN ALON: Sulaw. What makes you think she will go far in the tournament?

RANDY: I don't know if she'll go far in the tournament. But she catches my eye. *Beep.* She's smoking hot. Isn't that what you asked me? Zel, you really need to step it up. You're embarrassing yourself tonight. *Beep. Boop.*

ZELARIOUS ZAN ALON: She *is* a fierce combatant, no doubt about it. But don't forget about the entrant from that messed-up sphere we call Earth—Seamus "Potato Lips" O'Hoolihan.

RANDY: He's nasty, for sure. *Beep.* And ugly. *Boop.* And probably drunk.

ZELARIOUS ZAN ALON: Quite possibly, Randy, quite possibly. We have some intriguing first round matchups. How about Yvonne "The Furry Mountain of Moon Colony #1" Angerdlarnek going one-on-one with Reginald the Mega-Troll? That should be explosive.

Randy: And what about Maxx Gemstarr? *Beep.* He's hunky enough to cause my gears to spin the other way. *Boop.*

Zelarious Zan Alon: He sure is a handsome man. And a favorite to win the entire tournament. Watch out for the Universe's Favorite Bounty Hunter. But don't forget about the two big mysteries.

Randy: Ooooooh. *Boop.*

Zelarious Zan Alon: First, and to be honest, what I'm most excited about, is to see this unknown Combatant 2 from Jungafallow III. All we know is that he was awarded their government's invitation to the tournament and he's seconded by the esteemed Prince Korzo-Tapor. I know the prince personally and he wouldn't endorse anything less than a sure-fire winner. And, lastly, the wild card entrant and winner of the melee, Duke LaGrange—a bounty hunter.

Randy: Who? *Beep.*

Zelarious Zan Alon: Exactly, another mystery indeed. When we return, the entrances will begin. Now a word from Willie's World of Galactic Winnebagos—Where the Universe is Our Home, So Make it Yours... Now with Flushing Toilets Compatible with up to Eighty-Five Species!

[WILLIE'S WORLD OF GALACTIC WINNEBAGOS COMMERCIAL PLAYS.]

Zelarious Zan Alon: Welcome back, fight fans from across the universe. It's about time to see our combatants! I'm really excited, Randy.

Randy: *Beep.* Me too, Zel. *Beep.*

Zelarious Zan Alon: The lights are down and the trumpets are blasting. The crowd is in a frenzy. I haven't heard anything this loud and indistinguishable since the Trampling Death Robots' holiday album. This is quite a sight to behold. Wait a second, Randy. The first door is opening, and we have our first entrant into the Tournament of the Shield of the Colossal Calamari. It's Not Very Good at Math.

RANDY: But is it good at fighting? *Boop. Beep.*

ZELARIOUS ZAN ALON: No, Randy, that's his name. Not Very Good at Math. He's the representative of Zylantia and a renowned pirate lord back on his home planet.

RANDY: *Beep.* What a dumb name, Zel. *Boop.* Who are these Zylantian pirates anyways? Beep. I've never heard of them. *Boop.*

ZELARIOUS ZAN ALON: I can tell, Randy. Zylantia is a harsh cloud-covered world filled with villainy and treachery, with overtones of male chauvinism. Amongst this collection of vile scum, those that successfully earn a spot on a pirate vessel are considered royalty. Due to their affinity for theft and general terror, Zylantian pirates always have substantial disposable income. These blood-soaked nest eggs allow them to travel off-world to engage with other races and, if they're lucky, learn new ways to lie, cheat, steal, and torture.

RANDY: And they have four arms. *Beep.*

ZELARIOUS ZAN ALON: Great observation, Randy. They can utilize all four hands to slice, stab, and claw at their opponents. They are a devious race, no doubt. Just look at Not Very Good at Math. He's taunting the crowd with two arms, stroking his icy-white mustache with another, and... What's that other hand doing?

RANDY: That's even too gross for me to comment on, Zel. *Beep. Boop.* And what about that funny name?

ZELARIOUS ZAN ALON: It's customary on Zylantia that a child does not receive a proper name given to them by their biological parents. In fact, parenting is a bit of a lost art on Zylantia. Names just sort of evolve based on characteristics, traits, behaviors, or really stupid things that you do. Famous Zylantians include Pointy Elbows, Dried Spit on Mouth, Really Small Eyes, Trips More than Average Zylantian, and the universally-acclaimed chef that invented "never-ending mayonnaise," Mother Looks Like Dirt Bug.

RANDY: *Beep.* Looks like our second contestant is coming out now. *Boop.* It's my personal favorite! Wives, hide your husbands, because Sulaw is here. *Beep.*

ZELARIOUS ZAN ALON: That's right, Sulaw is the next competitor in the Grand Entrance. And wow, she's a fan favorite. Listen to these fans! Listen to those cheers!

RANDY: *Beep.* That's the sound of drool hitting the ground, Zel. *Boop.*

ZELARIOUS ZAN ALON: She's not just a pretty face, Randy. She's an accomplished warrior from Hiritai. Her tribe is the current ruling group, which makes her one important woman. Look at her now, paying respect to the Psitakki as she walks to her pedestal. What a class act. She knows honor. And how beautiful is that *chunki?*

RANDY: *Boop.* She looks pretty damn fit to me. *Beep.*

ZELARIOUS ZAN ALON: No, you crazy robot. *Chunki* is the golden material fashioned to form her breastplate and twirled around her waist like a skirt. The interconnected rings covering the midriff and fastened to the shiny brassiere and kilt are also made from the impenetrable *chunki*. But, as is common with the Hiritai warriors, her legs—muscular legs, at that—and feet are exposed. If you grow up in the harsh terrain of Hiritai, your feet become as tough as any cobbler's creation.

RANDY: *Beep.* You know a lot about these Hiritai women, Zel. *Boop.* Think you can introduce me to Sulaw?

ZELARIOUS ZAN ALON: You wouldn't want that,

Randy. The Hiritai hate men. They *loathe* men. They view them as tiny-brained, sex-driven nuisances. They put up with them for procreation until they can figure out a solution to eliminate them entirely. I've heard nearly a third of the gross national product goes towards male eradication technology. But as much as they hate men, they love parties. And being the center of attention—a trait that anthropologists believe they inherited from their ancient Earth ancestors. A Hiritai may take a husband for the sake of having a bitchin' bachelorette party and wedding and, before the honeymoon is over, the husband will either be subjected to a life of slavery in the Hiritai mines, or killed simply for being in the way. Once again, anthropologists see numerous similarities to their Earth-bound relatives.

RANDY: *Boop.* Well, I'm a robot, Zel.

ZELARIOUS ZAN ALON: You might have a chance, then.

RANDY: *Boop.* And I'm not really into gross generalizations of gender tendencies and furthering outdated stereotypes that demean entire populations. *Beep.*

ZELARIOUS ZAN ALON: You are quite the progressive, Randy. Oh wow, Randy, look at that. Did you see that? Not Very Good at Math and Sulaw are having a bit of a stare down. The crowd is eating this up. They meet in the first round, you know. Going to be quite the battle.

RANDY: *Beep.* Who's that coming out now? *Boop.* Or rather, slithering out. *Beep.*

ZELARIOUS ZAN ALON: That's the infamous Tor-torta of Krawn. The serpent people of Krawn are widely known for their advancements in two major industries: the torture industry and soybean harvesting. They lack hind legs, but they are quite agile slithering around. The arms on their upper torsos are ridiculously strong, as they are their primary means of locomotion. And they're covered in nasty spikes.

RANDY: *Beep.* He's pretty gross, Zel. Does he have any special skills? *Beep.*

ZELARIOUS ZAN ALON: Just wait a second... watch this.

RANDY: Oh wow! *Beep.* He can breathe fire! That's got to help his chances! *Beep.*

ZELARIOUS ZAN ALON: But he has a tough challenge in front of him. The representative from Earth is a bad dude.

RANDY: *Beep.* Aren't most people from Earth 'bad dudes'? *Beep.*

ZELARIOUS ZAN ALON: I think that might be a bit of an exaggeration, but this guy here comes from the heart of the gang wars in Ireland—New Tokyo, to be exact. Seamus "Potato Lips" O'Hoolihan.

RANDY: Beep. Why do they call him—never mind. I see. *Beep.*

ZELARIOUS ZAN ALON: Yes, he's not your average Earther. His mutation has given him abnormal strength and mass. Including on his face. I've heard of O'Hoolihan's exploits as a street tough before he became the chief enforcer for the Irish. You don't want to mess with this guy.

RANDY: *Beep.* Was he born this way? *Boop.*

ZELARIOUS ZAN ALON: He was, Randy.

RANDY: *Beep.* That had to be a painful birth. I feel sorry for his mother. Hopefully, she had good birthing hips. *Beep.* But the crowd seems to love him. I guess when you bring out two mugs of beer and toast the crowd, what's not to like? *Boop.*

ZELARIOUS ZAN ALON: No doubt! His legendary drinking adventures rival that of his fighting prowess. He and Tor-torta should be an interesting bout. Look who's out next. The biggest competitor in the field, it's Reginald!

RANDY: *Beep.* You aren't kidding, Zel. This Mega-troll is massive. How can anyone beat this guy? *Boop.*

ZELARIOUS ZAN ALON: He will be a tough out, that's for sure. Look at him saunter to the pedestal. Four steps and he's there. You know what, I don't think the pedestal will support him. He's a true goliath. But, Randy, they grow them big in the Silver Mountains of Mrelock.

RANDY: *Beep.* And stupid. *Beep.*

ZELARIOUS ZAN ALON: You're right, Randy. The Mega-Trolls aren't known for their mental dexterity and intelligence—but when you're that size and that strong, it makes up for areas where you're lacking. Look at Reginald playing to the crowd! His pounding of the chest signifies that he's very appreciative of the fans, and those primal screams are his way of saying that he's going to give it his all in this tournament.

RANDY: You're fluent in Mega-Troll? *Boop.*

ZELARIOUS ZAN ALON: His opponent is one of the crowd favorites. Wait for this cheer.

RANDY: *Beep.* They do love this lady! *Beep.*

ZELARIOUS ZAN ALON: I wouldn't be surprised if this is the second or third loudest ovation today. There she is, ladies and gentlemen, Yvonne "The Furry Mountain of Moon Colony #1" Angerdlarnek! She's quite impressive.

RANDY: *Beep.* Even I know not to mess with an anthropomorphic musk ox from any of the moons around Gartosh. Their fighting skill is known throughout the cosmos. *Beep.*

ZELARIOUS ZAN ALON: And Yvonne is the best. She won Miss Bovine Boxer over Lilly Arnaq last cycle in a hard-fought contest. She's a no-frills competitor and I'm curious to see how that plays out in the Tournament of the

Shield of the Colossal Calamari. She's going with no weapon and will rely on her mastery of the pugilistic arts.

RANDY: *Beep.* And her boxing. *Beep.*

ZELARIOUS ZAN ALON: Yvonne versus Reginald the Mega-Troll should be a fascinating and hard-hitting matchup. I can't wait for that one. And the next two fighters will round out the first bracket. A lot of us are anxious for this one as well.

RANDY: *Beep.* Look at this guy! He's rolling out from the holding area. I haven't seen anything like that before. *Beep.*

ZELARIOUS ZAN ALON: Randy, that's Kitar! He's showing off his patented rolling spike attack. His race, from the Olamandrian System, represents one of the few successful porcupinoid races in the entire universe.

RANDY: *Beep.* Why do you think that they have such a problem sustaining a civilization?

ZELARIOUS ZAN ALON: There's been a lot of debate about that, Randy. Most scholars seem to think it has to do with their inability to reproduce without sustaining major puncture wounds.

RANDY: *Boop. Beep.* I seem to do fine reproducing with my massive spike. *Beep.*

ZELARIOUS ZAN ALON: As much as Kitar is a legitimate contender for the Shield, I think most in attendance are more curious about this next entrant—Jungafallow III's mysterious Combatant 2.

RANDY: *Beep.* He sure is taking his time. *Beep.*

ZELARIOUS ZAN ALON: I know. Where are you, Combatant 2? The universe is waiting.

RANDY: *Beep. Boop.* I don't see anyone or any thing. I'm sure the backstage staff isn't happy about him missing his cue. *Beep.*

ZELARIOUS ZAN ALON: Hold up, Randy. I'm getting

an update from backstage. One of the producers is telling me that Combatant 2 is delayed. It looks like we'll have to come back to him. Let's not hold up the broadcast any longer. Who's next? Hey, I recognize that guy.

RANDY: *Beep.* How do you know it's a guy? It looks like a big pile of mush.

ZELARIOUS ZAN ALON: That's because it's Jin-Jin-Jin; he's a Globuloid from Hobunk Alpha. And man, is he going to be a tricky one to beat!

RANDY: *Beep.* Seems a bit soft. *Beep.*

ZELARIOUS ZAN ALON: By design, Randy. It's hard to knock out a Globuloid due to their nebulous form. But they pack a mighty powerful wallop. They've been known to squeeze the life out of prey—and rival mates. It's still a bit of a primitive world on Hobunk Alpha. But it's cycles ahead of Hobunk Beta.

RANDY: *Beep.* I don't think the crowd knows what to think about this guy. *Beep.*

ZELARIOUS ZAN ALON: They'll get a treat watching him duke it out. He trained under the legendary Nin-Jin-Nin, the Grand Victor of Slimo. Slimo, of course, being the primary martial arts discipline of those species lacking a tangible bone structure. The celluloid classes really love them some Slimo.

RANDY: *Beep.* And who does the hunk of gelatin get in round one? *Beep.*

ZELARIOUS ZAN ALON: Have you ever met a Goother Rat?

RANDY: *Beep.* I have not, Zel. *Beep.*

ZELARIOUS ZAN ALON: Consider yourself a lucky little android, because they are diabolical critters from the swamps of Gurlf. And this guy is no different. This is Gha. And that's his stone-tipped flail, the weapon of choice down home in the swamps. I believe he hails from Swamp Blorg in Gurlf, an especially tough marsh. He should feel quite at home with the Psitakki.

RANDY: He has to be our smallest competitor, Zel. *Beep. Boop. Beep.*

ZELARIOUS ZAN ALON: Yes, Randy, but don't let his size fool you. It will be interesting to see if the Goother Rat and the Jungafallowian entry meet at some point in the tournament. You know, there's bad blood there.

RANDY: Why? *Beep.*

ZELARIOUS ZAN ALON: I'm glad you asked. Goother Rats aren't only native to Gurlf. In fact, their lesser-evolved brethren are all over the universe, including Jungafallow III. But the fascinating part is that most astrozoologists believe they originated on Jungafallow III.

RANDY: How did they get to Gurlf? *Boop.*

ZELARIOUS ZAN ALON: The Jungafallowians tried to colonize the insignificant swamp planet we now know as Gurlf, but gave up after they deemed it just too damn disgusting.

RANDY: *Beep.* It has to be nasty for a Jungafallowian to say that. *Beep.*

ZELARIOUS ZAN ALON: Take my word, it's a bubbling ball of gaseous sludge. But a family of Goothers, who were being kept as pets by the landing party, escaped. A few millennia later, they developed speech, written language, quasi-complex social structures, and moderate levels of technology, including space travel up to one hundred light years. Back on Jungafallow III, they're still kept as pets or raised for their pelts.

RANDY: *Beep.* No love lost between these two then, huh, Zel? *Boop.*

ZELARIOUS ZAN ALON: It gets better. About two thousand cycles ago, a Gurlfian priest was blown off course and landed in the Jungafallowian system. When he voyaged back to Gurlf, he shared what he had witnessed to his people. He even brought back one of the lesser-evolved Goother Rats.

RANDY: *Beep.* What happened?

ZELARIOUS ZAN ALON: Immediately, five of the planet's religions toppled. The ruling parties demanded an invasion of Jungafallow to rescue their proto-cousins. But cooler heads eventually prevailed.

RANDY: *Beep.* Sounds like a Gurlfian probably won't be inviting a Jungafallowian to his birthday party anytime soon. *Beep.*

ZELARIOUS ZAN ALON: I think you're right, Randy. But let's not lose sight of Gha. He's a particularly angry and violent Goother. He medaled in four straight Gurlfian marsh-hopping events, but shunned the endorsements and a lifetime of celebrity in order to see the universe. Well, the nearest one hundred light years, at least. But, as it is with many space travelers, he grew bored and decided to enter the glamorous world of underground cage fighting. His success earned him a spot in this tournament.

RANDY: *Beep.* That's an impressive rat. *Boop.* And he seems pretty skilled with that twirly thing. *Beep.*

ZELARIOUS ZAN ALON: Yes, the rock-tipped flail or, as the Gurlfians call it, rock-on-the-end-of-a-rope-attached-to-a-pole.

RANDY: *Beep.* A creative bunch, no doubt. *Boop.*

ZELARIOUS ZAN ALON: We've spent so much time on Gha, we have two more coming out now. These two will be battling in round one, and I for one can't wait. Almost at his pedestal is Jorb of Karr.

RANDY: He looks like a giant sludge monster. *Beep. Beep.*

ZELARIOUS ZAN ALON: ...that spits acid, Randy. A giant sludge monster that spits acid. Not much is known about these creatures. No gender. Just that they are made of sludge and spit acid. He has a bit more structure than Jin-Jin-Jin, the Globuloid, but he's also a lot more sedentary. If he can connect with that green saliva, it's game over.

Randy: *Beep. Boop.* What about his opponent? He seems to have the fans jazzed up! *Beep.*

Zelarious Zan Alon: Oh yes, our only contestant that flies. It's a real treat to have him here. That's Glux Xyphormog II—a royal guardsmen of the Queen Mother of Planet F.

Randy: The Mother F'er? *Beep.*

Zelarious Zan Alon: As you can see, Planet F is home to a dominant insectoid species. We have millions of those in the galaxy, but the F'ers are regarded as the most honorable and chivalrous in their sector. Glux splits his time between training in combat, protecting the royal Queen Mother, and helping sire her legions of offspring.

Randy: *Beep.* My kind of gig, Zel. *Beep.*

Zelarious Zan Alon: Not only can Glux whizz past you with his aerial attacks, he's also an elite-level master with the signature weapon of the royal guard, the two-sided halberd. It's a deadly tool. But in round one, he will have to find a way to avoid that toxic drool of Jorb.

Randy: Oh, Zel. *Beep.* I forgot about this guy! I know him. *Beep.* That's the Grand Blademaster of Gyork! *Beep.*

Zelarious Zan Alon: You've done your homework, Randy. You are absolutely correct. The Grand Blademaster of Gyork is a swordsman like no other.

Randy: *Beep.* Yeah, it looks like he's made of sword parts. *Beep.*

Zelarious Zan Alon: When a Gyorkian wins the title of Grand Blademaster, not only does he have to forego his given name to become referred to as the Grand Blademaster of Gyork, but he also has to embed bits and pieces of swords into his skin surgically. He's a walking armory.

Randy: *Beep.* How does he... you know? *Beep.*

Zelarious Zan Alon: Let's just say that when you earn the designation of Grand Blademaster of Gyork, you take an involuntary vow of celibacy.

Randy: Ouch. *Boop.*

Zelarious Zan Alon: Exactly the point.

Randy: *Beep.* Good one, Zel. *Boop.*

Zelarious Zan Alon: What? Oh, Randy. Get your head out of the gutter. But, unlike the porcupinoids of the Olamandrian System, only a chosen few have this issue— not the entire race. So, the race has a chance to make it.

Randy: *Beep.* I think he's my new pick to win this entire tournament. *Beep.* Give me the Grand Blademaster of Gyork. Who does he fight in round one?

Zelarious Zan Alon: Get ready for the answer to that very question, Randy. This place is about to go crazy!

Randy: Who? Who is it? *Beep. Boop.*

Zelarious Zan Alon: Listen to that music. He's the only one with custom entrance theme music. And look at those lasers. This is quite a show.

Randy: Is it... *Beep* ...is it?

Zelarious Zan Alon: Yes, here he is, ladies and gentlemen! But mostly ladies. The Universe's Favorite Bounty Hunter, Maxx Gemstarr!

Randy: *Beep.* I change my mind, Zel! I change my mind! *Boop.* Maxx is my pick. Not the Gyorkian. Maxx is my guy! *Beep.*

Zelarious Zan Alon: Calm down, Randy. Calm down. Maxx is quite the specimen. Not only does he have super strength, but he's as cunning a competitor as you'll see. One strike from Maxx's power gauntlets and you're going to be down for the count.

Randy: *Beep.* I haven't heard this many females swoon since I posed in the Mister Nuts and Bolts Calendar last year. *Beep.*

Zelarious Zan Alon: They do love him. And he loves them. He knows how to put on a show. And look at this! He's walking down the aisle and shaking the other competitors' hands—or whatever they have resembling hands. This guy here is classy, Randy. We all could learn a few things from him.

Randy: *Beep.* If I was running from the law and he was after me, I would just give up. *Beep.*

Zelarious Zan Alon: Many do! Oh, hold the phone, we have an update. We have the final pairing about to come out—one of them is the hometown favorite, Gjrazzel. And afterwards, Combatant 2 will come out and greet the crowd. Seems that he was running a bit late.

Randy: This next guy intrigues me, Zel. *Beep.*

Zelarious Zan Alon: And why is that?

Randy: He won the melee match, right? *Boop. Beep.*

Zelarious Zan Alon: That's correct.

Randy: It was a pretty lucky win if you ask me. *Beep.*

Zelarious Zan Alon: He did have some good fortune on his side, thanks to an explosively suicidal Blop.

Randy: Can he have the same type of luck against Gjrazzel? *Beep.*

Zelarious Zan Alon: We will have to wait and see— but I know one thing: he will not have the crowd support. Listen to these boos and hisses greeting Duke LaGreen, a bounty hunter. Hold up, something from backstage. Yes. Yes. Sorry, ladies and gentlemen, it's Duke La*Grange*, a bounty hunter.

Randy: *Beep.* Where's he from, Zel? He looks like another Earther. *Beep. Beep.*

Zelarious Zan Alon: Actually, he's from Nova

Texas. It was once an Earth colony but gained independence many cycles ago.

Randy: I know it, Zel. *Beep*. They have a great planetary anthem. *Boop*. What are Duke's chances?

Zelarious Zan Alon: He's definitely the underdog in the field. Apparently, he's well known in bounty hunter circles, but I can't say that I know much about him.

Randy: He's no Maxx Gemstarr, that's for sure. *Boop*.

Zelarious Zan Alon: No one is, Randy. I'm not sure what this Duke LaGrange is good at, but maybe that can be an advantage up against the hometown hero, Gjrazzel.

Randy: *Beep*. Duke's having a little trouble getting up on the pedestal, Zel. *Beep*. He looks hungover. *Beep*.

Zelarious Zan Alon: I doubt he would drink before a battle with the likes of Gjrazzel. But if anyone can recognize a drunk shaking off the cobwebs after a particularly rowdy night of the drink, it's you, Randy.

Randy: *Beep*. You're too nice, Zel. *Beep*.

Zelarious Zan Alon: Speaking of Gjrazzel, it looks like he's about to enter the arena. To our viewers at home, Randy and I are going to stop talking for a moment for you to be able to soak in the spectacle that we are about to witness. Thousands upon thousands of fans—mostly Psitakki—are going to go absolutely crazy for this fighter. He's a descendent of the first champion and savior of his planet, Grozzel, and one of the most feared combatants in this part of the universe. I give you... Gjrazzel!

[BROADCAST FIZZLES. BLACK SCREEN. DEAD AIR. BROADCAST RETURNS.]

Zelarious Zan Alon: Oh my gods! What is going on? We need help now!

Randy: *Beep*. I think Gjrazzel may be dead! *Beep*.

Zelarious Zan Alon: He was just thrown out of the waiting room as though he was a tenth of his size. He's not moving! He's not moving!

Randy: Zel, look! *Beep. Beep.*

Zelarious Zan Alon: That has to be... No... It can't be...

Randy: *Beep. Boop.* Is that— *Beep.*

Zelarious Zan Alon: That has to be Combatant 2. Yes, it is! Look who's next to him—Prince Korzo-Tapor. I've never seen anything like him.

Randy: He's bigger than the Mega-Troll! *Boop.*

Zelarious Zan Alon: He's exactly that. A Mega-Troll-sized Jungafallowian. He has to be an experiment gone wrong. The crowd is throwing objects into the arena. I wouldn't advise that. Some of the other competitors are surrounding him. Keeping him at bay. The medical staff are tending to Gjrazzel. It doesn't look good, friends. I'm speechless.

Randy: How can anyone stop this monster? *Beep.* Will Gjrazzel be able to compete? *Boop.*

Zelarious Zan Alon: All great questions, Randy. And you'll have to tune in tonight to find out. The one hundredth and final Tournament of the Shield of the Colossal Calamari begins in a few hours! Don't miss it. The madness! The carnage! We need reinforcements!

[BROADCAST FADES TO BLACK.]

CHAPTER 14

A FEISTY CORNER MAN

"THIS ISN'T FAIR! DISQUALIFY THAT overgrown bastard," shouted a short Psitakki built like a brick house as he charged through a door in the back-stage area. Duke assumed this was Gjrazzel's corner man.

"What just happened?" screamed the broadcast's producer as he steamrolled his way into the gathering. "That brute ruined my show. Exalted Grand Shaman, I expect you to do what needs to be done."

"Yeah," began the stout corner man, "disqualify him! Execute him if you have to. He deserves a date with the Chief Interrogator General at the very least."

"And what of Gjrazzel?" asked Grand Shaman Klorzzel calmly.

"He advances, of course," replied the corner man as if there were no other correct answer.

"I meant how is he doing?" explained the Grand Shaman.

"Oh, he'll live," responded the irate corner man. "I think so, at least. But he should advance, regardless."

"Hey, wait a minute, guys," interjected Duke. "Why am

I being punished for what this two-headed oaf did to the kid?"

"I don't have any time for you," snorted Gjrazzel's trainer. "Consider yourself lucky that you don't have to fight Gjrazzel. You should gladly do the right thing and let him advance. It's the only way you would survive this thing anyways."

"Maybe. Or maybe I might just win the entire thing," Duke boasted.

All eyes rested on the Nova Texan. *They don't think I'm serious*, he thought.

The corner man started to laugh. It was a deep, visceral laugh that almost took him off his feet.

"Now now," the Shaman stepped in, "I appreciate confidence in a fighter. This one here—"

"Duke LaGrange."

"Yes, Duke LaGrange has confidence. I will give him that."

"But he obviously lacks smarts," added the diminutive cephalopodan. "Do the right thing, human."

"Or what, short stack? What are you doing to do?"

The corner man's face lit up with rage. His fists clenched and his teeth ground together audibly. He lunged at the bounty hunter but his progress was quickly impeded by the Shaman's staff. The corner man halted his attack immediately.

"Lower your weapons," the Shaman said, pointing his staff at Duke and Ishiro'shea. "No need for that now."

"Can we get back to what's actually important?" yelled the producer. "I'm broadcasting this garbage to half the universe and I don't even know what's going or *when* it's going on. I don't like surprises in my programming schedule. This tournament is our big bet ratings-wise, and now I don't even know if we have a full slate. If I get fired over this, Shaman—"

"Calm down," said Prince Korzo-Tapor, emerging from behind the Shaman. "You should be thanking us."

"I'm glad you came, Prince," said the Shaman.

Korzo-Tapor bowed.

"What do you mean I should be thanking you?" the producer protested. "You ruined my show. Maybe my career."

"Check the early ratings."

The producer pulled out a device from his belt. He input a few codes and a holographic image materialized over the instrument. He turned his back and walked a few paces away from the group. After a few moments, he turned back to the gathering, his eyes wide and the corners of his mouth turned up.

"You see," began the prince. "Controversy creates cash. Or in this case, ratings. And ratings create cash. You're welcome."

"We have a show to shoot. I'll get everyone ready. We're on in a few."

The producer ran out of the room, shouting, "Places, places, places!" to anyone in earshot.

"You're lucky the Shaman's here," said the corner man, "otherwise I would tear you apart, Jungafallowian."

"There will be time for that later," said the prince, "but, I will admit, you might have to get through my friend first. He's resting after his difficult scuffle with your man, Gjrazzel." He chuckled. "Who am I kidding? He didn't even break a sweat with your pathetic excuse of a champion."

The enraged Psitakki's muscles twitched and pulsated. He charged again. The Shaman once again prevented him from carrying through with his attack—however, this time, the Shaman's staff landed across the corner man's face. He hit the ground with a muted thud. As he scuttled to his feet, two of the Shaman's personal guards appeared and apprehended the feisty corner man. Korzo-Tapor's smirk only seemed to anger him more as he struggled to free himself from the grip of the two guards.

"I will not tolerate this," proclaimed the Shaman. "The final Tournament of the Shield of the Colossal Calamari will not be defamed by this behavior. Nor will it be derailed by the actions of Combatant 2."

"But honorable Grand Shaman—" the prince began, but he was silenced by the tip of the Shaman's staff.

"I'm disgusted by what I'm about to say," he began, "but I will not alter the rules or bylaws of this sacred competition, despite some of its participants doing their best to do so. What occurs outside of the tournament's bracket—be it in a bar or in the Grand Entrance—will not affect the competition itself. It is my final decision to allow Combatant 2 to compete as scheduled. As for Gjrazzel, if he can continue, he will face Duke LaGrange tonight at their scheduled time. If he cannot compete—and based on these injuries, I assume that to be the case—the Nova Texan will advance in the tournament."

"Unbelievable," barked the corner man. "You should be ashamed. How can you call yourself a Psitakki? Grozzel is turning over in his grave." He spit at the feet of the Grand Shaman.

Without even a gesture from the Shaman, the guards hauled the corner man away.

The prince bowed towards the Grand Shaman and began to walk away.

"Jungafallowian," shouted the Grand Shaman, "I won't be as lenient on you and your fighter if you push the limits again. This is your final warning."

"To a fair and entertaining event," said Prince Korzo-Tapor, bowing repeatedly.

As the Jungafallowian walked past Duke and Ishiro'shea, he paused. Both of his heads were so close to the bounty hunters that Duke could make out the markings on each individual scale of the royal reptiloid.

"Look at you, Duke. Seems like we did you a favor as well. You can thank me later."

"I don't want your help."

"Maybe not. But you *need* it. I'm sure we will run into each other again. Good luck."

CHAPTER 15

THE SNAKE AND THE MUTANT IRISHMAN

S TILL HUNGOVER FROM HIS NIGHT out at the Pondscum Tavern, Duke stretched out on the floor of the pre-fight holding room to try and sleep off the lingering headache. He couldn't help but dwell on his predicament. He wasn't unhappy about the possibility of advancing without a fight, but he also knew that the crowd wasn't going to be kind to whomever was on the receiving end of such good fortune. It was especially worrisome that his good fortune was the direct result of the bad fortune suffered by their home world's favorite son. And what if Gjrazzel tried to fight? The bouts had been moved around so that they were now last on the schedule; maybe they thought the extra time would be enough for Gjrazzel to heal.

He couldn't get comfortable enough to rest. His mind was racing with an eclectic menagerie of memories. The moment he closed his eyes, images of Mazilda and Maxx crept in, followed by the prince and the behemoth Jungafallowian, and snippets of the other combatants in the tournament. *How many different ways could I die at the hands of these crazies?* He kept going back to Mazilda and trying to figure out what she saw in Maxx. The Chief Interrogator

General. The Grand Shaman. The annoying producer and the hotheaded corner man. The bartender who was confident that Duke wouldn't make it out of the tournament alive. The Four I's surrounding Joe's. They all peeked into Duke's mind as he tried to relax.

"Hey Ish, turn on the view screen when you can. I think the fights are starting. If I can't sleep, I might as well scout my competition."

The ninja turned on the monitor. The broadcast was just getting underway.

"That Randy guy is great," laughed Duke.

Ishiro'shea nodded in agreement.

The opening bout of the tournament pitted the Earth representative, Seamus "Potato Lips" O'Hoolihan of New Tokyo, Ireland, against Tor-torta of Krawn.

"Man, we really need to talk to O'Hoolihan," Duke said to Ishiro'shea. "Let's hope this snake guy doesn't burn him to a crisp."

The two beings made their way to the center of the arena as they were introduced to rousing ovations. The Psitakki referee appeared to be giving them the rules and then backed away. The bellowing howl of a ceremonial horn signaled the start of the altercation and the official start to the tournament.

Tor-torta slithered back on his tail and pressed his chest down to the arena floor. He tried to get as much distance between him and O'Hoolihan's dreaded shillelagh. The Irish mutant twirled the club around but didn't charge. Tor-torta encircled O'Hoolihan and then lunged with a fang-first strike. The serpent's bite narrowly missed O'Hoolihan and forced him to stumble backwards awkwardly. As the Irishman fell, the Krawn native rose high on his tail and came down hard, leading with his spike-covered forearm. Seamus moved and countered with a glancing shillelagh strike to the back of the head. Tor-torta rolled a few paces but seemed uninjured.

The two danced and bobbed and weaved for some time. O'Hoolihan consistently tried to stay clear of Tor-torta's head—not only could he tear large chunks of flesh out with a single chomp, he had the ability to breath fire. One direct hit and Seamus would be done. *Well* done.

The slowly developing chess match between the two fighters suddenly turned into a slight advantage for Tor-torta when he tripped O'Hoolihan with his tail. He let loose a fireball that narrowly missed the Irishman but managed to dislodge his shillelagh, which fell to the arena floor engulfed in flames. The Krawnee wasted no time and pounced on his fallen opponent. His muscular tail wrapped around the waist and legs of the Irish gang thug and pinned him to the ground. He punched and clawed but Tor-torta showed no signs of stress. O'Hoolihan reached into his vest pocket and pulled out a knife. He stabbed Tor-torta—which got the serpent warrior's attention—but the action wasn't damaging enough for Tor-torta to release his grasp. He tightened his grip and Seamus flailed to the ground. Tor-torta removed the knife and tossed it aside. He gestured to the crowd; they responded with cheers, signaling their approval of the impending death blow.

The injured Earth mutant reached into his vest again. He threw out a chain, some brass knuckles, a pair of dice, and some other items that weren't distinguishable on the broadcast. They all piled up next to the shillelagh, now almost entirely covered in Tor-torta's flame. A tiny flask also spilled to the floor. Duke recognized that immediately. Seamus grabbed the vessel and downed the contents.

To make this less painful, thought Duke.

O'Hoolihan smashed the empty flask into a collection of sharp shards. He started to stab his captor's tail over and over. Tor-torta noticed this and prepared for his final death strike. The frill from his shoulders to the top of his head expanded, showcasing an imposing display. His mouth widened and he thrust his torso towards the Irishman still pinned against the arena floor.

As Tor-torta attacked, O'Hoolihan grabbed the fiery shillelagh and blew a mouthful of whisky onto the club. The fireball that emerged from the stick engulfed Tor-torta's face and upper body instantaneously. He released his vice grip on O'Hoolihan and squirmed around the arena floor, screaming in a high-pitched shrill. His pain was reflected on the faces of all in attendance. He was blinded and burning alive. In his chaotic scramble, he inched close to O'Hoolihan. The Irishman struck hard with the shillelagh, smacking Tor-torta's face. The serpent collapsed to the floor. Medics ran to the Krawnee and doused him with water to extinguish the flames. After a few moments, it was apparent that Tor-torta was closer to death than he was to continuing in the tournament.

The referee raised the hand of Potato Lips. The riotous crowd shook the arena with their passionate screams and chaotic gyrations. It was clear that the fans loved the extreme violence. The bar for such violence had been set high following the quick-thinking carnage of the Irish gang member.

Duke turned and locked eyes with his partner.

"What did I get myself into, Ish?"

CHAPTER 16

RECORDS ARE MADE TO BE BROKEN

DUKE AND ISHIRO'SHEA WATCHED THE other first round battles from the confines of their holding room. Each was more savage and unbridled as the one before. In the opposite side of the bracket, they witnessed the femme fatale, Sulaw, overpower and outsmart the devious four-armed Zylantian pirate, Not Very Good at Math. True to his chauvinistic nature, the Zylantian would not acknowledge that the Hiritai was the more powerful and skilled competitor and in the end he paid for it. However, Not Very Good at Math escaped with only two broken arms; had Sulaw given in to her hate-fueled desire, he would have been crushed unmercifully.

The third contest pitted Yvonne "The Furry Mountain of Moon Colony #1" Angerdlarnek against Reginald, the Mega-Troll from the Silver Mountains of Mrelock. Duke and Ishiro'shea were worried for their Gartoshian friend; Reginald stood taller than any combatant in the field, save for the Jungafallowian entry. On numerous occasions at the Pondscum Tavern they had heard, or rather overheard, about Yvonne's fighting aptitude. She was a definite favorite, but it was hard to overlook the behemoth brute that stood opposite her in the arena, swinging a massive steel mace.

Size does matter occasionally, thought Duke.

When the ceremonial horn sounded, Reginald tossed aside his mace and rampaged weaponless towards the musk ox.

Yvonne has the brains advantage, concluded the bounty hunter.

The Gartoshian hadn't brought a weapon into the arena, relying solely on her boxing abilities. But how would fisticuffs fare against an ogre four times her size—no matter how skilled the puncher? As Reginald rumbled toward her, Yvonne sidestepped the Mrelockian. Due to his massive size, his momentum drove him into the arena wall with a crash. He turned and sat up, resting his back against the barricade. It was obvious that he was dazed. Yvonne pounced, leaping to his midsection and unleashing a furious barrage of rights, lefts, and uppercuts. Blood flew from the Mega-Troll's lips and nose, splattering plasma across a section of spectators. They loved it. Reginald swiped his left arm, lifting Yvonne into the air, then planted her a quarter of the way across the arena floor. That single blow would have killed most sentient species, but Yvonne regained her composure and prepared for another attack. Reginald and Yvonne locked eyes and the Mega-Troll charged again. This time Yvonne didn't wait around. She picked up speed and headed on a direct collision course with the beast.

What is she thinking? She'd have a better chance surviving a headlong crash into a dwarf planet.

Reginald let out a primal yell as he closed the gap between himself and Yvonne. At the last moment before contact, Yvonne leapt into the air, leading with her horns. Just as Duke had seen—or rather, heard—Lilly crack the sternum of a Jungafallowian back at Cyborg Joe's a few months back, he witnessed the awesome power of a Gartoshian musk ox. Yvonne blasted Reginald square in the nose with her cranium-first attack. She fell back to the ground. Reginald collapsed with an elongated moan. He was knocked out. Yvonne showed no signs of movement either.

Slowly, she lifted her hand. The crowd, noticing her efforts, began to cheer and scream for her to get to her feet. The Psitakki referee had already ruled Reginald out of the contest, it was now just a matter of whether Yvonne would advance—or no one would. The referee surveyed the injured boxer intently. Some members of the crowd chanted "Y-vonne," some chanted "Fur-ry-Mount-ain," others screamed "Go Musk Ox, Go"—it came out a garbled mess, but it seemed as though Yvonne appreciated the support. She raised herself onto all fours and tried to stand. She wavered and fell back down. She tried again. She winced as she strained to muster the strength to stand. Her balance wavered but, finally, she made it upright. The referee signaled for the horn and raised Yvonne's hand in victory.

"Ish, I think she deserves a drink after that one," said Duke. "Who goes head-to-head with a Mega-Troll... and wins? I do hope she heals quickly."

Ishiro'shea nodded in agreement.

The next two quarterfinal matches were no less intense in their dangerous dance of devastation. Glux Xyphormog II, a Royal Guardsman of the queen of Planet F, used his ability to fly to give him an advantage over Jorb, the sludge monster of Karr. Though Jorb had the edge in strength and a noteworthy special ability—spitting deadly acid at his opponent—it was Glux's quick thinking and aerial acrobatics that allowed him to prevail over the bipedal mound of waste. Jorb managed to dissolve the midsection of the insectoid's double-sided halberd, but he couldn't quite connect with his projectile saliva when the guardsman took to the air. In fact, Jorb's poor aim forced many spectators to evacuate; syrupy lumps of corrosive phlegm went astray and landed in the seats. It was an attempt to bring down Glux as he flew directly overhead that led to Jorb's demise. His acidic spew missed the insectoid and came splashing down on his own face. Jorb, writhing in agony at the pain caused by his own venom, screamed his submission and was escorted from the tournament immediately.

In the longest bout of the opening round, Gha, the Gurlfian Goother Rat, met up with Jin-Jin-Jin, the Globuloid from Hobunk Alpha. Gha's flail did little damage to the surprisingly quick-moving mound of shapeless goo. Conversely, Jin-Jin-Jin's attempts to capture and squeeze the fleet-footed rodent into a premature death were futile. The match was so heated and hotly contested that it spilled out of the arena and into the locker room. The brawlers knocked down lockers and reporters and anything else that got in their way. The producer's legion of cameras caught every moment of the heart-stopping contest. It raged on, leaving the back room and heading out into the streets and exhibition area. The pair battled through concessions stands, kiosks selling memorabilia commemorating the event, and sponsors' booths hyping the latest and greatest in their respective industries. It was in one of the sponsors' stalls that the duel reached its dramatic conclusion. Jin-Jin-Jin managed to catch Gha in his nebulous clutches after the Gurlfian slipped on a puddle of nacho cheese sauce. He hurled Gha over a Psitakki military recruitment table, passed a stand stocked with souvenir shields, and into the side of one of the Willie's World of Galactic Winnebagos showroom floor models. The collision rocked the massive vehicle and almost tipped it over. Gha retreated into the Winnebago, seemingly to collect his thoughts and reevaluate his strategy against the fighter from Hobunk Alpha. Jin-Jin-Jin followed. The exact details of what happened next were known only to the two competitors. Inside a Winnebago in the exhibit hall adjacent to the arena had not been on the producer's list of areas to station a camera. After some shaking within the automobile, Gha emerged, raising his hand in victory. The Psitakki referee entered the vehicle and, after some moments surveying, returned and declared the Goother Rat the victor. The violent thuds and thumps coming from the vehicle's septic receptacle laid to rest any concerns that the claims of the flushing prowess of Willie's World of Galactic Winnebagos were anything less than one hundred percent accurate.

It had to be the tournament's first ever victory by flushing, thought Duke.

Duke turned from the screen to catch a glimpse of the producer hurrying by his room. The bounty hunter shot his head out of the door. "Hey!" he screamed.

The producer stopped in his tracks, turned around, and sent a menacing gaze towards Duke.

"What, Mr. LaGrange?" he barked.

"It's almost time for my match. Any updates on my opponent?"

The Psitakki didn't answer. He threw his hands in the air and scurried off, presumably to do something more important. Duke heard a faint mumbling about Winnebagos as the producer stormed away.

"Looks like we still don't know if I have to actually fight anyone tonight," complained Duke. "Ish, who's up next?"

Ishiro'shea made a face that could only mean one thing. *Maxx Gemstarr.*

The crowd was still restless after the last match had ended up leaving the actual arena. Given the prices that tickets fetched, the vibe in the arena was trending towards disappointment. Then the festering malaise simply stopped. Dead in its tracks, it stopped. Wonder, excitement, and unadulterated joy regained control over the collective in mere seconds.

That damn music. I hate that damn music. And those lasers.

There was no denying that Gemstarr knew how to make an entrance. He was a showman. Duke would argue that he wasn't much of an actual bounty hunter in practice, but he was great at marketing himself.

The crowd was rocking. The entire building felt as if it was moving off its foundation and rolling along the Psitakki countryside. Maxx ate it up. He motioned to each part of the arena, elevating the volume of their cheers to a fever pitch. He made victorious gestures, flexed his impressive muscles, and pointed to his power gauntlets. Each carefully planned movement received a bigger ovation than the one before. Duke was disgusted.

The Grand Blademaster of Gyork was shocked when he stepped out in front of the audience and was pelted with a loud chorus of boos and derogatory chants. He seemed visibly rattled by the reception. The swordsman flashed the two steel blades surgically implanted to the top of his hand, and started to taunt the crowd. They screamed louder and louder. He then drew his two shining broadswords from each thigh and raised them above his head. The two sets of blades, one set in his hands and the other *in* his hands, formed an "L" at the end of each arm. In response to this impressive display, trash and bottles rained down on the Gyorkian. Most ricocheted off without any damage, but a tub of piping hot nachos landed square on his face. Duke wondered if it was from the same batch that almost cost the Goother Rat his bout against Jin-Jin-Jin. The crowd broke into laughter as the Blademaster dropped his swords and stumbled about in panic.

The horns sounded and the match officially began. Maxx Gemstarr leapt in front of the Gyorkian and connected squarely with his power gauntlet to the swordsman's chest. He flew back across the arena and crashed into the retaining wall. Even before the referee could call the match in favor of Maxx, he was celebrating in the first row celebrity boxes, shaking hands and posing for photographs.

The loudspeaker rang out: "Maxx Gemstarr has just set a new tournament record for the quickest victory—ten seconds."

Maxx's iconic theme music filled the arena as what seemed like the entire planet cheered uncontrollably.

I really hate that guy.

Maxx's music halted suddenly. A familiar voice echoed throughout.

"Who gave that guy a mic?" Duke asked his ninja friend.

"Congratulations, Maxx Gemstarr," Prince Korzo-Tapor shouted to all those in the arena. "Impressive indeed. A new record, I hear. However, my friend, records are made to be broken, even brand new ones. And I guarantee that we will break this record. Now."

The audience was trying to digest both the interruption by the Jungafallowian prince and his bold claim.

"Ten seconds," he began, "is quite jaw-dropping. But eight seconds is even more magnificent. Am I right? My Combatant 2 will accomplish this feat against our opponent, or..."

"Or what?" shouted Maxx Gemstarr from the front row.

"Ah, Mr. Gemstarr, if we fail, we will forfeit."

The buzz in the stands was deafening. No one knew what to make of the enigmatic royal.

Combatant 2 stomped in to thunderous boos. His position as the most hated entity on Psitakki had been all but settled when he had taken out Gjrazzel during the Grand Entrance. Now, it appeared he was trying to become the most hated entity in the entire universe by upstaging Maxx Gemstarr.

"Of course, the bet is off if our opponent doesn't show," the devious prince stated. "I haven't seen the Olamandrian weakling since my friend here laid waste to that worthless squid."

An avalanche of refuse spilled down on the massive Jungafallowian. He didn't even notice it.

"You simpletons are putting up a better fight than our original opponent would have anyways," the prince continued. "Is that the best you got? Trash? Garbage? I guess it's befitting of Psitakki. Nothing but a bunch of swamp-dwelling pieces of trash."

The crowd erupted as Kitar busted through a holding cell door and charged directly at Combatant 2. He was coiled, with his spikes exposed, and rolling at breakneck speed towards the two-headed brute. The horn sounded as he approached the Jungafallowian and catapulted his spinning body—a living saw blade. Combatant 2 threw out his right hand and connected with the Olamandrian's body. Kitar collapsed and fell limp, sprawled out on the arena floor at the gargantuan creature's feet. The referee signaled the end of the round.

"Ladies and gentlemen, we have a new tournament record. Combatant 2 has defeated Kitar in six seconds."

The crowd was stunned. Not a single murmur could be heard amidst the thousands in attendance.

"Like I said, records are made to be broken," Korzo-

Tapor began. "Except this new one, maybe." He walked over to Kitar and kicked his paralyzed body. "Get this off of our arena floor."

Three referees ran over to drag the Olamandrian away.

"Your new champion. Fear him. Marvel at him. Worship him. He will not be stopped!" Korzo-Tapor's maniacal laugh permeated throughout the stadium. When it stopped there was an eerie silence. Nobody in the audience could argue with what they had just witnessed.

Duke looked at Ishiro'shea.

"How are we going to beat that thing? How's *anyone* going to beat that thing?"

The ninja shrugged.

Well, shit.

CHAPTER 17

FIGHT OR FUNERAL

"YOU'RE UP NEXT, LAGRANGE," SHOUTED the producer.

"So, wait. I'm fighting? Gjrazzel's recovered?"

"Sure, I guess. Probably. I'm just shooting whatever happens out there, so if it's a fight or a funeral, it's going to be broadcast across the universe," the Psitakki snarked. "A funeral would be sure to mix it up a bit."

"How respectful."

"Just be ready. When your name is called, follow this lighted pathway to the stadium entrance. When the big door opens..."

"Let me guess. Walk through it."

"I forgot that I'm dealing with a certified genius," jabbed the producer. "And you over there?"

Ishiro'shea did not acknowledge the Psitakki's finger pointed in his direction.

"What about Ishiro?"

"He's your corner man, right?"

"Yep."

"Right outside the door, there are a few steps that lead to a platform. He can watch the fight from there and throw in the towel if needed."

"That won't be necessary."

"You're right, you'll probably just die."

Duke wanted to respond with a witty line, but his mind was entirely blank.

The producer huffed. "Lights. Path. Door. Fight."

"Got it," Duke replied.

"And, for the love of the Colossal Calamari, try and do something that's interesting. You won't have a flammable Blop to save you this time around."

The producer stormed off, barking orders at any being he passed until he disappeared into the depths of the stadium catacombs.

The bounty hunter turned to Ishiro'shea. "Gotta give credit to Gjrazzel. He's a tough bastard to try and fight after what that Jungafallowian did to him." Duke paused. "So, any plans spring to mind? I probably should have a strategy going into this thing. To be honest, Ish, I sorta didn't think Gjrazzel would bounce back so quickly."

Ishiro'shea pondered.

"If I win, who do we fight next?"

Ishiro'shea flapped his arms, simulating wings.

"Ah, the bug. Great. A stick-twirling squid, then a giant bee-man with a double-sided halberd. Did I mention how much I hate this tournament?"

The crowd had been silent following the massacre caused by Prince Korzo-Tapor's Combatant 2. Now they began to collect themselves and isolated cheers began to swell from the arena. In short order, it was clear that they were ready for the next and final fight of the evening. Most importantly, they were ready to see if their local hero had recovered enough to wage mortal war against the long-shot melee winner for the honor of Psitakki.

The cries of "Gjrazzel" rang out. The speaker crackled

and a booming voice proclaimed, "First combatant in our final fight, from Nova Texas, Duke LaGrog, a bounty hunter."

"It's LaGrange!" Duke screamed as he walked out to the loudest jeers of the tournament. "How hard is that to remember? LaGrange! You get Glux Xyphormog's name right every time. C'mon!"

Debris fell from the rafters to line the arena floor. Duke ducked and swerved to avoid being struck by stray bottles or bricks.

The announcer began again. "And now, from right here on Psitakki, our grand champion and a direct descendant of Grozzel the Great, the master of the tarzantia tree staff, our hero, our hope, the greatest being in the universe, Gjrazzel!"

The collective adulation was almost sonic; Duke had to focus to keep his balance as the decibel level reached a point that would burst many an eardrum. Gjrazzel did not make his way out.

The crowd grew louder. And louder. Then it started to subside, turning to a hopeless clamor that verged on becoming entirely pitiful. Emerging from the dark, limping noticeably, was the brave Psitakki champion. His tarzantia staff was being used as a crutch. His head and left eye were bandaged. A brace covered his back and waist; he was barely able to move. But he approached Duke with an unwavering determination. *He's going to try and fight*, realized the Nova Texan. *He's actually going to try and fight. Holy hedgehogs.*

The referee met the two combatants in the center of the arena. He looked over Gjrazzel. Then Duke.

He's going to let us fight. This officiating bastard is going to let this half-dead guy fight.

"You probably know the rules," the referee began, "but, just in case, there aren't really any rules outside of no guns or projectiles. Or magic." He locked eyes with Duke. "No guns, okay? No matter how bad it's going. Just give up if you are getting beat to a pulp. Do not use a gun."

"I got it," snapped Duke.

"I know how you Earthers like to use guns," the referee continued.

"I'm not from Earth. I'm from Nova Texas. Do you not listen to the damn introductions?"

"I want a clean fight. No, I just want an exciting fight. So go crazy."

Duke turned his attention to Gjrazzel. He had to be heavily medicated; his eyes were glassy and vacant, a sliver of drool dripped from the right corner of his mouth and off one of his upper lip tentacles.

"Man, you don't have to do this," Duke pleaded. "You're in no condition to fight."

Gjrazzel just grumbled a particularly gurgly grumble.

"Seriously, it's not your fault. You're going to get your-self killed."

"Am I?" Gjrazzel replied softly. "Or is it you, Duke LaGrand, that's going to get killed?"

Why is this so confusing?

"It's LaGrange," he said in a defeated tone. As the last syllable passed Duke's lips, Gjrazzel hoisted himself into the air, supported by his tarzantia tree staff, and struck the bounty hunter with a left thrust kick to the upper chest. Duke stumbled back and fell to one knee.

The horn sounded.

Gjrazzel hopped towards him and repeated the same maneuver. The second kick knocked Duke to the arena floor. A third sent him crashing into the perimeter wall, where he crumpled to his backside.

"Whoa, there, Gjrazzel," Duke yelled. "I'm not going to fight you. You can barely walk."

"Then this makes your current predicament even more embarrassing."

Duke didn't disagree. Nor did the fans. Their hurrahs turned into laughter.

As Duke got to his feet, Gjrazzel approached and, for a fourth time, catapulted himself in the air. However, instead of kicking the bounty hunter, he wrapped his legs around Duke's neck. He tightened his grip. Duke struggled. Gasps of air were becoming increasingly difficult to obtain. His vision grew blurry.

Duke heard a voice. A female voice. It was telling him to hold on. It was then yelling Ishiro'shea's name. And Ol' Betsy's name. This struck Duke as odd. He always envisioned that the last words that he heard would be female but they wouldn't be screaming at Ishiro'shea and his gun. He opened his eyes and he saw Mazilda shouting something at Ishiro'shea.

She wants him to shoot Gjrazzel, Duke thought.

"No," the bounty hunter screamed in a muffled and indistinguishable bellow.

Ishiro'shea locked eyes with the bounty hunter and threw Ol' Betsy at him. It was a perfect toss. Duke caught it by the barrel and swung it at the tarzantia tree staff. It fell to the ground, along with its owner. Gjrazzel released his legs from Duke's throat. Duke choked as he tried to regain normal breathing.

Gjrazzel slowly made his way to his feet and picked up the staff. He swung it wildly, but Duke ducked and it crashed into the perimeter wall. By reflex alone, Duke stabbed the butt end of Ol' Betsy at Gjrazzel, connecting flush with his jaw. The cracking sound echoed through the arena.

Gjrazzel staggered and collapsed. The arena fell silent.

A noiseless hysteria was building within the arena. Duke could feel it. He didn't like it.

From the other side of the stadium, a diminutive figure stormed at Duke. As he drew nearer, his identity became clear. It was Gjrazzel's trainer.

Not this guy again.

His screaming became more intelligible as he approached. "Disqualify him! He used a gun! Guns are outlawed!"

The crowd recognized the possible loophole and many started fervently supporting the claims with boisterous chants. It was clear that Duke knocking out the courageous local hero was not the desired outcome of the masses. And the masses started to jump the barricade and spill onto the arena floor.

Not good.

The huddled mass moved towards the bounty hunter with hate and murder in their eyes. Duke was frozen.

He felt both of his arms tightly pinned and his body pulled backwards. He was hurled into the entryway, back first. Ishiro'shea grabbed Ol' Betsy and aimed it at the horde of attackers. He didn't shoot, but it slowed them enough for Mazilda to hit a button on the side wall, closing the door.

"Did I win?"

"I think so. But you aren't going to be a crowd favorite anytime soon," replied Mazilda.

CHAPTER 18

GOOD CONVERSATION

"MR. LAGRANGE, I CAN'T LET you in. I'm sorry."

"And why is that?"

"Because these folks will want to kill you after what happened at the arena," answered the barkeep at the Pond-scum Tavern. "I just can't let you in."

"So, kid, you want to be known as the guy that refused service to the first ever being to not only survive, but win a match in this holiest of holy tournaments after escaping from the melee?"

The Psitakki pondered this for a minute.

"Yes, but..."

"Never mind. I'll find somewhere else," replied Duke.

"There aren't any other bars, Mr. LaGrange. This is it."

"I will find someone willing to give me a drink. And I'll be sure to mention how you slandered the good name of Grozzel the Great by turning away someone who risks his life in the name of that great Psitakki warrior. I wouldn't be surprised if you get a few reporters in here asking some tough, hard-hitting questions before the night's done. Good luck."

Duke and Ishiro'shea turned around and slowly walked away from the tavern's entrance.

"Wait! Hold up!"

Duke paused, then pivoted to face the young bartender.

"Yes?" he asked, barely able to conceal a mischievous smirk.

"I have an idea."

"And that would be?"

"We have a back room. I'll bring you drinks personally. Just don't tell any reporters, okay? I won't tell the patrons that you're here, there won't be a ruckus, and you will get your drinks."

"I'm assuming they're on the house for this trouble that you've put us through and how I'm basically a celebrity now."

The bartender was visibly flustered. It was obvious that he wasn't used to beings like Duke LaGrange.

"I will see what I can do."

"And one more thing."

"Yes?"

"If Seamus O'Hoolihan comes in... You know him, right?"

"Yes, Mr. LaGrange. Potato Lips."

"Yes, Potato Lips. If he comes in, tell him to meet us in the back room. I want to talk to him. And the drinks will be on me. Well, I guess they will be on you. But you get the idea."

"What if he says no?"

"He's Irish. He won't turn down a free round."

"Yes, Mr. LaGrange, I will let him know. And let's get you to the private room before the crowd really starts to pour in. Follow me."

After traversing winding back hallways, dimly lit and smelling of exotic booze, Duke and Ishiro'shea entered a compact, square room. It was lit by torches and a single gas light fixture that hung from the center of the ceiling. The room was cool and draughty, but comfortable. There were a few barrels along the edge of the wall and a wooden bar in one corner.

"Please have a seat," said the bartender.

He bounced to the corner and opened up a barrel. He snatched two glasses from the counter of the wooden bar and scooped them into the barrel. They emerged with a glorious golden liquid.

Glyptodian Summer Ale.

"Why have you been hiding this from us? Who needs Light of God when you have the refreshing, full-bodied delight that is Glyptodian Summer Ale?"

Duke could see Ishiro'shea's smile from behind his mask.

"I thought that you might like it," said the bartender. "I hear it's quite popular in other parts of the universe. It's not a big seller here."

"Are all of these barrels full of it?"

"Yes."

"Looks like we won't be needing your services tonight. Just leave us to the beer and our own company."

The Psitakki exited the private drinking cellar.

"Things are starting to look up, Ish. Glyptodian Summer Ale, avoiding unnecessary skirmishes with locals, and—if we're lucky—a chance to ask Seamus a few questions about your parents and that photo."

Ishiro'shea raised his mug and the two clinked glasses.

The ale slid down Duke's throat, seeming to touch every part of his insides. He couldn't help but think about Cyborg Joe's.

"Reminds me of home."

"Get out of my way, boy," Prince Korzo-Tapor sneered as he pushed the Psitakki bartender away from the doorway.

"I'm sorry, Mr. LaGrange," the barkeeper stammered. "I told him that he couldn't come back here, but he—"

"It's fine," said Duke. "At least I know that the prince here isn't mad at me for beating Gjrazzel."

"Very true, Duke. It was quite an impressive win. I mean, it was impressive if you look beyond the fact that Gjrazzel was partially blind, couldn't stand on his own accord, and he was significantly concussed. But, hey, a win is a win."

"Thanks."

The Jungafallowian bowed.

"What do you want?"

"It seems that, like you, I'm not the most revered being on this rock. I just wanted to have a few drinks without being harassed. I had a feeling that you were in the same boat."

Duke huffed.

"Fine, what can it hurt?"

"That's the spirit, old boy. Oh, is that Glyptodian Summer Ale?"

Duke grimaced. "No, it's some local sludge. I would just order something from the bar."

The prince leapt over and grabbed Duke's mug in one seamless motion. Both reptiloid heads converged on the glass and took a whiff of its distinct aroma.

"I'm disappointed, Duke. I thought you would have recognized that this is Glyptodian. It's pretty apparent."

"I guess I'm a bit rusty," Duke said dejectedly.

"I love this vintage. Bartender, go fetch me two glasses. I

think I will stick to the same stuff as Duke and Ishiro'shea here."

The Psitakki bartender left the room and returned moments later with two empty glasses for the prince. He walked over to the barrel and scooped ale until both mugs were overflowing with the golden liquid.

"Now run along, boy," the prince said condescendingly.

"What do you want? Really," asked Duke.

"Why do I have to *want* anything? Outside of good drink and good conversation with good company, of course."

Duke rolled his eyes. Then he grinned.

"Fine then, Prince. I have a question for you. You know, just regular ol' conversation between friends."

"Go ahead."

"What was the attack on Gjrazzel all about?"

"I thought you would appreciate that unfortunate event."

"It was a pretty underhanded move, if you ask me."

"I don't remember needing to ask you, Duke. But I had my reasons. It was not unprovoked."

"Really?" Duke asked. "Gjrazzel didn't strike me as someone that would get involved with any extracurricular activities, especially before the biggest day of his life."

The prince didn't answer right away. He seemed to be planning how he was going to respond to Duke's question. "He was being somewhat..."

"Yes?" interjected Duke impatiently.

"...snoopy."

"About what?"

"I think that falls outside of the realm of good conversation."

Duke opened his mouth to respond, but the memory of Gjrazzel asking about the whereabouts of Korzo-Tapor and if he was somehow involved with him crept into his mind.

Is the prince telling the truth? There's definitely a connection.

"Fair point, Prince. So, answer me this."

"Yes?"

"Why are you here? Why are you, well, why is your pet project, fighting in this tournament?"

The prince chuckled. "Surely you are aware of our fighting reputation on Jungafallow III, Duke? If I recall, didn't you pick a fight with two overly eager Death Robots fans back at Joe's about a month or so ago? I believe it was the prelude to our first encounter."

"Okay, so you like to fight. Once again, not you, but your friend."

"Naturally. I find physical altercations to be somewhat primitive and undignified. And illogical. That doesn't mean that I don't like to watch them, however. We all have our guilty pleasures."

"So this whole ordeal is just in the name of Jungafallowian pride and your weird fetish?"

"Yes. And don't forget ego. I like to be a winner."

"Sorry, K. T., I'm not buying it. Not one bit."

The Korzo head took a big sip. The Tapor head followed suit. They both turned inward and eyeballed each other, as if discussing telepathically what to say next. To Duke's knowledge, Jungafallowians had no such ability, but when you share the same body for dozens of cycles, it's likely some silent language develops naturally between heads.

"Let's say you're correct, LaGrange, and I'm here for some alternative and sinister reasons."

"Fine, I'm correct."

"Cute. Why would I ever tell you? You, after all, are a sworn enemy to the Trampling Death Robots—a band, nay, a cultural phenomenon that I hold in high esteem. You are a bounty hunter and, despite the recent legal hurdles around that particular trade, it's still a profession with which someone like myself tends not to get too close and snuggly. Lastly, you are a participant in this noble tournament and, no matter how improbable, it's not impossible that you will face my precious Combatant 2 in the finals. Should I go on?"

It was Duke's turn to take an elongated sip of Summer ale. He turned to Ishiro'shea. He could sense that the prince knew they were mocking him. "Yes, please go on."

The prince appeared shocked by Duke's response.

"Let me think," he began.

"What about your boss?" interrupted the bounty hunter.

"My boss?"

"The good Admiral. Lothario LePaco. The scourge of the cosmos."

The snarky and pretentious expression that Korzo-Tapor wore on both of his faces became nondescript blankness. His right arm lowered from the table and out of view of the bounty hunting duo.

"I'm not sure I know what you mean," said the prince unconvincingly.

"Princey, c'mon. We've seen the tattoo. We know you are working for LePaco. And it's my keen assumption that he has more to do with you being here with this overgrown monstrosity than the spirit of competition."

Duke leaned back in his chair and folded his arms behind his head. He smiled a victorious "caught you red-handed" type of grin.

"I give it to you, Duke LaGrange," Korzo-Tapor began submissively, "you have seen through my ruse."

"You probably should have covered up the ink, man."

"I wasn't expecting anyone here to know the mark."

"Really? It's LePaco. He's probably the most known super criminal in the universe."

"Yes, but only those 'in the know' would have any clue about what this tattoo means—law enforcement at the senior levels only, other criminals, and..."

"Bounty hunters," Duke said, finishing the sentence.

"Yes. Most of them, at least. I'm not sure Gemstarr knows. He is, after all, a bounty hunter in name only."

"And an asshole in practice."

"Are you not a fan of his work?"

"Stop changing the subject, Prince. You're working for LePaco, fine. So are a billion other degenerates. But why did he send you here? Why does he care about this tournament? It has to be important for you to publicly humiliate Gjrazzel. That's a message if I ever saw one."

Prince Korzo-Tapor stood up and headed over to the barrels containing the Summer ale. He pushed them aside and peered behind the makeshift bar in the corner.

"I'm looking for something a bit stronger."

Got him right where I want him, thought Duke.

"Nothing," the prince said sullenly. "This will have to do."

He dropped both mugs into the barrel and pulled out another round of beer. He sat back down.

"I don't know why I'm telling you this."

"Because you know that if you don't, Ishiro'shea and I will make it our primary mission to find out what LePaco's up to, and likely cause more harm to you than if you flat-out told us."

"There's some logic in that statement. Somewhere."

"And I know LePaco, so this plan is probably so far in motion that telling me won't even make a bit of difference," Duke said in a bit of blatant ego-stroking.

"I wasn't expecting you to give my boss so much credit."

"Look, I hate the guy. I would introduce him to the business end of Ol' Betsy if given a chance—but he's the greatest criminal that I've ever seen. I'm not going to bring him to justice by figuring out some side job scheme on Psitakki. No offense."

"None taken," replied the prince.

"So call me intrigued. I'll get my shot at the admiral one of these days. I don't think this is it. You satisfying my curiosity about your mission for the admiral, in exchange for Ishiro and I staying out of your business regarding said mission."

The Jungafallowian royal seemed to relax. He downed both mugs of beer in single gulps. The Korzo head's eyes shrank as he leaned in.

"LePaco's been out of commission for some time, right?"

"Yes, he was running the risk of being a ghost in our trade. He was a few steps away from being nothing but a legend," replied Duke.

"Let's just say that he felt that he was having some trust issues within his inner circle," said the Korzo head.

"Paranoia?"

"I don't know. I wouldn't classify myself as inner circle. But maybe a little. So he decided to take a break to revamp his network. Rebuild, or refortify in this case, his empire. And he needed to start with the muscle."

"Believable, so far."

"We did some experiments on... let's call them the 'fringe' of Jungafallowian III society."

"There's a joke to be had, but for the sake of the story, I'll refrain," Duke quipped.

"Much obliged," the prince acknowledged. "The results were a mixed bag but then we found our star pupil, Combatant 2. He was bigger, stronger, and more obedient than all of the others. We sent him in the middle of a Trampling Death Robots fan convention with a shirt that read 'I've Heard Better Music in Elevators than at a Trampling Death Robots Concert.'"

"Don't get me started on elevator music," Duke replied, thinking of his long overdue project on the *Deus*.

"As you can guess, the thousands of die-hard TDR fanatics rushed Combatant 2 without thinking twice."

"What happened?"

"He single-handedly disposed of them all. The first ten or fifteen went down in a flash and the rest ran away. It was a roaring success."

"And so why bring him here? He passed your test. LePaco should have been happy with that."

"I'm not the admiral, so this next part is conjecture."

"Sure."

"The admiral wants everyone to know what he has under his employ. If Combatant 2 wins the Tournament of the Whatever It Is—and we have thousands of these enforcers across the universe—people will tend not to be as quick to double-cross or try and pull one over on the admiral."

"He's advertising his newfound power."

"In the most delicate and subtle way, of course," the prince added. "The Gjrazzel episode just added to our reputation."

"And if Combatant 2 loses?"

The Tapor head belted out a laugh that echoed throughout the secret drinking den. The Korzo head simply smiled.

"We don't think that will be an issue. We are quite confident..."

"Hey, there you are," chimed in a female voice from the doorway.

"Mazilda, what are you doing here?" asked Duke.

She paused and sneered at the Jungafallowian.

"What is *he* doing here?" she asked aggressively. "The company you're keeping has really gone downhill."

"An upgrade from you, my dear, there is no doubt," said the prince with a sneer. "And how is your new boyfriend, Gemstarr? Any new poses that he's practicing and planning to break out in the tournament? Or is he at his intellectual limit for flexing routines? I'm shocked he has time to take another girlfriend. I hope his mirror isn't jealous."

A laugh slipped through Duke's defenses. Mazilda treated him to a glance as piercing as any of her throwing daggers.

"Come sit down, Mazilda," offered Duke. "The prince has been sharing some interesting tidbits."

"I would rather—" began Mazilda.

"No need to finish that sentence, Miss Cloax. I was just finishing up my chat with Duke and Ishiro'shea and then I need to check in on Combatant 2. We need to strategize for our next big matchup with that Earth mutant."

The prince stood up and bowed disingenuously to Mazilda. She did not reciprocate the gesture.

"Thank you for the good drinks and good conversation, Duke. I hope to do this again soon," the prince said as he exited the room.

Mazilda sat down in the chair recently occupied by the Jungafallowian. She pounded her fists on the table, knocking over one of the empty glass mugs. "What was that about?"

"The prince was feeding us some garbage about why LePaco sent him here."

"Admiral LePaco?"

CHAPTER 19

PO-TAY-TO, PO-TAH-TO

"HE DOES APPEAR TO BE holding something back," Mazilda began, "and it's no surprise. He's a murderous reprobate that would sell out his own mother for a few extra seconds of power and a boost to his bank account."

"No arguments there," replied Duke.

"But what do you think he's hiding?"

"No idea. I have a feeling Gjrazzel knew something."

"The Psitakki?"

"Yes, the prince said he was being 'snoopy.' For some reason, I think he regretted telling us that part. I think Gjrazzel was on to his game, whatever that game is."

"What are you going to do now?"

"Nothing," Duke replied matter-of-factly.

"What?"

"I'm not here to deal with anything LePaco has cooking. I'm sure I'll have a chance at him real soon but, for now, based on what you shared with us, this tournament is about two things. Number one... staying alive."

"Number two?"

"Finding out about Ishiro's parents."

At this, the ninja perked up from his alcohol-induced trance. He raised his empty glass.

"Cheers, Ish. We'll find them. I made Seamus an offer he can't refuse."

"And what was that?" asked Mazilda.

"A free round."

"What makes you think he's going to even come into the Pondscum Tavern on the eve of his fight with Combatant 2?"

Duke smiled and kicked back once again in his chair.

"Oh, Mazilda. He's Irish."

"That's playing to stereotypes a bit."

Duke nodded his head in Ishiro'shea's general direction.

"It's still insensitive," Mazilda added.

"But most importantly, he's about to have to face that Jungafallowian science experiment. What else would one do with that looming in front of 'em?"

Mazilda pondered this for a moment, then seemed to submit to Duke's logic.

"Oh, by the way," started Duke, "to what do we owe the pleasure of your company this evening? And without the galaxy's favorite bounty hunter, nonetheless."

"The *universe's* favorite bounty hunter," Mazilda jabbed back.

"Right."

"Honestly, I thought you could use a little help. Do you know anything about your next opponent?"

"Yes, I do actually. Quite a lot, in fact."

"I'm all ears," Mazilda replied.

"He can fly."

"Great."

A booming voice redirected their attention to the door. The Psitakki bartender was already a few paces into the room; the voice didn't belong to him. No, it was a hulking brute of a man. More accurately, a hulking brute of a mutant man.

"Howya. What's the story here? I'm trying to get fluthered off this purple stuff and this eejit fella tells me someone's offering to buy me a few rounds. He takes me down to this kip of a room and now I sees you lot. What ya' playing at? Not codding me, eh?"

Duke looked at Mazilda in confusion.

"You understand that, Ishiro?" asked Duke.

The ninja shrugged.

"I mean you *are* half Irish, right?" questioned Duke.

Seamus "Potato Lips" O'Hoolihan wasn't the easiest person to understand. Duke surmised that much of this was due to the unusual mutation that caused his lips to balloon to the size of, well, potatoes. But giant lips or no giant lips, Duke didn't have the faintest clue what O'Hoolihan was saying.

"Come again, Mr. Lips?" asked the bounty hunter.

"I said..." Seamus started.

"He asked what do you want," said the Psitakki barkeep.

"Yeah, wut he said," Seamus agreed.

Duke looked to his half-Irish sidekick. Ishiro'shea concurred with the Psitakki's interpretation.

"Have a seat, please. I promised you some booze and I shall deliver."

"Got any of the black stuff?"

"Black stuff?"

"I take it that he means a local stout from his native land," chimed in the Psitakki. "Do you want me to stay and translate?"

"We got this, I'm sure you have customers that need that purple junk," snapped Duke.

"That purple drink is right manky. It will get you

locked, no doubt, but it sent me to the jacks for two whole days. Know wut I mean?"

"I..." Duke stuttered, "...do not. But I'm sure I'll figure it out with some context clues in due time."

The Psitakki rolled his eyes and exited.

"It's not your black stuff but this ain't half bad," Duke said pointing to the barrels of Glyptodian Summer Ale. "Ever been to Cyborg Joe's?"

"No, but I knows of it. Everyone does. Best place in the Andromeda to get totally landers when you're out on the tear, I hear. Up to your neck in floozies, from what I've been told."

Duke stood up and grabbed an empty mug from the corner bar. He inspected it to make sure it wasn't covered in too much grime.

Clean enough, Duke concluded. He dipped it in the barrel of Glyptodian Summer Ale.

"Well, this stuff is a best seller."

Duke slid the glass along the table and it halted in front of the Irish mutant. He downed the entire beer in one gulp, then wiped his mouth with his forearm.

"Not bad. A female's drink but it'll do for now, as long as it's free."

"What is that supposed to mean?" Mazilda snapped.

"It lacks a man's strength."

The female bounty hunter stood up rapidly, knocking her chair to the ground.

"Come again, you drunk..."

"Sit down, Mazilda. We don't invite people in and then insult them," Duke said, trying to extinguish the potentially flammable situation.

"I didn't invite this buffoon in. You did."

Seamus remained sitting in his chair, unfazed by Mazilda's show of aggression. Ishiro'shea slid the refilled mug back in front of O'Hoolihan, who smiled and nodded to the ninja.

"The reason we asked you here has nothing to do with the tournament at hand," said Duke. "I know you have a big fight tomorrow with the Jungafallowian, so we won't keep you long."

Seamus' eyes widened as if he had totally forgotten about his opponent in the next round.

"See, my dear friend here," Duke began, "is Ishiro'shea."

The Irish mutant did not react. After a few moments of awkward silence, he simply shrugged.

"Ishiro'shea. *The* Ishiro'shea."

Seamus's expression of ignorance didn't change.

"The two people that you are looking for, those are his parents."

"I don't have any idea what you're talking about. You are codding me, aren't ya?"

"We know you're looking for them. *Why* are you looking for them? And where are they?"

Seamus stood up and slammed his mug down on the table. "Look, I don't know what you're talking about. Alright? I'm here to win this tournament. Not find anyone's parents."

As he turned to exit the room, Mazilda was already at the door and slammed it shut.

"Does this look familiar?"

Seamus seemed to recognize the photo immediately.

"How'd you get that?"

"It doesn't matter," said Mazilda. "What do you know about these two?"

"You're telling me that this little guy over there is their son? You must think that I'm not the full shilling."

"He is," added Duke. "He is a descendant of the

Nobunaga clan on his mother's side. His father is, well, 'The Father.'"

"No way."

When Mazilda turned around, her face was mere inches from Seamus'. One of her trusty blades was close enough to shave his amber beard clean off.

"Put that away!" Duke screamed. "Sorry, Seamus."

"You heard what he said, lass. Best not be pissin' me off."

"Is that so?"

Without so much as a sound, Ishiro'shea placed himself between Mazilda and the Irish mutant, defusing the situation.

"Seamus, I swear to Nova Texas that he is," said Duke. "He's taken a vow of silence until he finds them again. They shipped him off when he was a young boy, to avoid the conflict."

"If this was true, which I don't believe, but say it were true, why do you think I'm tracking them down?"

"Really?" asked Mazilda, shaking her head. "We have your damn photos, you drunk bastard."

"That doesn't prove anything," Seamus argued, his arms folded in defiance. He sat down and finished off the rest of his beer.

At least he's not trying to leave, thought Duke. *Maybe we can get something out of this conversation yet.*

"Seamus, can we move past this? We know you're looking for them. Why?"

"Let's pretend that I am looking for these two people."

"Okay, we'll pretend."

"Great. I'm not looking for them both."

"You aren't?" asked Mazilda.

"No, not as such. I'm looking for—" Seamus caught himself. "—assuming we're still pretending and all, that is?"

"Yes."

"I'm looking for the man."

"The Father?"

"Yes, the Father. His bird is just trash that's in our way. The Father—we know this to be true, mind you—was corrupted by this demon witch here and brainwashed. I'm going to save him."

Duke looked over at Ishiro'shea. He could tell that the ninja was boiling internally at the thought of a mutant calling his mother a 'demon witch.' Duke motioned to him to calm down. He acquiesced.

They were all sitting at the table now, and a calmness permeated through the gathering for the first time.

"So, your aim is to bring back the Father to Earth and try and un-brainwash him?" asked Duke.

"Yes. He was our greatest leader. A man of God but also a man of war. Brilliant he was. He is. I hope he is still, that is."

"But why this tournament?" asked Mazilda eagerly. "If they're out there in the cosmos and you have this photo, why are you here instead of there?"

O'Hoolihan stewed on this question for a while. He looked around as if his interrogators had the answer hidden on their faces. His face became as red as his hair. "That's for my own knowin'. I think I'm done here."

"What?" cried Duke.

"I'm done. I'm not even sure why I told you as much as I did." He glanced at Mazilda. "Oh yeah, 'cause that floozie held a knife to my throat."

Mazilda reached for her dagger again, but Ishiro'shea grabbed her arm in mid-motion to halt the action. Seamus nodded at Ishiro'shea in a sign of thanks.

"It's about leavin' time for me. Thanks for the woman's brew."

"But we can help you," Duke shouted in a last-ditch effort.

The monstrous mutant slowly turned his misshapen face around and glared at the bounty hunter. "And how are you going to help me? You, obviously, don't have nothin' that I don't... Just my photograph that you stole. You aren't any closer to understandin' where it was taken than I am. Besides, your reasons for trackin' them don't line up with mine. Those aren't ideal partnerin' conditions, if you ask me."

"True. But we have something that you don't."

"And what's that?"

"Bait."

Seamus' eyes swelled. He opened his mouth to speak, then promptly closed it.

Is he... thinking? Duke wondered.

"Bait, you say?"

"Their long-lost child. Instead of you tracking them down, this could potentially help them come to you. Assuming the word gets to them. I'm sure that you have some channels to help spread this enticing nugget of information. If they've been so good at hiding, they've got to be tapping into some back alley, seedy underbelly types. Those folks tend to pick up all of the information and sift through it until they find something profitable. This has profitability written all over it."

"If it works and they get wind of their son and, let's say, they find me..."

"Us," corrected Duke.

"They find us," Seamus said with a grimace. "What then? How do I get what I want and you get what you want?"

"All that we want is for Ishiro'shea to be reunited with his parents. I don't see how that conflicts with your goals."

"What if he wants to defend his banshee of a mother?"

"If she's as awful as you say she is, Ishiro'shea will see it too. Maybe she was the reason that he was cast aside and removed from his home. His presence might just strengthen the Father's conviction and help you."

Duke knew his argument was flimsy. He was banking on Seamus' lack of critical thinking to push this partnership through.

The Irishman folded his arms and grumbled gibberish to himself. Then he concluded, "I'll think about it. It does make sense."

Duke smiled. Mazilda rolled her eyes at the mutant's stupidity.

"After my next fight, let's chat again," said O'Hoolihan. "I might have some more information by then anyways."

"What information?"

"We have some folks working on that photo and identifying the whereabouts."

"Cross-referencing some of the background images, I'd suspect," said Mazilda. "Angles of the light, barely visible serial numbers on items, type of soil or pavement. They can be used to trim the possibilities down to a few systems and maybe a hundred or so planets."

"Sure, I guess," responded Seamus, with much less enthusiasm. "All I know is that I should have some more information tomorrow."

"And why are you in the tournament?" Mazilda asked pointedly.

"Like I said, I have my reasons."

"Seamus, if we are going to work together for both of our benefits, we need to be open and honest," pleaded Duke.

Potato Lips sighed again.

"Fine. We heard some chatter that someone else here was hot on the heels of the Father and his witch queen."

"Do you think that was us?"

"Nope. I was entered in this tournament long before you crashed into the Shaman's table. Someone else."

"Who?" asked Mazilda.

"No idea. I thought it was that Jungafallowian but I haven't found anything on him. If he knows something, he's good at being discrete."

"There are a lot of unsavory types here," concluded Duke. "We will keep our eyes out, Seamus. You will be the first person we alert if we catch on to something."

Duke stood up and walked over to O'Hoolihan. He extended his hand. The mutant brute squeezed it so hard that Duke swore he heard a bone crack.

"Quite a grip there, Seamus."

The mutant conjured up a misshapen smile.

"Let's go find us Ishiro'shea's father."

"*The* Father," Seamus replied.

"Right, a father, the Father. Po-tay-to, po-tah-to."

Seamus snarled. He had clearly never heard that expression.

RANDY AND ZEL... AGAIN

[BROADCAST OPENS ON THE ANNOUNCERS' BOOTH.]

ZELARIOUS ZAN ALON: Fight fans, welcome back to the Tournament of the Shield of the Colossal Calamari! It's day two—well, day three if you count the melee night—and this is shaping up to be the greatest event in the tournament's rich history. We've had upsets. We've had death-defying feats of strength. We've had surprise attacks. And we've seen a record broken—and then broken again moments later. It has been nothing short of amazing!

RANDY: *Beep.* Yep. *Boop.*

ZELARIOUS ZAN ALON: You are truly the most dynamic color man in the business, Randy. And what a day we have planned. In the opening round, we witnessed Sulaw, the beautiful Hiritai warrior advance over Not Very Good at Math from Zylantia, and she will now take on Yvonne "The Furry Mountain of Moon Colony #1" Angerdlarnek. The Furry Mountain was able to overcome a very game Reginald the Mega-Troll.

RANDY: *Beep.* Finally, some girl-on-girl action. *Beep.*

ZELARIOUS ZAN ALON: I predict it will be the hardest-hitting bout of the evening. They are both fierce combatants and have a real shot to win the entire tournament. The winner of that slugfest will meet the winner of the match between Seamus "Potato Lips" O'Hoolihan of Earth and Combatant 2, the Jungafallowian, in the next round.

RANDY: *Beep.* Yikes. Not exactly an easy path for any of them in that bracket, Zel. *Beep.*

ZELARIOUS ZAN ALON: Agreed. Potato Lips disposed of Tor-torta of Krawn with his own flames, in one of the most dramatic finishes in the first round. Combatant 2 made waves across the universe by attacking Gjrazzel, the hometown hero, during the Grand Entrance. He then proceeded to shatter Maxx Gemstarr's record for quickest victory mere moments after Gemstarr set it. He leveled the poor Kitar in a mere six seconds.

RANDY: *Boop. Boop.* I'm not sure that he can be stopped, Zel. Not even by that mutant Irish thug. *Beep.*

ZELARIOUS ZAN ALON: But you know who probably benefitted most from Combatant 2's unprecedented attack on Gjrazzel?

RANDY: The unknown bum, Duke LaGrout. *Beep.*

ZELARIOUS ZAN ALON: You are absolutely right. The lightly-thought-of bounty hunter, Duke LaGrange of Nova Texas. He was able to take advantage of a hobbled and blinded Gjrazzel to win. Despite Gjrazzel's physical limitations and injuries, LaGrange still had to push the rules and regulations to sneak out a victory.

RANDY: *Beep.* I think he should be disqualified. The rules clearly say no firearms. *Beep. Boop.*

ZELARIOUS ZAN ALON: Most are on your side, Randy, especially those in attendance. But the Shaman did clear his use of the butt of the gun, so LaGrange does advance. But we can't underscore enough the valiant and noble effort made by Gjrazzel in this tournament. What a true champion.

RANDY: *Beep.* And damn LaGregg. *Boop. Boop.*

ZELARIOUS ZAN ALON: He doesn't get a free pass, however. He now has to square off against the winged warrior from Planet F, Glux Xyphormog II, who was able to get a win over Jorb, the sludge monster from Karr, by using his own acidic spit against him.

RANDY: That was some nifty flying, Zel. *Beep. Beep.*

ZELARIOUS ZAN ALON: Indeed. He did lose his prized two-sided halberd in the battle, but I'm sure that he will be ready for the Nova Texan. And the crowd will be solidly behind the Royal Guardsman from Planet F.

RANDY: *Beep.* I know I will be. *Beep.*

ZELARIOUS ZAN ALON: I think we're supposed to be impartial, Randy.

RANDY: *Beep.* Screw that. Duke can go "Glux" off. *Beep.* See what I did there? *Boop.*

ZELARIOUS ZAN ALON: I did, Randy, yes I did. Finally, the round will end with Maxx Gemstarr, fresh off of a sub-ten-second victory over a Gyorkian Blademaster—impressive stuff—and the feisty Gurlfian Goother Rat, Gha. Gha had one of the more unconventional wins in the tournament—and no one is happier than one of our key sponsors, Willie's World of Galactic Winnebagos. It's a real testament to the flushing power of a Willie's brand Winnebago.

RANDY: *Beep.* I wonder if Jin-Jin-Jin ever escaped? *Boop.*

ZELARIOUS ZAN ALON: I'm not sure. And I don't want to be there when he does, that's for sure.

RANDY: I'm really excited, Zel. *Beep.* This is going to be a crazy day. Who's up first? *Beep.*

ZELARIOUS ZAN ALON: It looks like we are going to see your guy, Glux Xyphormog II, try and end the upset streak caused by Duke LaGrange, the bounty hunter from Nova Texas.

RANDY: *Beep.* I hate that guy. *Beep.*

ZELARIOUS ZAN ALON: But first a word from our sponsors.

[UNCLE TOFU'S ADVENTURE LAND COMMERCIAL PLAYS.]

[WILLIE'S WORLD OF GALACTIC WINNEBAGOS COMMERCIAL PLAYS.]

[THE BROADCAST OPENS TO A WIDE SHOT OF THE ARENA.]

ZELARIOUS ZAN ALON: We have the best sponsors, don't we, Randy?

RANDY: *Beep.* Yes, edible roller coasters and toilets with the suck force of a black hole. Hard to beat it, Zel. *Beep.*

ZELARIOUS ZAN ALON: Despite the early exit of their favorite son, Gjrazzel, the crowd is packed and buzzing with excitement today.

RANDY: *Boop. Boop.* The *unfair* exit of Gjrazzel, Zel. *Beep.*

ZELARIOUS ZAN ALON: The lights are dimming and the trumpets are sounding. Here's our first competitor. It's Glux Xyphormog II! They love him and... Whoa! Look at that! Those are some impressive aerial moves!

RANDY: *Beep.* No doubt. It's hard not to root for this crazy insect. *Beep.*

ZELARIOUS ZAN ALON: They sure are behind him in this fight. However, I'm not sure if it has to do with their love for this insectoid warrior or their hatred for our next fighter. Here he is, ladies and gentlemen—and greeted by a rousing chorus of hate-filled heckles. I'm not sure what those hand gestures mean on his home world, but I have a feeling that the crowd isn't appreciating it.

Randy: *Beep.* I'll give it right back to him. *Beep.*

Zelarious Zan Alon: Get your hand back in here, Randy. Don't stoop to his level. Let's send it down and get an official introduction for these two.

Arena PA Announcer: Ladies and gentlemen and beings from all corners of the universe, welcome to the quarterfinal round of the Tournament of the Shield of the Colossal Calamari! This match is the opening contest of the day and will be a fight to the finish. Introducing first, from the majestic world of Planet F, a member of the most prestigious military unit on the planet—the Queen's Royal Guard —he's the master of the double-sided halberd and has sired over three hundred and forty thousand royal larvae for the Mother of the Empire, the queen herself. It's my honor to introduce the being that defeated Jorb, the sludge beast of Karr—this is Glux Xyphormog II!

[THE CROWD GOES CRAZY.]

Arena PA Announcer: And his opponent, from the harsh and barren world of Nova Texas, a two-bit offshoot of everyone's least-favorite planet, Earth. He's an unheralded bounty hunter that takes advantage of other's misfortune and uses illegal weapons to knock out injured competitors. He also claims to be a playboy—whatever that is. He's the melee victor—which he also won by pure luck. It's my job to have to introduce Duke LaGrunge.

ARENA PA ANNOUNCER: Correction. Duke LaGrange.

ZELARIOUS ZAN ALON: The Nova Texan seems to have irked the arena's PA announcer, even.

RANDY: *Beep.* Now that's impressive. *Beep.*

ZELARIOUS ZAN ALON: Now on to the match itself. I really don't see how LaGrange can pull this one off. It's an uphill battle for sure. First off, Glux is healthy. He doesn't have his two-sided halberd, but he has a standard-issue variety and he's still lethal with it. Second, Glux can fly. Third, he trains every day of his life and is constantly in danger's bullseye as one of the most revered soldiers of the imperial force. Fourth...

RANDY: *Beep.* We get it. This is going to be a blood bath. We can finally be done with this LaGoop character. *Beep.*

ZELARIOUS ZAN ALON: The referee is reminding these two contestants of the rules, or lack thereof.

RANDY: *Boop.* There are barely any rules, but LaGrotch still managed to break them. *Beep.*

ZELARIOUS ZAN ALON: To be fair to Duke, Randy, the decision was made that his use of the gun was legal. We have to move on, no matter how despicable this guy is. But, he doesn't have the gun with him now. It looks like he was given one of the house clubs, a pretty basic bludgeoning instrument; I don't see a talent like Glux Xyphormog falling victim to something as basic as a wooden stick.

RANDY: *Beep.* Let's go, Glux! *Beep.*

ZELARIOUS ZAN ALON: They both have retreated back to their sides of the arena and we are about to get this on.

RANDY: *Beep.* I think this will be a quick one, Zel. *Beep. Boop. Beep.*

ZELARIOUS ZAN ALON: And Glux is on the attack! He

just ran across the arena and now he's laying into Duke with the halberd. Or trying to. LaGrange seems to be blocking it pretty successfully with his club. Oh, wait! He's down on his backside. Glux is not letting up! He just missed LaGrange on that jab. Duke gets to the barrier and gets to his feet. Another halberd strike just misses. Oh, this does not look good for the Nova Texan.

RANDY: I can't believe he's dodging these! *Beep. Boop.* Get him, Glux! *Beep.*

ZELARIOUS ZAN ALON: What a kick by the Royal Guardsman! Duke is on his back again. Here we go! Glux is up in the air, hovering, there he goes... Duke moves! The halberd is stuck in the ground. It's not moving at all. LaGrange swings the club and connects. He then uses it to smash the halberd in two.

RANDY: *Beep.* Glux is not having much luck with halberds in this tournament, Zel. But I think he's fine. That love tap by LaGrout didn't do any damage. *Beep.*

ZELARIOUS ZAN ALON: You're right. It did appear to be a glancing blow. Glux recollects himself and charges again, Duke swats at him. No avail. Again. Nothing. It's obvious that the bounty hunter won't be able to slow down Xyphormog that way. Another sweep by Glux, and Duke swings. Glux grasps LaGrange's forearm in mid-swing with his foot. I have never seen that before in my life. He snatches the club and flies above the reach of the bounty hunter. Glux throws the club into the audience!

RANDY: *Beep.* He wants to make this a one-on-one battle. No weapons. Just the epic struggle between humanoid and insectoid. And I don't like LaDork's chances. *Beep.*

ZELARIOUS ZAN ALON: Okay, Randy, now you aren't even trying anymore.

RANDY: *Beep.* What? *Boop.*

Zelarious Zan Alon: Another diving attack by Glux, and he tackles the bounty hunter. They roll for a few paces and disengage. Another swift thrust kick by Glux and Duke hits the ground. He takes flight and charges the downed bounty hunter. He connects again! This is not looking good for Duke LaGrange. Glux hovers, Duke is up... and back down again. This time a kick to the back of the head. This could be the beginning of the end for the Nova Texan.

Randy: *Beep.* Finish him. *Beep.*

Zelarious Zan Alon: Glux swoops in and grabs the bounty hunter between his legs. Oh, I think I know what's happening now. Glux is lifting the woozy LaGrange in the air. He's going to dangle him high above the arena. Duke will have to either embarrass himself by giving up, watched on by a viewing audience of billions and effectively ruining what little reputation he may have in the outside world. Or plummet to his death.

Randy: *Beep.* A squishy death, Zel. *Boop.*

Zelarious Zan Alon: Right you are, my tiny metal compadre. Very squishy indeed. Glux is gaining elevation. LaGrange isn't moving. He might be out cold.

Randy: *Beep.* So if he's out cold, that means he likely won't answer, huh? *Beep. Boop.* So, that means Glux will have to...

Zelarious Zan Alon: Send him to splat city.

Randy: *Beep.* Alright! *Boop. Boop. Beep.*

Zelarious Zan Alon: They're high in the rafters now. The crowd is loving this. As impressive as Glux's fighting ability is, the fact that he can carry a full-sized humanoid to these heights using only his legs is a testament to his strength and conditioning.

Randy: *Boop.* No wonder the queen loves this guy so much. *Beep.*

Zelarious Zan Alon: Here we go. Glux appears to be asking the motionless bounty hunter to tap out. Give up. Submit. I don't see any signs of life from LaGrange.

Randy: *Beep.* Is that eye opening? *Beep.*

Zelarious Zan Alon: Oh wow, fight fans! Shocking. LaGrange was playing dead. He just swung his body upwards and kicked Glux square in the jaw. That's a pretty sneaky move and shows that Duke may have some fight in him. He's now firmly grabbing Glux by his ankles but he's still dangling from the height of the upper deck. He's playing with fire. Glux is trying to shake him, but Duke is holding on. He's moved up and now has a firm grip on Glux's left thigh. He's trying to mount the insectoid. Glux starts a speedy dive to try and shake the rogue from his body, but the Nova Texan is hanging on. I've definitely never seen this before.

Randy: *Beep.* They're going to hit some spectators! Watch out! *Boop.*

Zelarious Zan Alon: You're right. Glux is accelerating down to the arena floor at an uncontrollable speed. Duke has a full mount now. He's riding Glux like some sort of Mrelockian skybeast. It's affecting Glux, too. He can't seem to steady his flight, he's all out of sorts. LaGrange is holding on for dear life. They just swooped mere inches above the heads of the patrons in the lower sections.

Randy: *Beep.* If they crash into the stands, advantage Glux. *Beep.*

Zelarious Zan Alon: No doubt. I bet that a large portion of those in attendance would love a crack at Duke LaGrange. They just flew over the head of Duke's corner man.

Randy: *Beep.* That tiny masked fella is his corner man? *Boop.*

Zelarious Zan Alon: Yes. Ishiro'shea, from Earth. Apparently, he's a skilled martial artist.

Randy: *Beep.* Maybe he should have joined up instead of LaGrease. *Beep.*

Zelarious Zan Alon: That's what most insiders have told me, Randy. Another swoop over the crowd, narrowly missing Ishiro'shea again. Duke reached down and appeared to slap a fan in that section!

Randy: *Beep.* Figures! Just when I thought that I couldn't hate someone more, he does that! *Beep. Boop.*

Zelarious Zan Alon: What's this? Does Duke have a knife? It looks like a tiny dagger. Where did that come from?

Randy: *Beep.* Did he steal it from that fan? *Beep.*

Zelarious Zan Alon: Oh no—he's shredding Xyphormog's wings. They're going down! LaGrange is on top. This is going to be loud!

Randy: *Boop.* Damn. *Beep.* [Randy's commentary censored on the broadcast.] *Beep.*

Zelarious Zan Alon: You can't say that on air, Randy. It's a mess down against the barrier. The two crashed headlong into the wall at full speed. The referees are checking on it. I can't believe this. I'm speechless.

Randy: *Boop.* [More censored commentary.] *Beep.*

Zelarious Zan Alon: Glux Xyphormog is not responding. He's out cold. I can't believe that I'm about to say this—

Randy: *Beep.* Then don't. *Beep.*

Zelarious Zan Alon: Duke LaGrange wins.

Randy: *Beep.* [More censored commentary.] *Beep.*

Zelarious Zan Alon: Duke LaGrange advances to the semifinals of the Tournament of the Shield of the Colossal Calamari. Fight fans, do you believe in miracles?

CHAPTER 21

MAXX AND THE RAT

DUKE DIDN'T CARE TOO MUCH for the taste of his own blood. Nor did he particularly like the taste of anyone's blood. The one possible exception being the blood of the Awlravian Jumping Cow, whose plasma is a common drink amongst Awlrav's inhabitants and whose milk is a toxic poison. The Awlravian Jumping Cow's blood is a prominent ingredient in the mixed drink Coagulation Celebration, a festive signature cocktail at Cyborg Joe's Grill N' Go & The Why Not Saloon on Planet Kelt. Unfortunately for Duke, his blood didn't come with a free party hat and edible confetti.

"That was a close one," said Mazilda.

"Thanks. And thanks for the assist," said Duke, wiping blood from his mouth with his forearm.

"Those morons on the broadcast thought I was some random fan that you were taunting. Can you believe that?"

Is she mad that they thought I was cheating—or that they didn't recognize her? Duke wondered.

"Hey now, I like those guys. Randy is awesome. Easily my favorite broadcaster."

"You probably shouldn't listen to the replays then," smirked Mazilda.

"Oh," Duke responded with a frown.

Ishiro'shea patched up some of the bounty hunter's cuts.

"Ouch. That stings. You know what you're doing?"

"Toughen up, pansy," said Mazilda. "You don't want one of those cuts to open up in the next round."

"Who are my options again?"

"Shut up, Duke, you know damn well that it's Maxx."

"Or the Goother Rat. He's pretty squirrelly. The rat might get lucky and have Maxx flush himself down a toilet," Duke laughed. "Where is ol' Maxxy-poo anyways? Shouldn't you be with him?"

"We're on after Yvonne and Sulaw. He likes his alone time before a fight."

"I'm surprised he doesn't need your help to wriggle into that getup of his," said the Nova Texan, rolling his eyes.

"I do like how he looks in that," Mazilda whispered to herself. Her focus drifted noticeably.

"Whatever," replied Duke. "He's still a big dumb animal."

"A *sexy* big dumb animal."

"If you're into that sort of thing."

"Most women with eyes are, Duke."

"Only if they also lack taste," he jabbed. "But seriously Mazilda, thanks for the help. It was like..."

"Old times," she said, finishing his thought.

"Yes, old times. Good times. I don't exactly know *why* you're helping me. Helping us, really. But Ishiro'shea and I are thankful."

Mazilda seemed to blush, at least as much as could be discerned from her pale yellow skin. She grabbed Duke by the shoulders and planted a kiss on his cheek. She hugged Ishiro'shea and kissed him on the top of his head.

"I'm glad that we reconnected."

The loudspeakers started to boom, shaking the back rooms of the arena.

"The next match is up already, I should probably get back to Maxx. I'll see you tonight. Hopefully, Seamus can give us some more info."

"See you tonight."

Following a quick patch job on some of Duke's more noticeable scrapes, he and Ishiro'shea lounged in their personal holding room to watch the other bouts unfold. Duke flipped on the monitor to the broadcast; a fight was already in progress.

Yvonne "The Furry Mountain of Moon Colony #1" Angerdlarnek was panting, her thick fur matted and a single stream of blood dripping down from the corner of her mouth. Her opponent, Sulaw of the Hiritai, was breathing heavily as well, and a bulbous purple knot swelled under her left eye. The dirt from the arena floor caked her back and thighs. The two combatants were circling each other, waiting for an opening for another series of attacks. Sulaw snarled at the Gartoshian musk ox.

Somehow, she makes bloodied, dirty, and beaten-up look damn good, thought Duke.

Sulaw darted at Yvonne's sturdy legs, trying to take her down and grab a mounted position. However, Yvonne fended off the athletic Hiritai with a swift knee strike to the shoulder. Sulaw tumbled down and rolled out of striking distance. Neither woman had a weapon. This was not shocking in Yvonne's case, as she tended to rely on her boxing prowess. Duke hypothesized that Yvonne had been able to dislodge Sulaw's weapon earlier in the match. *Advantage Yvonne*, concluded the bounty hunter.

The match became a series of chess-like moves. Neither fighter gained much of an advantage until Sulaw aggressively charged Yvonne nearly an hour into the encounter. She sprinted at full speed toward the musk ox, which prompted Yvonne to start her deadly head butt charge, the move that had leveled the behemoth Mega-Troll in the opening round. Sulaw miraculously avoided the collision in midair; as she flew over the Yvonne by a good arm's length, she snagged her right horn and forced the Gartoshian to lose control and fall into a mid-flight spin. Yvonne crashed to the ground with a massive thud, then rolled near to the barrier wall.

"She totally duped her, Ish. I don't know if this is making me concerned or aroused," said Duke.

Sulaw walked over to the injured Yvonne, now on her hands and knees. Sulaw looked at the crowd and made gestures, inviting a choice: should she finish her off respectfully or in a blaze of unfiltered violence? They chose the latter.

The Hiritai took a few paces back, then began a stroll towards Yvonne; as she came closer, she picked up speed.

"She's going to punt her in the head," shouted Duke to Ishiro'shea.

As Sulaw's right leg began to swing, Yvonne jumped in the air and came down with a powerful right cross across Sulaw's jaw. The cracking of the jawbone echoed throughout the arena. The Hiritai warrior collapsed immediately. There was no chance of her getting up.

The referee made the easy call to end it. Yvonne fell to a knee, her fatigue visible. She managed a wave to the appreciative, bloodthirsty crowd but then she needed help from Psitakki officials to make it to the back.

"Now that Sulaw's out of the tournament, do you think I should ask her to drinks?" asked Duke.

Ishiro'shea did not respond.

As was customary on the broadcast, after a fight concluded, the programming jumped to some pre-taped fluff pieces hyping up each fighter's background, resume, their unique path to the tournament, and any general badassery that could be attached to their name. Not surprisingly, Maxx Gemstarr had the longest and most elaborate video montage of any of the competitors. Even less surprising, it was during Maxx's vignette that Duke decided to take a much-needed nap.

When the bounty hunter awoke, the next contest had already begun— Maxx "The Universe's Favorite Bounty Hunter" Gemstarr versus Gha, the Goother Rat from Gurlf.

"What'd I miss?" asked Duke.

Ishiro'shea pointed to Gha on the monitor and then made a motion that signified the Goother Rat was nearing his end. At a second glance, Duke realized what Ishiro meant. Gha was beaten badly. Instead of his customary frantic movement, he was sluggishly moping around, trying—unsuccessfully—to dodge Gemstarr's strikes. Maxx eventually caught Gha, hoisted him over his head and tossed him across the arena. He posed for the crowd; they cheered at his superiority over his opponent. However, this gave Gha enough time to retrieve his flail which had, presumably, been cast aside by Gemstarr at some point in the fight. The flail sat right under the designated corner man station, where Mazilda stood cheering on her man. As Maxx continued to delight the crowd, Gha hit him from behind with the flail. The muscular bounty hunter tumbled over as the crowd collectively gasped. Gha swung again, narrowly missing Maxx as he rolled away rather clumsily. Gha landed a vicious swing on Maxx's backside, causing a mild chuckle in the audience. Gha connected again.

Is the Goother Rat going to pull this off?

Another powerful flail whip crashed down across the chest of Gemstarr and sent him to the ground. Gha pounced on top of the prey. As Gha mounted him, Maxx tried to block the Gurlfian's punches, scratches, and bites. However, some of Gha's offense was getting through; Maxx was in trouble.

In his whirlwind assault, Gha must have forgot about Maxx's power gauntlets—surgically implanted forearm guards that packed enough wallop to level an especially bulky tanker that's been submerged in cement and placed behind a heavily fortified lead-lined wall. When you get hit flush with a Maxx Gemstarr forearm strike, it's like being punched in the face with an iron fist powered by a jet engine.

Maxx's forearm radiated an electric neon blue.

Move away, Gha! Get off him, shouted Duke internally. *His arm thingy...*

The bounty hunter smashed both power gauntlets against the torso of the Goother Rat. Gha flew up into the air, then crashed into the top of the barrier wall, narrowly missing the VIP suites. Smoke puffed from his wiry fur, and his eyes rolled back into his head. He was toast.

Damn.

As Maxx celebrated, thanking his fans with yet another flexing routine, Duke saw Mazilda applauding from the corner man station. He didn't like it.

After more packages and some expert analysis by well-known fighters attending the event, the last quarterfinal began. Seamus "Potato Lips" O'Hoolihan entered first, to a rousing ovation. The audience roared even louder as he downed two mugs of beer at the same time. Just as loudly as they had cheered Seamus, they hissed and jeered the Jungafallowian responsible for injuring Gjrazzel. Combatant 2 didn't even seem to notice. His corner man, Prince Korzo-Tapor, did—however, he seemed to relish it. He taunted the crowd with as much vigor as his gigantic minion physically abused his opponents.

"Hey, Ish. I think there's someone they hate more than me," Duke observed. "Let's hope that it's not both of us in the finale—we might have an empty house."

Ishiro'shea was squarely focused on the monitor.

"Don't worry, he just has to live. He doesn't have to win. Even if he's in a hospital bed, we will make sure to get the information that we need. We just have to wait until the fight is over and then we will..."

Ishiro'shea's planted his face firmly into his open palm.

Seamus "Potato Lips" O'Hoolihan was sprawled out in the middle of the arena, his shillelagh broken in half next to him, with a Psitakki referee standing over him. He had been knocked unconscious in only a matter of seconds. Combatant 2 raised his arms in victory and trash filled the arena floor just as quickly.

"At least he's alive. They're bringing out a stretcher; better than a gravedigger."

Ishiro'shea reluctantly nodded his head in agreement.

"Did you see Maxx tonight?" a voice said. "Wasn't he spectacular?"

"Oh hey, Mazilda. No, he's just a lucky bastard. I thought that little rodent had him beat."

"No chance," she countered. "He's—"

"What are you doing back here?" Duke said, cutting her off, which appeared to surprise Mazilda. "I have to fight your boyfriend tomorrow, remember."

"I thought you'd be happy about that?"

"Happy about getting a chance to embarrass that fake? Yes. I can't think of anything better. In fact, it makes this entire ordeal worthwhile."

"Then why are getting so snippy with me?"

"I'm not super jazzed about fighting Maxx with *you* in his corner."

"How sweet..."

"No, not 'how sweet.' As long as we've known each other, as much as we've cared for each other, I know you'll do anything needed to win. So, until after the fight, maybe we take a break from our side project related to Ishiro's parents."

"Duke? C'mon," Mazilda pleaded.

"Look, you're here with that..." Duke began, but he was stopped by Ishiro'shea, who pointed to the exit as a crowd of people made their way from the arena to the backstage area.

"Sorry, Mazilda, stay right there."

"I thought you wanted me to leave?"

"Okay, leave. Do whatever. We have to go see something."

She pivoted and saw the passing stretcher, upon which lay a beaten Seamus O'Hoolihan. She stepped aside and let Ishiro'shea pass. Then she stepped in front of Duke.

"I get that you don't want me here before the match. It's a bit paranoid, but whatever. But don't keep me away from talking to Seamus with you. I'm as invested in tracking down Ish's parents as you."

"Fine," Duke said reluctantly.

As they approached the stretcher, Duke could see that Seamus was fastened down but his eyes were wide open.

"Seamus," Duke began, trying to keep pace with the medical team carrying the downed Irishman.

"Hey, mate. I got my arse kicked by that guy."

"A lucky shot," chimed in Mazilda.

"Funny one, lass," Seamus said. "Good luck if you have to scrap with 'im, Duke."

"How are you feeling?"

"I've been better. Not sure why they have me strapped down like this, it's like they've never seen someone get knocked out before. I'm sure they'll give me some headache meds and send me on my way."

"That's good. It looked pretty brutal. Glad to see that you're not badly damaged."

"No more than normal."

"I know this isn't the perfect time—" Duke began.

He was cut off by Mazilda. "Any new news on the Father?"

"Actually, yes. Let's meet up at the Pondscum after I get done with these morons. I have some news that you might find quite interesting."

"Like what?" Mazilda asked assertively.

Seamus smiled back at her. He turned to face Duke. "Talk to you in a bit, mate."

CHAPTER 22

DUKE, ISHIRO'SHEA, AND MAZILDA SAT around the table in the back room of the Pondscum Tavern. They had instructed the bartender to usher Potato Lips discreetly to them when he arrived. They had no timetable but, with a few unopened barrels of Glyptodian Summer Ale lining the back wall of the room, they weren't in any rush.

"I'm still not sure about you being here," Duke said to Mazilda. "I mean, at least not tonight, on the eve of the epic battle of bounty hunting legends. Well, one bounty hunting legend and one jerk that couldn't bounty hunt his way out of a paper bag."

"You're a legend now?" Mazilda quipped, rolling her eyes.

"Well, we aren't going to let any of our strategy slip out."

"Strategy? *You* have a strategy? I thought you were allergic to strategy, to planning, and to anything that requires you to do something that can't be classified as wingin' it."

"Why does that surprise you? We've won three matches

here. If I recall, I'm the first one ever to do that after being stuck in that damn melee. First one ever. In a million years. *One million years.*"

"So, if *I* recall, your strategy has actually been: one, hide behind an explosive Blop with a death wish; two, hope that the grand champion of Psitakki gets maliciously attacked outside the tournament so he will be half-blind, concussed, and crippled; and three, ride around on the back of a flying insect and get a dagger handed to you by your ex-girlfriend so you can clip his wings and crash him into a wall?"

Duke pondered this for a moment. He smiled. "Pretty much, more or less."

"You're such an ass."

"Speaking of asses," Duke responded as he nodded towards the door.

"Maxx, baby, what are you doing here?"

Gemstarr wasn't smiling, which concerned Duke because he assumed that Maxx's face was permanently fixed into an affable expression, ready for publicity shots and whatnot. Maxx pushed away the Psitakki bartender, who apologized from the hallway. He eventually gave up and ran back to the front of the house.

"What am *I* doing here?" Maxx said. "Shouldn't I be asking you the same thing, Mazilda?"

"We talked about this, Maxx," she said softly through gritted teeth.

"Fraternizing with my next opponent? We talked about no such thing. You're already on thin ice after your debacle earlier."

"Do tell?" Duke interjected with a sly grin.

Mazilda's face grew red. She glared at the Nova Texan.

"Did you see my last fight, LaGrange?" Maxx said.

"I did. You better not try to start a career as an exterminator given how you struggled with that rat, Maxxy."

"Yeah, the match would've been over if I had a corner man with half a brain."

"Hey," Mazilda's voice rose above the others. "I said I was sorry for not picking up that flail when it was beside my seat."

"Any corner man worth their weight would've known to do that. Because of you, I had to repair a suit and get five stitches."

Wait, five stitches in his suit? Duke asked himself.

"Mazilda, you're lucky that I'm Maxx Gemstarr."

"So lucky," Duke whispered to Mazilda, out of Maxx's earshot.

It was clear that she wasn't happy with either of them.

"Do you know who I am, Mazilda?" Maxx said. "You're lucky to be the woman standing next to me. No more of those sneaky, bush league assassin gigs for you anymore. And why is that? Because of me. So, leave these two morons to themselves and let's go."

Mazilda took a deep breath.

Oh, she's going to kill him, thought Duke. *Hey, maybe I'll get a free pass to the finals.*

Mazilda reached down to her thigh.

Dagger to the face, coming up!

However, Mazilda didn't pull out one of her deadly throwing knives. She scooted the chair out gently and stood up. "Yes, Maxx. Sorry."

Duke and Ishiro'shea exchanged confused looks.

That's not the Mazilda that I knew.

"Wait a damn second, here. She might be scared of you, but I'm not," Duke proclaimed.

"Stop, Duke. Not worth it," Mazilda whispered so that only Duke would hear.

Duke ignored her.

"If she wants to stay with us, she can stay with us,"

Duke said. He removed his laser revolver from its holster and twirled it on his finger.

Maxx didn't seem too impressed. "And you're going to make me leave, are you? With that puny pea shooter?"

Duke then removed Ol' Betsy from his back. "How about *this* pea shooter?"

Maxx's eyes widened and he took a step back. "Hey now, Duke. No need to do anything stupid."

"If Mazilda wants to stay here with us until Seamus arrives, she's more than welcome to. She's not sharing any of your tricks or secrets because, quite frankly, I don't need them. Tomorrow I'm going to expose you as the fraud you are."

"Did you say Seamus? As in Seamus O'Hoolihan?" asked Maxx.

"Yes."

"Potato Lips?"

"Yes, Potato Lips."

"You haven't heard, have you?"

"Heard what?"

"He's dead."

"What are you talking about?"

"It's all over the news, man. How long have you been in here drinking?"

Duke didn't answer.

"What happened?" Mazilda chimed in.

"They don't know—only that when he was in the medical tent awaiting his final clearance so that he could leave, he fell on something sharp."

"Something sharp," asked Mazilda.

"Yeah, maybe a surgical tool. Or a knife. Or something. But it went right through his neck. Dead."

Ishiro'shea banged his fist on the table and sat down heavily.

"So you're probably going to be waiting around for some time," Maxx laughed.

No one joined in.

Duke slumped down in a chair despondently.

"I guess that you can come with me now, Mazilda. See you tomorrow, LaGrange," Maxx said with a subtle cackle in his voice.

"This doesn't make any sense," Duke said to his companion. "What are we missing?" He looked around the room. "Hey, where'd Mazilda go? Did she leave with Maxx?"

Ishiro'shea shrugged.

Duke strolled over to the door and peered into the hallway. He saw Maxx grasping Mazilda's arm as she struggled to keep up with his long strides.

"I don't need you, Mazilda," Maxx muttered. "You need me. Remember that. Okay? You're making me regret this relationship. Stop hanging out with those losers."

They turned the corner and were gone.

Ishiro'shea still sat at the table, gazing at its surface dolefully.

"We'll get to the bottom of this. Don't worry. This is just an inopportune setback. We're already better off than when we got dumped here. We just gotta get out of this tournament alive."

CHAPTER 23

I CAN'T LOSE

"YOU'RE UP FIRST TODAY, LAGRANGE," barked the producer.

"Are you ever in a good mood?" asked the bounty hunter.

"Not when I have to deal with the likes of you," replied the Psitakki.

"Hey! What did I do?"

"Nothing personal, LaGrange. I already told you that you're a ratings killer. In fact, the only way the ratings would improve is if you got killed."

"That can't be right. People love me."

"No, they *hate* you," corrected the producer. "Not love... hate. But it's not a 'We all want to see him beaten to a pulp' hate like the hate for Combatant 2. Yours is more of an 'Ugh, can someone just remove this guy from my screen?' hate. One gets me ratings. The other one gets me fired."

Duke didn't reply. He couldn't. He felt emasculated.

"But," the producer continued, "things are looking up."

"Fans are finally starting to get me now? Taking down that royal bug must've won me some fans."

"Nope, you're fighting Maxx Gemstarr. He's a ratings magnet. So, for once, I'm not dreading you gracing the airwaves. You know, I don't exactly get a do-over with this tournament."

"I hate Maxx Gemstarr," Duke shouted.

"You're the only who does. Any time he's on, most galaxies tune in."

"I hate him even more now."

"Regardless, try to last more than a few seconds. We need some drama."

Duke tipped his hat without answering and moved down the hallway to his holding room.

"Don't worry, Ish," Duke began as he hung his hat and holsters on the wall pegs. "I promise that we'll start investigating what happened to Seamus after the fight tonight. Win, lose, or draw, I promise."

The ninja shook his head and sat cross-legged on the floor. Duke flopped on the couch.

"You know, Seamus' mutation made his skin almost impenetrable. How could a tiny surgical instrument kill him? Even if he had areas that weren't as calloused, how impossible is it that he accidentally fell down and landed on something sharp enough to penetrate his skin in the exact location that would kill him? I'll answer it. It's *very* impossible."

Duke reclined on the couch and closed his eyes. He started to hum the Nova Texan planetary anthem. Within moments he was asleep.

"Wake up, LaGrange. You're on in a few."

"Man, that guy is annoying," Duke said to Ishiro'shea in between yawns.

Ishiro'shea stared at Duke.

"What? You don't think I'm taking this fight with Maxx seriously?"

The ninja nodded.

"I am, give me some credit. I just happen to know that I'm smarter, faster, and craftier than him. He's just a pile of muscles. One carefully placed punch and he's done. The Goother and the sword guy didn't even get a clean shot at him—his face, at least. I just have to avoid his magic wristband thingies. Easy enough."

Ishiro'shea looked disappointed.

"You don't think I can win? My own corner man? What do you think I should do?"

The ninja shrugged.

"Thanks, that's helpful," Duke replied sarcastically.

Duke splashed water on his face and partook in some mild calisthenics as his pre-fight preparations. He threw some punches into Ishiro's open hands. He felt good. He felt ready.

Finally, I get to kick that bastard's ass, once and for all, he thought.

As he made his way through the arena doors towards his designated area along the barrier, he was overwhelmed by the usual negative reception. He just ignored it this time. He didn't taunt. He was focused on his opponent, or at least the outcome that he desperately wanted.

The lights dimmed and the music and laser show that was Maxx Gemstarr's entrance filled the hall. It seemed more over-the-top from the floor of the arena. It engulfed the entire space; you would have had to hide in a lavatory deep in the bowels of the stadium to escape the reach of Maxx's introductory spectacle. Duke looked up at Ishiro'shea; the ninja was bobbing his head to the beat.

"Hey," Duke shouted. "You're on my team, remember."

Duke could see Ishiro's smirk under his mask.

Unlike the first two rounds, in which Maxx had sauntered out to the crowd's praise, only stopping to flex and pose, this time the Universe's Favorite Bounty Hunter rode in on a small decorative hovercraft. Lasers and lights pulsed from every nook and cranny of the ship. Smoke billowed from below until it almost covered the entire arena floor. By the time the hovercraft slowed to a stop, Duke estimated that only his hat would be visible to the crowd. Trailing behind Maxx were two lines of scantily-clad females from a dozen different systems. They all danced in a choreographed routine and, at its conclusion, hoisted up a banner that read: *You're our hero, Maxx! Beat Duke LaGreen. Love, the Gemstarrlets.*

"It's LaGrange," shouted Duke. "It's LaGrange! How hard is it?"

Not a single spectator acknowledged his plea. Their eyes were all fixated on the pomp and circumstance around the entrance of Maxx Gemstarr.

This is pointless, realized Duke.

As the public address announcer screamed Maxx's name, the roar from those in attendance nearly shattered the roof. It was truly deafening. It would have even made Gjrazzel's ovation seem pedestrian.

It's going to be so great to shut these people up and expose Maxx for the fraud that he is, Duke thought. But just as he finished that thought, another crept into his mind. *Holy hedgehogs, what if I actually lose? What if I lose to Maxx Gemstarr? I'll be banned from every reputable establishment in the whole of the universe. The Queen might even disown me as a patron.*

As the vents in the bottom of the arena floor sucked up the excess smoke produced by Maxx's hovercraft, Duke gulped nervously. Beads of sweat rolled down his forehead.

I can't lose. I can't lose. I can't lose.

His thoughts became more and more distracting as he approached the referee at the center.

"I can't lose. I can't lose. I can't lose," he mumbled aloud.

"Oh yes you can. You can. You can," Maxx replied in a velvety baritone. "And you will. And probably rather quickly and in a humiliating fashion."

The referee tried—unsuccessfully—to stifle a chuckle.

"What?" Duke said distractedly. "Shut up, Maxx."

"Ouch. Duke, you are on fire today."

The official laughed again, this time not even trying to hold it in. Duke glared at him and he clamped his mouth shut.

"You two know the rules," the referee began, "so I want..."

"We know what you want," Maxx interjected, "and I promise to give you and the universe what they want—Duke LaGrange out of this tournament."

"Works for me," the referee concluded and walked away.

The two combatants did not budge. Duke wiped the sweat from his brow but never broke eye contact.

"You know you're a loser, LaGrange."

"Loser can mean so many things. It's a big universe, lots of interpretations."

"Your jokes aren't going to save you today. Neither will a Blop or a Jungafallowian sneak attack or an insect that can't land. You are going to get really hurt. I'm going to make sure every bounty hunter, former bounty hunters, bounty hunters with expired licenses, wives of bounty hunters, and children contemplating an exciting career in the field of bounty hunting know that I was the one that broke you down and beat you to a pulp."

"What if I beat you?"

"What? Don't be ridiculous."

"Okay, let's say that you are the favorite."

"I am."

"Fine. And you should win. But you don't. Have you worked out how you're going to explain that to your fans? It's not like you lost to a Mega-Troll or a Jungafallowian giant or the greatest boxer on Gartosh. You would lose to another bounty hunter. And one that didn't even get a proper invitation. You won't be the Galaxy's Favorite Bounty Hunter anymore."

"It's the Universe's Favorite Bounty Hunter," replied Maxx.

"Whatever. You will just go back to being a muscled-up moron in spandex. You will go back to being the fraud that you are."

Maxx seemed to ponder this notion for a minute.

Go ahead, you big dumb animal. Get your mind thinking about something else. You only have so many brain cells, thought Duke.

Maxx came to attention. "Nope, don't think it can happen. There's no way that you can beat me, LaGrange. And it will be extra special knowing that Mazilda will be in my corner watching me decimate you."

Duke peeked around his rival's massive frame. "Where is Mazilda?"

Maxx turned around and realized that his girlfriend and corner man was not in her customary position.

"Trouble in paradise?"

"Shut up, LaGrange."

"Oh, and when I beat you, I'll make sure to add in an extra shot for how you've been treating her."

"I'm real scared," Gemstarr replied, expressing faux terror.

The Psitakki referee approached them at a full sprint. He stopped mere inches from the two combatants. "Guys, get back to your spots so we can start this thing," he ordered in between breaths.

The trumpets sounded. Duke LaGrange, one of the Andromeda Galaxy's most renowned bounty hunter play-boys, would finally get his crack at Maxx Gemstarr, the celebrity known to all as the Universe's Favorite Bounty Hunter.

CHAPTER 24

SEMIFINALS

A FEW MOMENTS INTO HIS bout, Duke realized that Maxx Gemstarr might be a fraud when it came to bounty hunting, but he was a more than capable scrapper. In fact, he could teach master classes in the art of asskicking. Duke was slowly becoming his worst pupil. Though he had managed to avoid a disastrous death blow from Maxx's power gauntlets, he was proving less successful at avoiding his fists, knees, and feet, all of which were introduced to Duke's body with unyielding force.

"Have you ever actually fought anyone before, LaGrange?"

"Shut up, Maxx," replied Duke. "You can't be all that tough if I'm still talking, huh?"

Maxx connected with a swift boot to Duke's chest, sending the Nova Texan to the dirt. Duke's vision was getting hazy and his hearing a bit muffled. But he was lucid enough to look up and see Gemstarr's expansive grin and hear the chorus of cheers from those in attendance. He struggled more and more for each breath. He was not only about to lose to Maxx Gemstarr, he was about to lose without landing a single punch. He was going to lose without even getting a fleck of dirt on Maxx's ridiculous spandex jumpsuit. He was about to be the laughing stock of the bounty hunting world.

"Don't you wish Mazilda was watching this?" Duke said, clutching his chest.

"Your distractions aren't going to work. I wish I could say that I've been wanting to do this for a while but to be honest, LaGrange, I kinda forgot about you."

The hulking Gemstarr stood over the reeling Nova Texan. Duke wasn't sure what was going to happen, but he knew it was going to hurt.

Then he had an idea, something that he hadn't thought of in quite some time.

"My dad taught me this one," Duke muttered.

As Maxx raised his foot to stomp on his face, Duke dug his fingers deep into the arena floor, shoveling up as much dirt as he could. He hurled it directly into Gemstarr's eyes. Maxx staggered back, wiping the soil from his eyes. His blindness was only temporary, so Duke leapt on his first opening in the contest.

Duke struck Maxx in the face with his right hand, followed by a knee to the midsection, and another right to his jaw. Gemstarr winced and dropped to a knee. He held up his muscular frame with his right arm. Duke had him wobbling and he needed to finish him off. He drove another fist into his kneeling opponent's jaw. Maxx absorbed the shot and didn't fall to the ground as Duke had hoped. Duke went in for another but Maxx rose up before the strike could land, swinging his elbow back and catching Duke flush. The Nova Texan was once again on his backside with the Universe's Favorite Bounty Hunter standing over him.

"I thought you were an orphan," said Gemstarr. "What dad teaches someone that dirty of a trick?"

Duke couldn't think of a witty comeback. He could

only think about his impending demise at the hands of someone that bastardized and profited off of the noble profession of bounty hunting. This was not going to be pretty.

"You've had your fun, now you say good night," Maxx declared softly. It was the first time that Duke LaGrange actually feared Maxx. *Maybe he isn't such a joke after all.*

Maxx raised his right hand in the air. The power gauntlet embedded in his forearm pulsed neon blue. Duke could hear a buzzing sound.

"Your time in this tournament is over!" screamed Maxx. Then, "What the—"

His arm began to spark and started to spasm in every direction.

"What's going on?" he shouted frantically.

His arm, driven by the gauntlet, whipped around his body in jerky motions. The motor in the out-of-control forearm guard was quite powerful; it twisted Maxx's entire body in a series of wild convulsions. It slammed him into the ground. Again. And again. The audience sat in total silence as the cries and pleas from the muscular bounty hunter rang throughout the arena.

Duke scooted to the barrier wall to avoid the flailing Gemstarr. He looked up at Ishiro'shea. Beside the ninja, in the area designated for the corner man, was Mazilda Cloax.

"What are you—" he began.

"Finish this clown," Mazilda hissed.

She handed Duke his favorite weapon, Ol' Betsy. The crowd started to complain—they obviously weren't quite over the controversial ending to the match against their home world hero, Gjrazzel.

Duke walked up to the clearly suffering Gemstarr. He was standing but struggling to keep his arm at bay; he was battered and bruised.

"This one is for Mazilda."

The butt of Ol' Betsy cracked Maxx in the face. He dropped to the arena floor like a felled tarzantia tree.

Duke looked back at a smiling Mazilda.

This was a good day.

The referee raised Duke's hand in victory. Then the bounty hunter collapsed, equal parts exhausted and overjoyed.

Duke was on the couch in his holding room, wet towels on his forehead.

"How long have I been out?"

"Not long, Mr. LaGrange," answered a Psitakki medic. "We're just here to make sure that you can continue. It seems you are just a bit dehydrated. We've stuck a few tubes here and here to get your fluids back up. Your species loses your fluids at such a rapid pace, very odd. I'm surprised that you can do *anything* athletic in nature."

"Thanks, doc."

"I'm done here, you've cleared my tests. Get some rest, Mr. LaGrange. You've got a big fight tomorrow. I hope your luck doesn't run out."

"Luck? That's talent."

The doctor did not respond. He closed up his medical kit and exited the room. A team of four other Psitakki trailed after him.

"Ish, where's Mazilda?"

The ninja shrugged.

"She helped us. She helped me. Not Maxx," Duke said, his eyes wide and his smile stretching across his face, nearly touching his jawline. "What do you think it means?"

Ishiro'shea repeated his shrug.

"Oh, wait a second, is Yvonne's fight on? I want her to waste that Jungafallowian monster. If she took out a Mega-Troll, she can take out this guy, right?"

Ishiro'shea turned on the monitor just as the fight was about to begin.

"This is going to be good."

The crowd was solidly behind the Gartoshian musk ox; Duke enjoyed the hate that Combatant 2 received from the fans. He was surprised how much he enjoyed not being the most hated competitor in the field. Prince Korzo-Tapor continued his taunting of the crowd both during the entrance and while standing in the corner man's box at the barrier wall.

Combatant 2 came out as the aggressor but Yvonne was able to avoid his clutches. She ducked under his lunges and frustrated the overgrown brute. After a missed attempt at a stomp, Yvonne landed a few hard body blows to the Jungafallowian's right side, just under his armpit. Due to his extreme height advantage, she had to reach a bit and it was clear her strikes didn't have their normal power—but they were enough to annoy Combatant 2. He lunged again and missed. Yvonne peppered him again on one side. He tried to counter with a big left hand but his swipe missed the musk ox. Yvonne connected a right cross to one of Combatant 2's heads. It appeared stunned but Combatant 2 didn't lose his balance. The fact that he didn't show much damage after the blow froze Yvonne—it appeared that she was trying to process the fact that he was still upright. It was enough of an opportunity for the Jungafallowian to grab her and hurl her across the arena.

Yvonne got to her feet having suffered only a few scrapes. Combatant 2 ran towards her. She did the same, lowering her head as she sped towards the gargantuan beast.

"This is what she knocked Reginald out with," screamed Duke in excitement. "Get 'em, Yvonne. Get—"

His words ceased but his mouth hung open.

The musk ox had leapt in the air, horns first, as she had during the earlier action. It was a tactic that appeared impossible to survive. Her cranium struck Combatant 2 squarely in the chest. Duke estimated that the collision could be heard in neighboring star systems. The crowd was silenced.

Not only did Combatant 2 survive, he stood firm. Yvonne was face-first in the arena dirt. She was out. The referee approached, but the Jungafallowian caught him and tossed him away. The referee hit the dirt with considerable force and rolled into the barrier wall.

He's not done with her, thought Duke.

The Jungafallowian hoisted up Yvonne by her throat. She dangled unconsciously from his grasp. He paraded her around the arena to rousing jeers. He motioned that he was going to crack her skull with his fist. The crowd grew even more restless.

"They can't let this happen," shouted Duke. He ripped off the tubes providing fluid to his body and stumbled to the door. Ishiro'shea followed close by, katana drawn. Duke exited through the tunnel and into the arena. The prince and Combatant 2 noticed the bounty hunters immediately. Korzo-Tapor already had the microphone in hand to address the arena.

"How sweet! Duke LaGrange, our next victim, is coming to watch the last few moments of life of the Furry Mountain of Moon Colony #1. He must be curious to see what is going to happen to him tomorrow."

"Let her go!" Duke screamed from the other side of the arena.

"What? What was that? I can't hear you, LaGrange,"

the prince said over the loudspeaker. "I guess we have to kill her now."

Ol' Betsy sang. The arena floor in front of Combatant 2 burst up. Only a gaping hole remained. At the edge of the crater, Combatant 2 remained as still as a statue, still clutching Yvonne by the neck.

"Drop her," Duke yelled at the prince.

"Even you aren't dumb enough to..."

In one motion, Duke had holstered Betsy and drew his laser revolver. He loosed one pulse. It cleaved the top of the microphone off.

Duke and the prince locked eyes. The stare down lasted for what seemed like ages. Korzo-Tapor broke off first and signaled to Combatant 2. He dropped Yvonne unceremoniously into the pit that Betsy had created. He marched to the prince's location.

"We will see you tomorrow, LaGrange," the prince snarled. "You're a dead man. Big mistake. Really big mistake."

Ishiro'shea ran to Yvonne's aid, signaling for the Psitakki medical teams.

Duke was caught off guard. The crowd was cheering him.

The Grand Shaman came over the public address speaker, attempting to calm the situation. He sent in his personal guards to separate Duke from the exiting prince and Combatant 2. The situation was diffused quickly. Duke couldn't help but think that this was the producer's idea.

The medical team carried off Yvonne. Ishiro'shea looked back at Duke with concern in his eyes.

"Go ahead and make sure she's fine. Meet you back at the Pondscum tonight."

Ishiro'shea gave him a thumbs-up.

It'll probably keep his mind off of the Seamus stuff, thought Duke.

The bounty hunter was ushered back to his holding room by the Shaman's guards.

"I'm fine, I'm fine. You can go," Duke protested.

They threw him forcefully into his room. His momentum caused him to fall ungraciously onto the couch.

"Thanks, appreciate the help, guys."

The guards did not acknowledge Duke. One of them slammed the door and Duke heard their footsteps as they marched away.

A knock followed shortly after.

"I'm in here. Not causing any trouble. You can go away. Thanks."

The door opened slowly. It wasn't a Psitakki guard.

"I'm fine with a little trouble."

Mazilda has never looked so beautiful.

CHAPTER 25

ONE MORE ADVENTURE

DUKE SWUNG THE DOOR OPEN to the backroom of the Pondscum Tavern. It crashed against the wall. His life-long companion, Ishiro'shea, looked up at him. Duke smiled. Ishiro'shea then glanced down at what Duke clutched in his hand: the hand of Mazilda Cloax. The ninja stood up and held a glass high in the air.

"How about you do a little less toasting and a bit more pouring," said Mazilda with a smile.

Ishiro's eyes brightened. He vaulted to the beer barrels that lined the back wall. Before Duke and Mazilda sat down, he had placed two full mugs of Glyptodian Summer Ale before them.

"It seems that, for the time being, the band is back together," proclaimed Duke.

"Let's just get you through tomorrow alive," Mazilda said.

"Sounds like a plan to me," Duke replied, hoisting up his glass for another round of celebratory cheers.

The three reminisced about past adventures and misadventures, from Mazilda single-handedly sinking a Zylantian pirate ship to Ishiro'shea's sword battles with the Shark-women of Freylonia to Duke's trials dealing with the Hiritai tribes. Mazilda didn't appear to care too much for those stories. They shared laughs and tears as they recalled the time that they'd spent together.

Duke was in the midst of recounting a particularly crazy adventure involving him and Ishiro'shea on a primitive world, a madman, and a magic orb, when their session was interrupted by an irate Prince Korzo-Tapor.

"Don't bother getting up," the prince shouted as he approached the table. All four of his eyes were enraged. One head spoke as the other cycled through a progression of snarls and scowls. "Nice to see you, Mazilda Cloax. Ditching yesterday's news for your new toy?"

"I'm actually her used toy," Duke said with a smirk. "I pre-date that goon I beat down."

"Regardless," the prince said, "you will *die* tomorrow. No bones about it. It's over, LaGrange. No one insults me in public like that. You'll wish that your shot had actually hit me."

"Where's your friend?" asked Duke.

"Combatant 2 is resting. Trying to invent new ways to destroy you."

"Neat."

"He's unstoppable. You saw him today. Not even your cow friend could faze him. He took her best shot and shrugged it off like a gust of wind."

"I'll admit, Prince, it was impressive. But I have a few tricks up my sleeve."

"We shall see, LaGrange. Tomorrow you die."

"You've said that already. If it's my last night, can you do me a favor and let me enjoy it with the best friend a man could have and the prettiest lady in the galaxy?"

Prince Korzo-Tapor looked around at the table and

laughed. He stormed to the doorway just as the Psitakki bartender was entering.

"Mr. LaGrange, the prince..." the bartender began, but then stopped at the sight of the Jungafallowian.

"A bit late there, barkeep, but no worries," said Duke. "The good prince was just leaving."

Korzo-Tapor left the room as the bartender apologized profusely.

"Stop," Duke said. "Go back and serve some drinks."

"So Duke, what are these tricks up your sleeve?" asked Mazilda.

"I got nothing."

Mazilda pulled out a pair of keys and dangled them in front of Duke.

"Lucky for you, I got something," she said smugly.

"What's that?" asked Duke. He snatched the keys and examined them. "Did you swipe these off the prince?"

Mazilda nodded.

"The emblem says Psitakki General Storage for Big Stuff and Really Big Stuff," read Duke.

"Hey, bartender, get back in here!" shouted Duke.

A few moments later, the bartender arrived.

"Do you know where this is? This General Storage place?" asked Duke.

The Psitakki glanced at the key and seemed to recognize the emblem immediately. "Yes, sir. It's just around the corner. It's a huge warehouse-type facility, heavily guarded. It's actually where we keep our surplus alcohol."

"Interesting," Duke began. "Why would a prince with unlimited funds, along with his prizefighter, be staying in a shady storage unit?"

"Interesting indeed," Mazilda agreed. "Maybe we pay him a visit?"

"I don't think you'll be able to get in," interjected the barkeep.

"We will if they think we're picking up some barrels of Glyptodian Summer Ale for you," said Duke slyly.

"I don't know."

"You don't want to be known as the bartender that prevented a finalist in the Tournament of the Shield of the Colossal Calamari from investigating a potential cheat..."

"Fine, fine. Just do it," the bartender said huffily. "I'll be happy when this damn tournament is over with."

That change of heart came on fairly quickly, Duke noticed.

The Psitakki tossed the key back to Duke and relayed a passcode for entrance into the bar's storage unit.

"If you get caught, I'm going to tell them that you robbed me at gunpoint."

"Fair enough," agreed Duke as the bartender exited the room. He turned to face his companions. "Ready for one more adventure?"

"But, promise me, after we see what's up with the prince and his brainwashed monster, we refocus our efforts on Ish's parents," Mazilda said.

"And Seamus," Duke added. "Yes. Of course we will. That's the most important mission, no doubt."

"What are we waiting for, then?"

This warehouse looks like a... well, a warehouse.

"I was expecting, I don't know, more," said Duke. "If the prince is brewing up something questionable, seems like he would've picked a place with a bit more, I don't know, pizazz."

"I think he wants to hide in plain sight," countered Mazilda. "Nothing about this place really makes you think 'Oh, hey, there might be a crazed sociopath with an unhinged monster under his control in here'. It's actually what I would've done."

Duke clicked his fingers against his chin. "Whatever. So do we knock?"

"Or should we try to get in with a bit less..." Mazilda started.

"Permission?"

"That's one way to put it."

"I think Ish has already made that decision for us."

They looked up to see the emerald-clad martial artist scaling the drab stone perimeter wall. He gave a thumbs-up, then turned around at the apex. Not a sound could be heard as he, presumably, landed safely on the other side.

"Odd. No alarms," noted Duke.

"I don't think burglary is a common practice on Psitakki. Probably don't see the need."

"Or it means that the real security is on the inside."

The rusted door that marked the side entrance opened slowly with a whine and a creak. Duke drew his laser revolver, Mazilda pulled out both of her throwing daggers. The moonlight caught the blade and twinkled.

"I really hope this is Ishiro," said Duke.

From the shadows emerged the stout ninja.

Thank you.

He waved them in cautiously; Mazilda closed the door softly behind them.

The trio came upon a second door that led into an interior building and, fortunately, it was unlocked. They proceeded down a stairwell. It was musty, with sporadic puddles of standing water, but it wasn't gross. It wasn't a cave. Duke wasn't a fan of caves, unless they were on

Oscavia. This dilapidated warehouse was an upgrade from the majority of caves.

"I woulda thought that there'd be at least one person here. It's a huge storage facility and no one is tending to their stuff? No picking up or loading up or piling in? We can't be the only ones here."

"That *is* odd, Duke. What's the prince's unit number again?"

"1314, right, Ish?"

Ishiro'shea nodded.

"That has to be around the corner to the right."

As the three approached the unit, it was clear that unit 1314 was one of the largest in the facility. It was the size of most of the single-family dwellings on Earth or Nova Texas.

"I don't get the property choice, but at least the prince has some space. Maybe he got a screamin' deal?"

"Or maybe he's hiding something that can help you win tomorrow? There has to be something that will shine some light on his dealings or weaknesses in that brute of his," Mazilda added.

"That's the plan. Let me see the key, little buddy."

The gunfire came out of nowhere. More accurately, it came from the two units on either side of 1314.

A trap.

Four Jungafallowians emerged from the depths of the storage boxes and opened fire on the trio. Ishiro'shea bolted behind a pile of metallic crates. Duke shoved Mazilda out of the way and they both rolled to an area covered by a stone barricade.

Duke rattled off a bevy of pulses.

"I got one," Duke yelled. "Three more. They're toting pretty heavy guns for Jungafallowian thugs."

"Maybe the prince loaded them up with the best from his armory. He seemed to have this planned out."

Duke did not respond. He peered up over the barricade. An errant shot crashed into the stone mere paces from his face, and sent a chunk hurtling into the air.

"That was close."

The bounty hunter let loose another salvo of pulses.

"Got another one. I think. He's at least wounded."

"How did he know we were here? And why don't you seem to care?"

"I have it under control," replied Duke nonchalantly.

"What are you talking about?"

Duke lobbied a smile in Mazilda's direction.

"I don't like that look, Duke."

"Watch this."

The bounty hunter stood up and aimed Betsy at one of the storage facilities. She sang a melodious tune of chaos.

"Let's go!" he shouted.

Mazilda didn't flinch. Duke grabbed her by her arm and lifted her into the air. A less nimble being would have landed irregularly, tripped, and smashed their face on the ground. But Mazilda was one of the deadliest assassins in the galaxy; definitely one of the deadliest that had come from the ranks of bounty hunting.

Duke slid Betsy back into her holster and grabbed his laser revolver. He fired into the ceiling.

"You aren't hitting anything!" Mazilda shouted as he dragged her through the smoke-filled corridor, dodging enemy fire.

"I just want them to chase me. Well, us."

"What?"

Duke pushed open the door that led to the exterior courtyard. He slammed it.

"Hurry, let's head to the Pondscum. They won't follow us there."

"What about Ishiro'shea?" Mazilda asked.

"All part of the plan, Mazilda."

"What plan?" she questioned the bounty hunter.

"*The* plan. The plan to lure these guys out after us and leave Ishiro there to figure out the real scoop."

"You honestly planned for an ambush?"

"Of course. The possibility of an ambush, at least. The prince is a smart guy. He'll have noticed his keys were gone. Once he didn't come back for them—like anyone that didn't have anything to hide would have done—I knew that he knew we would be heading that way."

"That's a bit of a convoluted plan. Even for you."

"What are you talking about? My plans are usually on the simple side. Shoot and run. And talk to a pretty alien if there's time."

The duo heard the interior door crashing into the stone wall.

"Let's go, Mazilda. Ishiro is going to do some digging and meet us back at the Pondscum in a few."

"If he's still alive."

CHAPTER 26

THE MAIN EVENT

DUKE LEANED UP AGAINST THE wall in his holding room. He twirled his pulse pistol on a finger, his gaze fixed on the floor.

"Hey, I'm worried about him too," Mazilda said softly. "But we're moments away from you having to fight that monster. He's crushed everyone that's he faced. Yvonne. That Olamandrian. Seamus. We need to come up with some sort of plan."

"I'm good," Duke muttered as he holstered his gun. "Ish will be here."

"I sure hope so. But whether he's here or not, it won't affect what happens in that arena. You need a plan, Duke. And what if..."

"What?"

"What if the worst happened?"

"That's easy. When I see the monster, I shoot the monster."

"The Psitakkis will be on you in no time. You'll spend the rest of your life with the Chief Interrogator General."

"You wouldn't rescue me?"

"Be serious."

"You wouldn't?"

The producer entered the room and broke the silence. "I can't believe you're still in this thing, LaGrange. But hey, ratings weren't too bad yesterday. Thanks to Gemstarr, of course. We're about ready for you. Where's your corner man?"

Duke pondered this question for a second. "I don't really know."

"I'm going to step in and handle the duties today," blurted Mazilda.

"Aren't you Maxx Gemstarr's girlfriend?" snapped the producer. "Well, this week, at least."

"I'm jumping ship for a winner," she replied.

"Oh. This is highly irregular," the Psitakki said.

"Think of it," Mazilda began, "even if the fight doesn't deliver..."

"It probably won't," the Psitakki interjected.

"Even if it doesn't, you can always spin a story about why Maxx's girlfriend is now with his hated rival, Duke LaGrange. Can you see it?"

The producer thought about this for a moment. A sly smile crept over his cephalopodan face. "Not sure that they'll believe LaGroin is Maxx's rival, but I do like the scandal, the intrigue. Gossip-rag angles do work. Everyone loves infidelity and scheming partners."

Duke stepped into the hallway. He looked around. No Ishiro'shea.

"Let's go do this," Duke said to the producer, without acknowledging the Psitakki's conversation with Mazilda.

The producer didn't respond. He turned his back to both Duke and Mazilda and tapped his headset. "What? What's going on? He's not what? I'm heading that way."

The Psitakki was clearly panicked. He glared at Duke.

"You know the way. Try and be somewhat entertaining. Or just die in a really exciting way."

"Isn't that what you told me last time?"

The producer scurried away frantically, screaming into his headset.

The Nova Texan looked up at the ceiling. It was pulsing with the vibrations coming from the arena. They wanted a finale worthy of the million-year history of the tournament. A finish worthy of the title "Tournament of the Shield of the Colossal Calamari."

The door slid open. The entire arena was pitch black. Suddenly lights and lasers beamed across the entire width of the stadium. Music boomed. It wasn't as elaborate an entrance as Maxx Gemstarr's—there were no Gemstarrlets or hovercrafts—but it was an upgrade over Duke's usual stroll into the arena amidst boos and debris slung by the fans.

The crowd gave Duke a healthy round of applause. Once again, it wasn't Maxx Gemstarr level, or even Sulaw or Yvonne or Glux. But it was probably on the same level as Jorb, or Tor-torta. Duke, for the first time since the Grand Entrance, tipped his hat to the fans.

"Introducing first, from the Earth colony of Nova Texas," the public address announcer began. "He's the greatest underdog story in the million-year history of the Tournament of the Shield of the Colossal Calamari; he's the first being to survive the melee match and win his first round contest; he's defeated the Royal Guardsman Glux Xyphormog II, he's defeated the Universe's Favorite Bounty Hunter, Maxx Gemstarr. He's the unexplainable and incomparable Duke LaGrange. A bounty hunter."

That's much better. Still no mention of Gjrazzel.

The announcer boomed, "And his opponent—"

He didn't continue. The microphone was simply cut off. Duke could sense the crowd growing curious.

From the entrance tunnel designated for Combatant 2 came another Jungafallowian. A much smaller Jungafallowian. A Jungafallowian that Duke LaGrange did not care for. And he had a hot microphone, wired into the public address system.

How does he keep getting hold of these microphones? Duke thought.

"What happened? Where is he? Where's Combatant 2? You know where he's at, don't you, LaGrange?"

Prince Korzo-Tapor was clearly not happy.

"That's funny, Prince. I had a question for you about a missing person, too," Duke shouted across the arena.

"What are you talking about, bounty hunter?"

This isn't going to go anywhere, concluded Duke.

The Jungafallowian prince turned to the Grand Shaman's box, halfway up a far section of seats.

"Shaman, disqualify this man! He kidnapped Combatant 2! I have it on good authority that he and his lackeys sabotaged my hotel last night and kidnapped Combatant 2."

"Hotel? Are you referring to that storage facility? The one with the armed thugs waiting to shoot us?"

The prince did not acknowledge Duke's dig. He continued to plead with the Grand Shaman. "This fraud has disgraced the name of this tournament, he's disgraced the Colossal Calamari, and he's disgraced the memory of Grozzel the Great. He's a black eye on the entire planet of Psitakki. You must deal with him. He must pay."

The Grand Shaman rose to his feet. His handlers and attendants followed suit. His robes flowed gently as he slid to the podium at the edge of his suite. From this pulpit, he could overlook the entire arena floor and address his people.

"Now, Prince Korzo-Tapor, I understand your complaint," he began, speaking into the microphone. "This is highly irregular, indeed. If what you say is true, that is."

"What do you mean?" hissed the prince.

"I have no proof that these accusations are true. It seems a bit far-fetched to think that anyone or anything could kidnap your impressive entrant. If anything, it takes some of the shine off of what was an unblemished reputation."

"He did. I don't know how, but he did."

"And," the Grand Shaman continued, "wasn't it you, mere days ago, that claimed that what happens outside of the tournament does not dictate the actions *in* the tournament? It was *your* Combatant 2 that injured Gjrazzel during the Grand Entrance. I allowed him to continue without penalty."

The recollection of this event caused a stir in the crowd. They began to cheer and applaud the Grand Shaman's train of thought.

He's a good politician, I'll give him that, thought Duke.

"Now why should I be so lenient towards you and Combatant 2, but not to Duke LaGrange?"

"Because Gjrazzel had that coming to him," Korzo-Tapor shouted.

The crowd's hatred reached a fever pitch. The Grand Shaman had to ask for them to calm down. It was apparent that even he sensed a riot about to unfold.

It was Korzo-Tapor that spoke next. "And we didn't try to make a mockery of the tournament. Did our personal dealings with Gjrazzel get a bit out of hand? Yes. But we didn't meticulously plan a kidnapping to disrupt the finals. This stain on evolution here... he did."

"A bit out of hand? My ass," shouted Duke from across the arena.

One of the prince's heads twisted back and flashed an intense glare at the bounty hunter.

"You do bring up some good points, my Jungafallowian friend," the Shaman began. The crowd started to rustle at this indication that he had had a change of heart. "But I do pride myself on being a fair leader."

The crowd veered back to cheering the Shaman.

He knows what he's doing.

"What to do?" the Shaman said with the voice of a true games master. "What should we do about this quandary? Do I send this bounty hunter to the Chief Interrogator General for a lifetime of torture and pain unparalleled in this sector of the galaxy, all on the word of my good friend, Prince Korzo-Tapor?"

The crowd moaned, groaned, and hissed.

"Or do I award the victory to Duke LaGrange? His ingenuity has allowed him to advance—in some cases, controversially—but he, to my knowledge, has broken no rules."

The audience applauded in favor of this course of action.

"Ah yes," the Shaman said, raising an index finger, "but, if Duke wins, then you are deprived of a final battle and a public beating at the hands of the Chief Interrogator. We do strive to give you your money's worth here on Psitakki."

The applause downgraded to only slightly positive murmurs, then into complete silence, then into gabbled conversation. A chant crept from the cheap seats in the upper regions of the stadium and into the areas of premium suites. It was gaining steam.

"Torture. Torture. Torture."

Both of the prince's heads turned back to the bounty hunter and smiled.

That turned fast.

"Calm down, my friends in attendance. No need to make a decision," the Shaman shouted in the voice of a great orator. "I've just received word from the back. It appears that Combatant 2 has arrived!"

"What?" shouted Korzo-Tapor. "Where?"

"It's obvious that Duke LaGrange did not kidnap his opponent," the Shaman continued, "and so, we have our main event!"

The crowd exploded.

Combatant 2 emerged from Duke's entrance tunnel slowly. Duke saw no signs of blood or bruises. He clearly hadn't been in combat.

Could he have killed Ishiro without even a scratch to show?

Combatant 2 trudged out slowly, to lukewarm applause. His plodding was so deliberate that Duke wasn't sure if he was actually moving. The fans clearly still hated him for what he had done to Gjrazzel, but he had shown up in time to provide them with a final fight, so had redeemed himself somewhat.

The prince stepped to the center of the arena floor and assumed the role of ringmaster. "Everyone in attendance, I present to you the greatest competitor in the history of this tournament. He's already set records that will outlast the universe itself. He's the destroyer of Kitar. He's the crusher of Seamus O'Hoolihan. He dominated and decimated Yvonne "The Furry Mountain of Moon Colony #1" Angerdlarnek. Now witness him obliterate Duke LaGrange in a matter of seconds and win a holy shield of Grozzel. He's the pride of Jungafallow III, he's Combatant 2!"

The ground rumbled and quaked as Combatant 2 crashed to the floor.

Duke was lifted into the air by the shock waves from the fallen monster. Korzo-Tapor, the closest to his collapsed entrant, fell awkwardly, dropping the microphone.

"No!" cried Korzo-Tapor. "This can't be. This can't be. Get up. Get up. Please."

The behemoth didn't move. But he did smoke. And he sizzled a bit. His back leg twitched irregularly. A single row of tiny explosions raced down his back. Slightly larger explosions followed all over the Jungafallowian's body. There was no blood, no exposed muscle tissue, no bones popping through the gaping gashes on his skin.

Metal.

"An android!" shouted the Grand Shaman.

"Duke, turn around, Duke!" screamed Mazilda.

"Holy hedgehogs!"

Stumbling towards Mazilda was Ishiro'shea. He was drunk. He toppled over the wall and hit the arena floor in the most un-ninja-like manner.

Duke ran over to his lifelong companion and knelt down. "You stupid bastard. You stupid drunk bastard. I thought I'd lost ya'."

Ishiro'shea gave him a groggy thumbs-up.

"You know Prince's guy is a frickin' robot?"

Ishiro'shea nodded.

"Wait. No? You didn't? Did you get the robot drunk?"

Another thumbs-up.

"And that's how you win at pit fighting with a drunk space ninja."

CHAPTER 27

FAIR AND SQUARE... FOR THE MOST PART

"I'M IMPRESSED, LITTLE BUDDY. I mean, I knew you could drink, like *really* drink, but to outdrink an android... That's next level, right there."

Ishiro'shea allowed a chesty belch to exit his body.

The Psitakki guards surrounded the buzzing carcass of Combatant 2 and the fuming Prince Korzo-Tapor.

"Get him!" bellowed the Grand Shaman from his perch. The guards tightened their circle around the Jungafallowian.

"If I were you, Shaman, I would tell them to back off," said Korzo-Tapor, still gripping the microphone.

"And why is that?"

"If you don't, you'll die."

"Is that right, Prince?"

"It is," said Korzo-Tapor, regaining an aura of calm. He flicked his finger at the Shaman, signaling for the Psitakki leader to turn around.

The guards stationed in the Shaman's suite had disappeared. In their place were two Jungafallowian thugs. Both pointed powerful blasters at his face.

"Now do you believe me?" asked the prince maniacally.

He jerked around to address Duke, Ishiro'shea, and Mazilda. "Put the gun down, LaGrange. If you as much as tickle me, my guys up there will splatter the Grand Shaman all over his adoring constituents."

"Why would I care about him?" asked Duke.

"C'mon, LaGrange, we both know that you won't cause political upheaval on another planet for the sake of escaping unharmed."

"I wouldn't?" Duke replied. "You think much higher of me than most, Prince. But you're wrong. I'm a survivalist, and an egotistical, self-centered one at that. I will most definitely do whatever is needed to save my skin, especially if it means the universe contains one less psychotic Jungafallowian."

"Fine, then, Duke. I'll give you some points for self-awareness. Fooled me. Go ahead and do it."

Prince Korzo-Tapor opened his arms as wide as possible, giving Duke a clear kill shot. "Kill me, bounty hunter."

The Grand Shaman screamed out from his stage, "Don't do it. We can work this out peacefully. Diplomatically."

"Go ahead, I'm waiting," the prince continued.

Duke begrudgingly placed his laser revolver back in its holster.

"That's what I thought," chuckled Korzo-Tapor. He turned his attention back to the Grand Shaman. "Here's what's going to happen. You're going to order everyone to drop their weapons. In fact, go ahead and do that now."

The Shaman signaled to the guards on the arena floor and stationed throughout the arena. They all complied.

"Then, I'm going to walk up to you, and you are—with a big smile on your face—going to award me the holy shield of Grozzel. Combatant 2 will be forever known as the last champion of this tournament. If I hear of you or anyone else saying otherwise, I will come back and personally disembowel you."

"Fine," the Shaman grumbled into his podium's microphone.

"Then you, me, and my two guards are going to proceed to my ship. If anyone tries anything funny, you get blown to a billion tiny Psitakki bits. Got it?"

Reluctantly, the Shaman shook his head in agreement.

"When we're safely in our ship, we'll throw you out of the cargo doors before takeoff, and we'll be out of your hair forever."

Solid plan, Duke concluded. *Probably what I would've done were I inclined to be a tyrannical villain.*

"What's the plan?" asked Mazilda in a hushed tone. "You are 'Mr. Plan' now, remember."

"No plan. I think we just let him get away. I mean, it's just a decorative shield. Frankly, I'm kinda impressed with the lengths he went to for an antique. I know some collectors get pretty intense over certain rare pieces; did you ever see *Attack of the Hobbyists?*"

"There's the Duke I know," Mazilda quipped.

"What's that supposed to mean?"

"Do you really think that the prince built a massive robot warrior that was undetectable to anyone as an actual android, traveled to one of the most deadly tournaments in the universe, and is staging what amounts to an assassination plot, all for a shield that's just really pretty to look at?"

Duke began to speak but was cut off.

"Don't answer that," Mazilda said. "You did, didn't you? Anyways, I'm inclined to believe that the shield probably means something. Something big. Maybe it has something to do with Ishiro's parents."

The ninja jolted out of his alcoholic daze at the mention of his parents.

"You went and woke him up, Mazilda, for a bunch of nonsense."

"Think about it. Seamus was looking for someone or something here that knew about Ishiro's parents."

"Yeah."

"The prince must've discovered something linking the shield and Ishiro's parent. So, he killed Seamus to get him out of the picture. He just assumed Combatant 2 would win without any mess and without attracting suspicion to the shield."

"But he didn't count on Duke LaGrange, trailblazer—"

"Stop it. But, yes, he didn't think there was anyone that could beat Combatant 2."

"Do you think that's why he attacked Gjrazzel, too? He did tell me that Gjrazzel was getting involved in business that wasn't his to get into."

"It's quite possible," Mazilda agreed.

"I guess that means that we *do* need a plan now," grumbled Duke. "Did I ever tell you that I'm not a huge fan of Psitakki?"

The trio peered up to watch Korzo-Tapor making his way up the stands to the Grand Shaman's box. None of the audience members tried to harm the prince, presumably for fear of being responsible for the Shaman's death. However, they did make some really nasty faces at him.

Duke pinched his temples with his thumb and middle finger. "I got nothing. Think, Duke, think."

"I'm not doing much better," added Mazilda.

"I wish the *Deus* was here," concluded Duke.

The prince had reached the Shaman's suite. "Open the case, oh great Shaman of Psitakki."

The Grand Shaman followed his orders. The glass casing atop its marble pedestal tilted open, revealing an ancient circular shield.

Not as glamorous as I would've thought.

Korzo-Tapor jerked the shield out of the case and placed it on his arm. Both heads grinned as they surveyed the priceless relic attached to his forearm.

"Grab the Shaman and bring him with us," the prince ordered his two stooges.

A wooden projectile whizzed through the air from behind the Shaman's chair in his box. The tarzantia staff struck Prince Korzo-Tapor directly in the chest. Duke could hear the Jungafallowian's bones crack on impact. It reminded him of a recent episode at Cyborg Joe's when he had been saved from another ruthless Jungafallowian by a stampeding anthropomorphic musk ox named Lilly Arnaq.

The botanical missile not only crushed the sternum of the two-headed royal, the force actually lifted him off the ground and tipped him over the edge of the Grand Shaman's suite. Prince Korzo-Tapor plummeted with extreme velocity towards the arena floor. His body lay sprawled out, lifeless, his outstretched arm still sporting its super-expensive piece of armor.

The two gun-toting henchmen whirled around, but didn't know who to shoot at. The Shaman, noticing the opening, dove under one of his chairs. Duke sent two pulses out. Each struck one of the Jungafallowian thugs, who both collapsed to the floor. Duke wasn't sure if he had killed them, as his vision was blocked by the railing, but he was confident that they were incapacitated.

Duke looked up to the box. Out of the shadows stepped a Psitakki covered in bandages, limping, and generally looking like he was in a whole lot of pain. He kicked away the guns from the immobile Jungafallowians.

"That's one tough bastard."

Gjrazzel exited the Shaman's box to a raucous ovation. As he descended the steps towards the arena floor he was mobbed by fans offering pats on the backs, pleas for hand-shakes and hugs, even the odd unsolicited kiss.

Mazilda grabbed Duke and Ishiro'shea by the hands and dragged them towards the corpse of Prince Korzo-Tapor. "That's your shield, Duke. Don't let Gjrazzel take it," she snapped.

"Surely he won't. He seems like a good guy. But he *is* making a beeline for it."

"Remember, he thinks you cheated," she argued. "These fans think you cheated. He will try and take it. Trust me."

Gjrazzel reached the prince's body at the same time as Duke, Mazilda, and Ishiro'shea. Neither side moved. Not a single muscle twitched amongst the two parties. The crowd, for the first time in many days, was totally silent, without a single murmur coming from the thousands in attendance.

It was Gjrazzel that moved first. He reached down and grabbed the shield. Duke unholstered his revolver. Mazilda readied a throwing dagger. Ishiro'shea drew his katana.

The Psitakki looked up at them. Duke noticed the confusion in his eyes. His body was beaten badly, after all, and he had no weapon, at least that the bounty hunter could see. The four remained in this position for some time, each assessing the situation and running the odds in their heads about what action-reaction combination would give them the best probability of survival.

Duke then put his gun away.

"What are you doing?" barked Mazilda.

He placed his hand on Ishiro'shea's katana, lowering it without any resistance.

"Mazilda, put away your knives."

"What? No."

"Please," Duke begged, never taking his eyes off of the Psitakki and the holy shield of Grozzel.

"I don't like this," she huffed as she placed her knives into her belt.

"Thank you," Gjrazzel said. "Thank you, Duke LaGrange, and his friends, for not letting this abomination ruin the legacy of our planet and its greatest hero."

Duke tipped his hat.

"I believe this is yours," Gjrazzel stated. He extended the shield to Duke. "You won, fair and square... for the most part."

Duke smiled at the Psitakki's addendum to his statement.

"Congratulations," Gjrazzel continued. "You honor the memory of my great-great-great-great-great-great..."

"I got it," Duke interrupted. "Your ancient ancestor."

The Nova Texan grabbed the shield and slid it onto his forearm. Gjrazzel put forth his hand. Duke took it and the pair shook hands to an eruption of hoots, applause, and other bodily sounds of a positive connotation. Gjrazzel raised the bounty hunter's hands in victory.

The Shaman stepped up to his podium.

"Duke LaGrange," he proclaimed, "the last champion of the Tournament of the Shield of the Colossal Calamari."

"See, I told you that I got this," Duke said to Mazilda with a wink.

She responded with a subtle shake of the head and a not-so-subtle roll of the eyes.

"I don't know about you," Duke began, "but I'm ready to celebrate."

Ishiro'shea extended two thumbs-up.

CHAPTER 28

A CRUEL REUNION

"SO HOW WAS I?"

MAZILDA slid closer to the bounty hunter and kissed him gently on the cheek.

"I've had better," she said with a laugh. She sprang out from the bed and walked over to a hutch in the corner of the room. She started to get dressed. "It's much nicer than the holding room, that's for sure."

"You're lucky you didn't see where Ish and I had to stay during the tournament."

"A dump?"

"That's putting it nicely. I don't even think *you* would be caught dead there with your clothes off."

Mazilda grabbed one of Duke's boots from beside the hutch and hurled it at him playfully. "Not funny, not at all."

"It's kinda amazing how much better your accommodations get when you win an ancient, quasi-religious combat tournament. I could get used to this," he said as he folded his arms behind his head. "Not a bad life. What's this joint called again?"

"The Palace Royale Hotel of..."

"Let me guess," Duke interjected. "...of the Colossal Calamari."

"Yep."

"And Ishiro got his own room! He never gets his own room."

"I'm glad you're happy."

"Are you sure you have to get dressed? Do you really have somewhere to be?"

"Are you sad, Mr. Champion of the Calamari?" Mazilda said, pouting. "Are you going to miss me?"

"Yes, of course," Duke said matter-of-factly. "Who, in their right mind, wouldn't miss a naked assassin of your skill set in their bed?"

Mazilda got back into the bed, only partially dressed. She crawled on top of Duke until her thighs were straddling his stomach.

"I think we have a bit more time," she whispered seductively. She bent down and kissed him. "How about we try this?"

"I'm game. Whatever it is, doesn't matter, I'm in. One hundred percent in!" Duke said eagerly.

"I sure missed your enthusiasm," Mazilda replied. "Let me grab something."

She hopped off of the Nova Texan and glided over to the hutch. She opened up a satchel and pulled out some shiny metallic objects. Within a blink, she was back in the bed and on top of Duke. She dangled the items in front of the bounty hunter.

"Handcuffs? You tart."

"I borrowed them from the Chief Interrogator General. I had an odd feeling that they'd come in handy, one way or another," she said.

"Not the most original idea, Mazilda, but on such short notice, it'll do."

She bent down and kissed him again.

"I promise you that this will be anything but unoriginal. You'll never have experienced anything like this before," she said assertively.

"Like I said, one hundred percent in."

She snapped his left wrist into a pair of the handcuffs, then cuffed it to the bedpost. She did the same to his right wrist using the second pair. She bent down again but didn't kiss him. Her lips were touching Duke's ear.

"I'm sorry, Duke," she whispered.

She vaulted off of the bed and headed back to the hutch.

"Very funny. Come back over here, you vixen."

"I'm sorry," Mazilda repeated.

"Not funny. You got me. This is original. Faking that you set me up in a not-so-innocent position. You win. Now come back over here!"

"I'm sorry," Mazilda repeated again as she finished getting dressed.

"No, don't put the clothes *on*. Mazilda, what's going on?"

She looked at him with a stern expression. As they locked eyes, her expression transformed into one of doubt, and then sadness.

She picked up the shield from the dresser and covered it in her cloak. She placed the bundle under her arm.

"This is what's going on," she said, signaling to the shield under her arm. "I really wished that you wouldn't have come here. It was a cruel reunion for both of us."

"Decidedly more cruel for one of us, obviously," Duke remarked.

"You have no idea what this is, do you? This is a power like you've never seen."

"You'd be surprised what I've seen recently when it

comes to powerful objects," Duke said, his thoughts drifting to his adventures on Neprius. "Why do you want it?"

"I don't. But my employer does."

"Your employer? What's going on, really? I thought you were going to help Ishiro and I find his parents."

Mazilda looked at the ground.

"This was all a lie," Duke shouted. "Us getting back together was a lie. Just a ruse."

She looked up. A tear fell from her eye.

"I'm sorry."

Before Duke could respond, Mazilda Cloax and the shield were out of the room.

I guess I should start screaming for help now.

"Don't judge me."

The green ninja remained silent as he worked on the handcuffs. Duke knew what he was thinking, though.

"You didn't sense it either. She fooled us both."

Ishiro'shea stopped working and glared at his bounty-hunting friend.

"Fine, she fooled me *more*."

The ninja went back to work on the handcuffs. They weren't releasing. Duke could sense Ishiro's frustration.

"Just cut 'em off. I'll worry about the pieces on my wrists later. If we're going to try and track her down, we better hurry."

Duke pulled his arms in as far as possible, creating a taut chain for Ishiro'shea to aim at. The bounty hunter closed his eyes. A gush of wind, a loud crack, and his left arm was free, then his right.

"Thanks, little buddy. We need to go now if we're ever to find her."

Ishiro'shea paused and tilted his head at Duke's half-clothed body.

"Yes, after I get dressed, of course."

The former Salutatorian from the College of Cohorts, Consorts, Co-Conspirators, and Other Assorted Sidekick Types darted to the door.

"You got an idea?"

Ishiro'shea returned a thumbs-up and then waved his hand for Duke to hurry up.

"Give me a second. I don't want to put Mazilda and her mysterious boss away forever in just my birthday suit."

Ishiro'shea and the now fully-clothed Duke sprinted down the hall and out of the Palace Royale Hotel of the Colossal Calamari, dodging reporters and children asking for autographs.

Ishiro'shea directed them down the road to the nearby auditorium that had hosted the Grand Shaman's pre-tournament gala. Behind the auditorium was the royal space dock for the use of the Shaman's guests. It was a lovely, albeit a tad gaudy, parking garage.

"Makes sense," Duke began. "She knew that you would rescue me and, likely, in short order. She wouldn't have let that happen if she was going to be lurking around here for a while, hiding out. She was heading directly for a pick-up and exit from Psitakki. And this *is* the closest place to park a ship. Let's just hope we aren't too late."

The sky above the spacecraft parking lot was a tranquil lavender color, without even a single cloud, open and clear —other than a titanic ship that was approaching rapidly.

"Wait a second—is that one of the Four I's ships?"

The bounty hunters looked at each other in terror.

"This is not an ideal situation, little buddy."

The spacecraft was of substantial girth. Upon its landing, the vessel took up a dozen spots allocated for an entire row of standard-sized commercial ships. It sported sleek lines and appeared to be made from a single slab of material, with no sign of rivets or junctions. It was beautiful. The only things that broke up the ship's clean facade were the multitude of guns, missile launchers, plasma cannons, and the like that covered nearly a fifth of the ship's surface. On the side, painted in white letters, perfectly sized and spaced so as to not detract from the awe of the armaments, yet not go unnoticed entirely, were the words: *Intergalactic Infrastructure Improvement, Incorporated.*

As Duke and Ishiro'shea approached, a rampway emerged from the underbelly of the Four I's battle cruiser.

A robed figure made her way out of the shadows of one of the Shaman's leisure ships and headed towards the ramp of the Four I's cruiser.

Ol' Betsy fired into the air. Mazilda stopped immediately. She turned around, still grasping the shield under her arm, though it was now unwrapped. Duke and Ishiro'shea marched towards her; she did not try to flee, nor grab her throwing daggers. From this distance, she could probably still kill them.

"You can't get away that easily," said Duke, still aiming Betsy at Mazilda.

"You shouldn't have come, Duke," Mazilda said. "Really."

"From your vantage point, agreed. If I didn't come, you'd have gotten away. And these bureaucratic nutjobs would get the shield. And that would be bad, I'm guessing."

"No. You shouldn't have come because there's absolutely no way that you can escape."

"You do realize that I'm the one with the sonic shotgun in this exchange, right?"

"It doesn't matter."

A crunching noise came from behind Mazilda. A dozen

Four I's soldiers marched out from the battle cruiser in perfectly straight lines. They were dressed in black tactical gear and each individual was indistinguishable from the next. When they reached the bottom of the ramp they fanned out behind Mazilda and pointed twelve automatic rifles at the bounty-hunting duo.

"See, Duke, it doesn't matter."

"Don't get too trigger-happy, guys. In fact, put your guns down or I blow up Mazilda and the shield."

There was no movement from either side.

"Hold," Mazilda commanded the group, motioning for them to lower their weapons. "So what do we do now, Duke? You know more of them will come and you'll either have to kill me or be killed. If you leave now, you can live to fight another day, in another battle."

"It seems that you forced me into *this* battle," Duke replied.

"And I'm giving you a way out. Go. Please. You weren't even supposed to be here. Maxx was my target."

"Gemstarr?"

"Yes, he was thought to be a favorite in the tournament and I just had to get close to him. Which, as you know, wasn't hard, considering he's a moron."

"Can't argue with that," Duke agreed.

"And the prince," Mazilda continued, "had the other side covered with his mechanized monster. Our employer felt pretty confident that one of those two would win the tournament and get the shield without any additional violence or notoriety. With no one expecting a thing, he would have a much longer runway to set things in motion."

"Wait? The prince was in this too? I knew he was lying about why he was here."

"I told him that his dumb machine wouldn't work. He was going to get caught."

"But you had us go after him. Remember the warehouse?"

Mazilda simply nodded.

"No... that was a setup," Duke said slowly. "You didn't steal any keys. You led us there to get ambushed and killed. How could you?"

"That wasn't my idea," said Mazilda, a note of pleading now in her voice. "But our employer thought it would be the easiest way to get the shield."

"That's why you didn't like the fact that Ish and I had a plan that you didn't know about."

"Yes, and it worked gloriously. I'll give you both credit. Leaving Ishiro there to investigate while the prince's goon chased us. But I still can't believe that he talked that android into having a beer with him."

"He's a good listener," Duke smirked. "And so I guess I was just your insurance policy once I beat Maxx."

Once again, Mazilda's silence gave Duke his answer.

"But you helped me beat Maxx in the tournament? Never mind, don't answer that. You thought I was an easier mark."

"With our past and all, it was..." Mazilda seemed to struggle to find the words, "...more natural."

"What if that bug would've beaten Maxx? Or the slime monsters? Would you've cozied up to them too?"

"I was going to make sure that wouldn't happen but, had it happened, possibly."

"I always thought I would be the one that sunk to these depths in my career—not you."

"You don't understand how persuasive my employer is and what he's promised me. If I get him this shield, I'll never have to work again. No more assassinations. No more hunting down or running from really nasty people. It will be over."

"This shield is that important to this cat, huh? Why?"

"I don't know. I really don't know."

"It's not like you to go into a mission and not know all of the details."

"I know it's not, but the pay and the promise made up for going without a few bits of information," she argued.

"A few bits? If they're offering as much as you say they are, you know it can't be good. Are you that selfish to put beings in jeopardy? An entire planet? An entire system? Just for a little rest and relaxation?"

"Wouldn't you?"

Duke pondered. He didn't like the accusatory tone, but he understood how his past actions might lead her to believe that was the case. However, Duke LaGrange was not a bad guy.

"No, I wouldn't."

"Then I'm sorry to disappoint such a noble warrior."

"Noble warriors," Duke corrected her. "Don't forget, Mazilda, you also lied to Ishiro'shea."

She has a soft spot for Ish, thought the bounty hunter. *Maybe she'll tell us some more.*

"I guess that's true," she replied.

"You even brought a phony photograph of Ishiro's parents to get us excited. That was possibly the cruellest thing that you did, ya' know."

"That wasn't a fake," Mazilda insisted. "It's real. And I really stole it from Potato Lips. He was after your parents, Ishiro, but not for the reasons he was telling you."

"How do you know this?" asked Duke.

"Because I'm after them too."

"Aren't you the busy girl," jabbed Duke.

"I thought you might have made some progress so I risked asking you. But you hadn't made any. Then I found out that Seamus *did* discover something."

"And he was going to tell us," Duke added.

"Maybe. And I couldn't have that happen."

"It was you. You killed him. Not Korzo-Tapor. You."

"It had to be done," Mazilda said drily. "Seamus was probably playing you both too. Don't you see?"

Duke shook his head in frustration and re-aimed Betsy at Mazilda. She tensed up.

"Please go, Duke."

"I can't go until I know why these Four I's guys want this shield. Guys, don't be shy. You tell me and Ish and we'll go."

"We don't know," Mazilda pleaded. "These guys don't know either."

"Aren't they your employers? And they don't know?"

"No, Mr. LaGrange, *I'm* her employer."

The soldiers parted to reveal a tall, slender humanoid wearing an outlandish uniform. Medals covered his pink jacket adorned with elaborate epaulettes. His tight trousers matched the color of his shoulder pads; they disappeared into knee-high boots that likely cost more than the spacecraft parked beside the battle cruiser. He sported an equally garish mustache that extended far beyond the width of his face, yet was still pencil thin.

He pointed an antiquated pulse pistol at Duke. The bounty hunter hadn't seen that model in many cycles but he knew that it packed a wallop. A sometimes inaccurate wallop, but a wallop nonetheless, compensating for its lack of precision with power. On the back of the hand that gripped the gun, Duke noticed a tattoo.

A fish with a mustache.

"Nice pink jacket," said Duke.

"It's salmon, actually."

CHAPTER 29

POOR, POOR DUKE LAGRANGE

"CAN I SAY 'WE MEET again'? I've always wanted to say that," Admiral Lothario LePaco said, plucking his thin mustache. It extended beyond his cheek and curled up into a tight spiral.

"I never pegged you for someone that asks permission for anything," replied Duke.

"How have you been, my old friend? It's been some time. We were quite the bounty-hunting royalty back in the day," LePaco said in a tone of reminiscence.

"You haven't been a bounty hunter in a long time, LePaco," Duke snapped.

"Once a bounty hunter, always a bounty hunter. Or something like that," LePaco countered.

"Have you even paid your dues to the Bounty Hunters Union?"

"Yeah... that's not a thing," LePaco said dismissively. "Please tell me you haven't been sending money to that scam? I wouldn't even stoop that low and I've done about every sinister deed in the book. Oh no, wait, you *have* been sending money to them. Poor Duke LaGrange. Poor, poor Duke LaGrange."

"Enough with the talk of the good ol' days, Lothario. What's going on? I have to admit, I'm a wee bit shocked that you're the leader of the Intergalactic Infrastructure—"

"No, no, no," the admiral interjected. "These guys? You think these guys are my grand plan? My opus of power? My—"

"Then what are you doing here?" Duke said, relishing the chance to interrupt LePaco in return. "With them."

"Oh, I've bought 'em. They do work *for* me."

Duke was perplexed.

"I'm sorry for maxing out the engine in that head of yours," said the admiral, "but the Four I's are just a company that helps me organize stuff."

"Stuff? As in planets and peoples and civilizations?"

"Yeah, stuff. They are a well-run organization that offers a service that I needed—so I bought them. They've been excellent. Outside of letting you escape from Tardasio 7. Mind you, those involved were severely punished."

"Why do you need to organize governments and planets?"

"When you plan to rule over the entire universe, you need a good infrastructure. And the word 'infrastructure' is right in their name. Look at the ship."

"I see it. How are you, pray tell, going to take over the entire universe?" Duke said with a laugh. "You're a slippery crook, I'll give you that. You've built up a nice seedy empire of crime and extortion, no doubt."

"Why thank you, Duke. That means a lot," LePaco said with a subtle bow.

"But running the universe? Taking over every system and galaxy that's been charted?"

"And those that we don't have charted," LePaco added. "Don't forget them."

"C'mon, that's crazy. Even for you. How would you even start?"

Duke glanced over at Mazilda. She was nudging her face at the object in her hands—the shield.

What's wrong with her? Duke thought as he watched Mazilda spasm, seemingly in his general direction.

"I'm glad you asked," LePaco said, "because I know a few things that you probably don't. I doubt many people in the whole of the universe know these things. Myself. A few trusted advisors. That booze-peddling wench, Queen Joe."

The inclusion of the Queen's name really vexed the Nova Texan. *How is she involved in this?*

"Shut up," Duke moaned.

Mazilda repeated her gesture but this time with a bit more vigor.

LePaco must have caught the action out of the corner of his eye. "What my associate is trying to tell you is that the Shield here is part of my plan. It looks ordinary to you, maybe a bit mystic and ancient, yeah, but on the whole, ordinary. However, it is, in fact, a crucial part in what could become the most powerful weapon in the universe."

"That shield?"

"Yes, this Shield. I'm not talking, 'Oh, look, he has a big laser' powerful; I'm talking 'This will rip down the very dimensional fabric of known time and space' powerful."

"Not buying it," Duke responded. "It's a shield."

"So, Duke, have you never seen an ordinary object—like a shield—prove to be more powerful than it appears? Could it have, I don't know, let's say magical powers? Have you seen anything recently that could be a boring old object one second, then a magical killing machine the next? Maybe something round?"

"Shut up, LePaco. I know what you're referencing. I'm to believe that the Orb that Controls Everything and Must

Be Respected is somehow related to this Holy Shield of Grozzel?"

"Intrinsically linked."

"You're insane."

"My mental well-being has nothing to do with the relationship between that Orb and this Shield," LePaco remarked. "It's very, very true, my old bounty hunting friend. Deep in your gut, you know it. You can feel it."

"I honestly cannot. But even if you were telling the truth..."

"I am."

"Even if you were telling the truth," Duke began again, "I've seen what the Orb can do. It's not pretty."

"No, but it's powerful," the admiral proclaimed with a twinkle in his eye and a smile on his face.

"Yes, and it corrupts those that are close to it. The bastard that controlled it on Neprius was turned from a halfway decent scientist into a ruthless, maniacal ass in no time. It turned a relatively good guy into a mini-you. He was so brainwashed and decimated by it, there was no way that he was going to do anything other than destroy that planet and himself along the way."

"So, you stole it from him. Good job, Duke the Savior."

"No, we killed him."

"You killed Ot Vangu?"

"How do you know Ot Vangu?"

The admiral's attitude became more serious. He held the aged pulse pistol a bit firmer, a bit straighter. "Then, Duke LaGrange, it seems that you killed my half-brother."

"Come again?" Duke responded.

"Ot was my half-brother. He moved to Earth when he was a child. We kept in touch but he never knew about my history, my career. And you killed him, in cold blood."

"Wait a damn second, you crazy bastard. I helped kill

Orbius—the person that the Orb turned Ot Vangu into. Your brother was dead long before I ever showed up. He didn't even recognize the name 'Ot Vangu.'"

LePaco stared off in the distance but the barrel of his gun never left its position.

Is he crying?

"His mysterious disappearance was the first domino to fall," the admiral began in a markedly more somber and reflective tone. "The residual energy left behind from that Orb was nothing that I had ever seen. No one had any idea, but I had a hunch. I searched and searched, researched and researched. A few rabbit holes later, I made a few key discoveries that led to a revolutionary hypothesis. It led me to my destiny. A way for me to rule the universe."

"You are one crazy bastard."

"The energy signals surfaced again. First at Cyborg Joe's, which was interesting considering Joe was there."

"She's always there. She owns it."

LePaco disregarded Duke's comment and continued.

"So I sent Prince Korzo-Tapor to investigate."

"He told me he was defending the honor of the Trampling Death Robots."

"What we he supposed to tell you, LaGrange? That he was there investigating the remnants of a super weapon on the dime of Lothario LePaco?" the admiral replied angrily.

"No, but..."

"Then it popped up again, not long after he said he destroyed you and your freaky ship. We analyzed it for quite some time. Of course, we had no idea that you had been sucked up into the damn thing. And now we know that it took you to my half-brother. And you killed him." The final statement was punctuated with a menacing growl.

"Slow down, LePaco. If you do anything stupid, I'll blast Mazilda and the Shield. And your dream will be over."

"Go ahead, shoot it," replied LePaco.

"What?" both Duke and Mazilda said in unison.

"That's a powerful gun, I know. Widowmaker? They don't make 'em like that anymore, ya' know. But it's not going to even dent this Shield."

"But I'll be splattered across the side of the ship," chimed in Mazilda.

"I told you it would be a dangerous mission," LePaco replied.

Mazilda dropped the Shield and sunk behind the wall of Four I's infantrymen.

"Ready... aim," LePaco began.

He didn't make it to the final command.

A swirling light appeared behind Duke. The light transitioned into a portal that was large enough to fly the *Deus Ex Machina* through. Which was good, because that's exactly what was coming through.

CHAPTER 30

THE THIRD PIECE

"OF COURSE YOUR SHIP SHOWS up. No way to escape and it shows up. You're gettin' kinda predictable, LaGrange," grumbled Admiral LePaco.

"Predictable just evened the odds, Admiral."

"Who's even driving that thing?" asked LePaco.

"It has a damn good autopilot setting."

"So, the stories of your legendary piloting, I see, are greatly exaggerated. The credit should be to the *Deus* herself?"

Duke chose not to take the admiral's bait. He kept Betsy firmly pointed at him.

Even when the *Deus Ex Machina* was fully out of the portal, it didn't close. The ship kept its exposed weaponry pointed directly at the admiral and his Four I's guards. The *Deus* hovered for a moment, then landed gently behind Duke and Ishiro'shea.

Who's that waving from the bridge? thought Duke. Earl? How did he... Never mind, best to not ask questions.

The side hatch opened. A faint melody emanated from the elevator bank. Ishiro'shea eyeballed Duke.

"I know, Ish, I'm going to change that music eventually."

Three individuals emerged from the *Deus*. The first was an athletically-built bipedal male carrying a glimmering broad sword. Po'l. The second was a wide-shouldered anthropomorphic musk ox from one of the moons of Gartosh, pounding her fist into her open palm as she approached. Lilly. The figure in the center of the trio sported no visible weapons. She was beautiful. He had known her for a long time and really enjoyed her martinis. Queen Joe.

"Well, today must be a special day," remarked the admiral. "On top of my favorite bounty-hunting odd couple, I get to meet a Miss Bovine runner-up and the always delightful proprietor of Cyborg Joe's."

The trio did not return the admiral's niceties.

"But *you* I don't know," LePaco said, pointing his gun at Po'l.

"Name's Po'l. From Neprius," the warrior said bluntly.

"I've heard the old expression 'bringing a knife to a gun fight,' but you're literally bringing a sword to an intergalactic battle cruiser fight," LePaco jested.

"I like my odds," Po'l responded, his focus on the admiral unwavering.

"Wait," LePaco began, "where did you say you're from?"

"Neprius."

"Ah yes, that's where the magic Orb was located, am I correct?"

"So what?" Po'l growled.

"You must've known my half-brother then?"

"I doubt it."

"I don't know. Does the name Ot Vangu ring a bell?"

"Orbius?" Po'l cried. "You were related to Orbius?"

"Well, Ot Vangu. Not sure why you lot keep calling him Orbius."

"We could call him by a more accurate name."

"And that would be?"

"Murderer. Tyrant. Dictator. Piece of..."

"I get it, Neprian. You didn't like him."

"Didn't like him? He killed too many of my friends and family to count. He tortured my people. I was glad when I got to see him shot down and the madness stop."

"You saw Duke kill my half-brother?"

"I saw Ja'a—" Po'l began.

Duke interrupted him. "Yes, he saw me do it. He saw me blast a hole in that bastard's chest so wide a three-headed ice wombat would fit through it."

Duke glanced back at Po'l. The Neprian seemed to understand Duke's intention.

"I guess I'll get to complete the circle and you can watch Ot Vangu's half-brother blow a hole through his murderer," LePaco proclaimed, his pulse pistol now aiming directly at Duke.

The Queen stepped forward.

"Enough of this, LePaco. This ends now," she said gently, but with a strong undercurrent of force.

"And you, my lovely Queen, are going to end this?"

"If need be. Tell your men to back down. And I'll take the Shield."

Duke was caught off guard. *So she does know about the Shield?*

LePaco seemed to notice Duke's reaction. "Go ahead, tell your friends about the Shield. About its powers. About how you knew where it was and sent Duke to his likely death to retrieve it."

"That's not true," she countered. "I do know about the Shield. And the shields before it that are forever lost in time.

I did know where it was. But I did not send Duke nor anyone to retrieve it. The last ninety-nine have come and gone without anyone trying to manipulate its power for evil. I had no reason to believe that this one would be any different."

"There wasn't a *me* around for the first ninety-nine," LePaco smirked.

"Why didn't you warn us, at least?" asked Duke.

"I didn't foresee any of this happening."

"Surely you saw Duke's little vacation to Neprius happening, right? You needed him to retrieve your precious Orb?"

"LePaco, you know nothing," the Queen snapped, "about the Shield, the Orb, anything."

"I know about the third piece. The Amplification Key."

Queen Joe paused. Duke couldn't see her, as he had his eyes and Betsy's barrel glued to LePaco, but he could sense her being shaken by that last comment.

"And I know where to find it," LePaco bragged. "What do you think about that, Queen?"

Duke felt a shadow creep over him. He turned, his attention shifting from LePaco and the Four I's soldiers.

Crackles and pops filled the air. The space surrounding Queen Joe turned from hazy gray puffs, to a smoky black cloud, to an obsidian wall of opaque gas that framed her entire body. Her eyes radiated a color Duke had never seen before.

"Admiral LePaco," began the Queen. Her voice had changed. The volume increased, but it became extremely distorted. Light emitted from her mouth as she spoke. "You will not leave here with the Shield."

LePaco was frozen in fear. His infantrymen began to retreat. Duke noticed Lilly and Po'l fall back as well, to avoid the growing ring of onyx gas. Seeing that he was no longer the main target for the admiral's pulse pistol, Duke stepped to one side to stand beside Ishiro'shea.

The admiral fired his pulse pistol directly at the Queen. The gaseous ring closed around her and seemed simply to reject the projectile. The cloud reopened to display an unharmed Queen Joe. The admiral tried the same tactic again, with the same result.

"What are you?" he whimpered.

"Hand me the Shield," she commanded with even more urgency.

LePaco shuffled over to the Shield and picked it up.

The explosion rocked the very ground that they were standing on. Duke looked back to see that the side of the *Deus Ex Machina* had been struck rather violently. And again. The Four I's battle cruiser was attacking.

Mazilda.

Queen Joe's appearance returned to its normal state, or what Duke considered her normal state. The artillery barrage had achieved what Mazilda likely wanted to accomplish: by the time they had collected themselves, Admiral LePaco was nowhere to be seen. Neither was the Shield.

"Let's get back to the ship," screamed Duke. "Before Mazilda turns the cannons on us."

The Four I's soldiers did not engage in a firefight. They fell back to their battle cruiser, providing a barrier to protect LePaco.

"No," replied the Queen. "I can't let him leave with that Shield."

Duke noticed that her eyes were still glowing. The protective gas wall was gone but her hands were still covered in the smoky substance. She raised the gaseous oven mitts, and bolts of electric fury shot out at the soldiers. Three of the men were lifted off the ground and deposited beyond the rows of ships. The remaining infantrymen accelerated in their retreat towards the ramp. The Queen sent another strike to the side of the battle cruiser. Its impact caused as much damage as any cannon that the *Deus* possessed.

"Queen, come back! They're gonna start firing at you," Duke screamed.

"The Shield," the Queen replied. "LePaco can't have the..."

The battle cruiser's cannon blew a small crater in front of the Queen. She was immediately displaced from where she had been standing, but, despite the force, she landed squarely on her feet. She hurled another strike. The battle cruiser rocked and wobbled. The ramp ascended back into the belly of the ship with the remaining Four I's soldiers clinging to it.

"Let them go!" Duke pleaded.

There was another blast from the battle cruiser. The Queen was sent across the loading dock but, again, landed safely on her feet.

Duke turned around and headed towards the *Deus*. As he reached the ship, he heard another explosion shake the Four I's battle cruiser. By the time that he reached the bridge, he could feel the return volley from the ship quake the foundations of the dock.

This isn't stable, thought Duke. *We need to leave now.*

"Buckle up and hold on," Duke advised Lilly, Earl, and Po'l. The *Deus* lifted into the air and hovered over the loading dock, level with the battle cruiser.

Ishiro'shea was already stationed in his usual seat and was nimbly dialing up commands on the control panel.

Phasers sung from the *Deus* and pierced the side of the battle cruiser.

The Queen followed suit with another blast.

"If we aren't leaving," Duke said, "let's at least bring this bastard down!"

Joe and the *Deus* tag-teamed another round of strikes.

"We got 'em," Duke muttered to himself.

Admiral LePaco and Mazilda did not counter with another shot. Instead, the lower hatches opened and a payload of explosives dropped from the innards of the ship.

"Joe!" screamed Duke.

The base of the multitiered dock crumbled immediately. The impact of the bombs caused the entire dock to fall in on itself like a giant sinkhole. It was reduced to a pile of twisted stone and infrastructure within seconds.

"No!" screamed Po'l.

Duke looked up. The battle cruiser was gone.

CHAPTER 31

RACE TO THE WARP STATION

"I REALLY HOPE WE CAN make up that time," Duke muttered to himself.

"Are you sure it was the right thing to do, leaving Earl and Lilly behind?" Po'l asked. "Shouldn't we have helped them find the Queen? If she's alive."

"Was it the right thing to do?" Duke repeated Po'l's question. "Yes, I think so. Doesn't make it less hard. But it was right. If she survived that blast—and if anyone could, it would be the Queen—they'll find her."

"I hope you're right," Po'l replied.

"Me too," said the bounty hunter in a hopeful tone. "Earl wasn't going to leave the Queen. Even if he saw her scattered across the planet by a photon explosion, he would try and pick up the pieces individually. If he's going to stay, it's only right that we leave someone there to protect him. He's big, but he's a bartender, not a fighter. And you know the Shaman is going to be sending folks in to see why his private loading dock is now a massive pile of rubble."

Ishiro'shea turned away from the control panel and offered a nod of agreement. Duke appreciated the support.

"But why couldn't we stay? All of us?" Po'l asked.

"We have to catch that ship."

"It has a pretty sizeable head start."

"Yes, but the *Deus*, I would bet, is a bit faster, and the battle cruiser took a good deal more damage. I think we can catch up to it before they get to the warp station. Assuming that they used the public warp station."

Po'l thought about this for a moment. He seemed to be struggling with the notion.

"But why the rush? Why do we have to stop them now?"

"I think the universe might depend on it," Duke replied, somewhat cryptically. And dramatically. He turned his attention to Ishiro'shea. "Anything, little buddy?"

He shook his head.

"Damn."

"What do you mean, 'save the universe'?" Po'l said, continuing his line of questioning.

"That Shield that he has..."

"Yeah."

"Well, it's obviously important. Joe risked her life to get it back from LePaco."

"I'll give you that."

"And we know the Orb That Controls Everything and Must Be Respected is somehow connected to it. LePaco is going after it now."

"And Cyborg Joe's is..." Po'l began.

"Defenseless. Empty. Wide open," Duke finished. "I've sent off a few emergency calls for aid and defense to other planets in the system. Surely, Kelt has some friendly neighbors that don't want to see Cyborg Joe's destroyed. It could buy us some more time."

"And?"

"Nothing," replied Duke.

The Neprian sunk down in the co-navigator chair

beside Ishiro'shea at the control panel. His dejection was palpable.

"That's why we are going to catch up," Duke said. "And destroy the ship."

"You would destroy the ship?"

"We have to," replied Duke.

"Even with Mazilda on it?" asked Po'l.

Duke paused. He took in lungfuls of air and exhaled slowly. His eyes couldn't meet Po'l's; he kept them firmly fixed on the ground.

"Yes. Even with Mazilda on it," he said solemnly. "She's the reason that we're in this mess. Whether she was truly that greedy or whether she was brainwashed or whatever, it is what it is. She's not more important than the whole universe."

Po'l raised himself up from the control panel and made his way to the circular barrier surrounding the captain's chair. He ducked under it to stand next to Duke. He placed his hand on Duke's back.

"You told me once that you felt that Mazilda was the one that got away. Maybe you *meant* to let her get away. Maybe you know, somehow, that her path was heading in a direction that wasn't right."

"Ya' know, Po'l, I think this is the first time that you've ever given me credit for anything," Duke replied.

"A lot has changed since I first met you in that cave outside of Dre'en. You still might be a bit of an ass for my liking but, as Uu'k called you, you could be my 'small doses friend.'"

Duke cracked a smile.

"Thanks, old friend."

Po'l nodded.

"Maybe I let the wrong one get away," Duke remarked.

"You mean you let her stay on a two-bit primitive rock," added Po'l.

Duke's smile grew as he gazed at the view screen.

Ishiro'shea sprang from his seat. The view screen blinked and beeped.

The battle cruiser.

"We got 'em. We can easily close this gap," Duke said joyously.

Po'l remained beside Duke, grasping the rail as they picked up speed.

"So tell me Duke, how do you know that LePaco's going to head to Joe's? How does he know that Joe has the Orb?"

"It's the same way he knew that it was at Joe's previously, when he sent Korzo-Tapor after me—the residual energy signature."

"It gives it off when it's just sitting there, lying around?"

"Not sure, but it does when it portals, I know that. And when we came back from Neprius, he picked it up. And it hasn't been used since and no other residual signatures were made, so he probably assumes—correctly—that it's still at Joe's. And he knows the Queen isn't there."

"Probably why the Four I's were there when you arrived."

"Seems to make sense," Duke remarked. "Speaking about those Four I's guys, I have a question for you."

"Yeah?"

"How did you get the *Deus* back? Don't get me wrong, I'm extremely happy that you guys did, but how? They seemed to pack a mighty punch. And they had an entire frickin' armada floating around the planet."

Po'l smiled.

"I have no idea."

"What?"

"I have no idea. No idea whatsoever."

"You weren't part of that specific mission?"

"Mission? There wasn't a mission."

"I'm not following you," Duke replied in confusion.

"There wasn't a mission to retrieve the *Deus*. It just started firing and broke free of the Four I's."

"I mean, it has done some interesting things in its day. Remember Vern?"

"We were sitting there—me, Queen Joe, Earl, and Lilly. Might have been a few others. I wouldn't say that we were officially planning or plotting or even scheming, but we were discussing the current situation. After you guys hopped through the portal and Joe sent those soldiers running away—the ones that could still run—we knew they'd be back. And they'd likely be a tad more angry. So we were chatting about how we could drive them away, what types of defenses the planet has, evacuation strategies, et cetera."

"The Queen thought they'd get more aggressive."

"She did. Something changed after you left. She became more and more worried. She didn't shake them off as another trivial nuisance."

"Interesting."

"But, as I was saying, we heard these explosions outside. Loudest thing I'd ever heard—well, until today. We ran out and the *Deus* was up in the air blasting down Four I's tanks, shooting up at the ships hovering close to the ground. It was insane."

"Who was piloting it?" asked Duke eagerly.

"No one. It was doing it alone."

Duke smiled and shook his head. Ishiro'shea turned back as he overheard the recounting of the episode.

Even Ish is shocked.

"Usually there's someone in the *Deus* when these things happen. And a big red button," Duke remarked.

"But after it broke away and sent those goons fleeing, it deposited itself in the field behind Cyborg Joe's. Of course, the Queen went to check it out. She returned sometime later, in a panic. Asked Lilly and I about going into a hostile environment on a rescue mission. I was bored, so I was like, 'I'm in.' Lilly wasn't as eager until she heard that it was on Psitakki."

"She probably thought Yvonne was in danger," Duke replied.

Po'l looked blank.

"Sorry, Po'l, never mind. We met someone that knew Lilly on Psitakki."

"Could be the reason. Not sure. Earl even volunteered to drive. So the Queen whipped up a portal out of thin air and then you know the rest."

"This damn ship," quipped the bounty hunter.

The view screen pulsed again.

"Well, Po'l, get ready. You're about to enjoy your first ever dogfight in space."

"I should probably go sit down, huh?"

CHAPTER 32

A FEW COINS SHORT

COMPARED TO MOST WARP STATIONS, the one nearest to Psitakki was somewhat pedestrian. Sure, it had a circular portal—commercial-grade—that was half the size of a moon suspended in the vast openness of space, but so did all the others. And the others typically had a much better rest stop with halfway decent eateries and shopping establishments. This one had a moderate-sized snack bar and a few floating kiosks full of bits and bobs of Psitakki-themed merchandise.

However, to Po'l's eyes, the gargantuan disk sitting against its starry backdrop was pretty spectacular. His culture hadn't even made it to the soufflé stage of civilization.

"Quick, Duke, we're going to lose them," screamed Po'l. "They're right near it."

"That's fine. We want them to portal out of here," Duke responded. "We're going to follow them."

"What? What if they're heading back to Kelt?"

"That's the plan."

"Won't we be deposited right in the middle of their armada?"

"Possibly. But it beats us shooting at them, missing, or even hitting them and the explosion cracking the exterior of the warp station's portal. Then, they die…"

"Which is good," said Po'l.

"…and we die. The entire planet of Psitakki dies. Possibly the majority of the system dies."

"Which is not good," Po'l said, correcting himself.

"Nope. But we can tail 'em in there. When we come out, we sneak up on them—when they're out of range of the exit portal, that is—and we attack. We'll just be old memories by the time they clear the portal. There's no chance they'll think we followed them."

Ishiro'shea tapped on the control panel to get Duke's attention. He pointed at the view screen. The Four I's battle cruiser was entering the portal. The *Deus* accelerated to maximum velocity.

"Are you sure this is safe?" asked Po'l. Duke noticed him clenching his stomach.

"What? You've portaled a lot, right? Didn't you go to all of those pleasure planets and on your little 'epic quests'? In fact, you portaled *here*, didn't you?"

"Yes, but those were just door-sized. And coming here happened so quickly; the Queen just kind of pushed us through a slightly larger door, that happened to be in the sky. We didn't race headlong into a flashing hole bigger than a planet."

"It's not that big. But, yeah, you might want to hold on to something. It can get a bit bumpy."

A blue light above the view screen blinked repeatedly. *Click.*

"What was that?" asked the Neprian.

"It's charging us to portal. I just hope that I've got enough…"

"What's happening?" asked Po'l. "Why are we slowing down?"

"Good question," said Duke. "Ish? What's going on?"

The *Deus* came to a sudden halt, despite Ishiro'shea's attempts to dial up maximum velocity.

An android popped up on the view screen. The robot was a pretty nondescript, standard-issue droid for the Department of Intergalactic Portal Stations. In other words, a titanium toll taker.

"Welcome to the Psitakki Warp Station and Portaling Center, I am Department of Intergalactic Portal Stations representative L43-EE49889. You can call me Wesley. We are very excited that you chose to take our portal directly to Planet Kelt. However, the account balance associated with this craft is not sufficient to fund the travel. Would you like to add funds to your account, Mr. Lafayette LaGrange?"

"Lafayette? No wonder you go by Duke," smirked Po'l.

"Yes, I'll add some cash, my good cybertronic friend," Duke answered.

The bounty hunter gave the robot five different account numbers, but none of them satisfied the monetary requirements.

If mindless procedural robots could appear frustrated, Wesley was at that point. "Mr. LaGrange, it has now been five attempts. I am going to have to ask you to power down your ship and exit the portal queue. You can return when sufficient payment is possible. I'm sorry and we hope to see you soon."

"Wait a second," Duke screamed at the view screen. "We're trying to save the universe. You let Admiral Lothario LePaco through your gate a few moments ago. You know Admiral LePaco, don't you? The most wanted man in the cosmos. And you let him through."

"He had sufficient payment. That is my only require-ment. Other concerns are not in my jurisdiction."

"We have to get through so that we can stop him from destroying the universe," Duke begged.

"If that's the case, I can let you through—" the robot began.

"Thank you," Duke replied.

"—once you have sufficient payment in your account," the robot concluded.

Ishiro'shea hopped up again and signaled out the front window. The portal was closing.

Holy hedgehogs, we must be the last one in the line for Kelt, Duke realized. *They're closing it.*

"We could sure use a nice giant red button right now!" Duke shouted at the ceiling of the *Deus*. "This would be one of those perfect times."

Nothing.

"Mr. LaGrange, please power down your vessel. The ship behind you wants to be on its way."

"Ish, turn on the comm and hail the ship behind us," commanded Duke. "Maybe they'll take an IOU or just help us out from the kindness of their hearts."

The ninja looked back at Duke with a sour expression.

"What?"

The view screen now displayed the ship behind them, which was also trying to leave Psitakki but heading some-where other than Kelt. It was a gorgeous state of the art vessel. Longer than the *Deus* but cylindrical and sleek. It was painted a bright yellow.

"Oh no. Hail him anyways. What can it hurt?"

Ishiro'shea hesitated.

"Yes, I'm sure," Duke groaned. "This is going to be painful."

The screen cut from the nagging robotic toll taker to the

bruised yet still very much handsome face of Maxx Gemstarr, the Universe's Favorite Bounty Hunter.

"Will you get your hunk of garbage out of my way so I can leave this awful system?" screamed Maxx.

"Hello to you, too," replied Duke. "Believe me, I want out of here as much as you do."

"Is that right? People started to turn on you once they found out that you cheated to beat me?"

"Not exactly. I promise I didn't do anything to you."

"My power gauntlets just malfunctioned on their own?"

"I didn't say that either," Duke countered, "I just said I didn't do it. You might have made another enemy on this trip."

Maxx thought about this and appeared to come up blank.

"And that is?"

"Think about it, Maxx. Who else was a tad peeved at you for how you treated them?"

He looked perplexed.

You really can't think of it, you oblivious son of a bitch?

"No idea, LaGrange."

"Mazilda, you idiot."

"Why would she be mad at me?"

"Because you treated her like garbage. Oh, and she was using you to get the Shield."

"You're insane, Duke. Now let me through."

"It's true, Maxx. Don't worry, she used me too. We're trying to track her down and kill her. She's working for Admiral LePaco."

"Now I know you're insane. He's dead. Or hiding. Or something. Why does he want the Shield? Why did Mazilda want it?"

"I don't have time for this. Let's just say that LePaco knows of a few artifacts of extreme power that, if he gets them all, can destroy everything. Mazilda helped him. She used you because you were the tournament's favorite."

"That's for damn sure," Maxx added.

"She sabotaged you because she decided I was easier to manipulate," Duke confessed begrudgingly.

"You're starting to make more sense now."

"I just need to get through the portal, but I'm a few coins short. Would you loan me some? Then I'll track down Mazilda and bring her to the justice that she deserves."

"So, you're admitting that you cheated to beat me, as that was the *only* way in the universe that you could've bested me. Then Mazilda made you look like a bigger fool than me. And now you're broke and need to borrow money from me. If I don't, the universe will likely end because of your gullibility and stupidity. Is that about right?"

The bounty hunter gritted his teeth. He gripped the guardrail around the captain's chair with so much force that he ripped the decorative padding.

I can do this, I can do this, I can do this, he repeated to himself.

"Is that pretty much the gist of it?" Maxx asked again.

"Yes, pretty much," Duke replied.

Gemstarr broke out into hysterical laughter.

"This is better than any Shield," Maxx said in between fits of hilarity. This went on for a few moments, then the screen went black.

"What just happened?" Po'l asked.

"I really don't know. But I didn't like it," Duke replied in the sullen tone of a broken man. "I feel like I've been robbed of my dignity. Not sure how much of that stuff I have left anymore."

The android reappeared on the screen.

"Thank you for your payment, Mr. LaGrange. Enjoy your travels to Kelt."

CHAPTER 33

COSMIC FLOTSAM

"**P**RETTY FUNKY, HUH?" ASKED DUKE.

"Different," Po'l replied. "A lot different than when the Queen brought us to Psitakki."

"Oh yeah, her portals are much more pleasant than these D.I.P.S. jobs. You need a ton more oomph to portal ships all day rather than us fleshy hunks of meat with the occasional *Deus* throw in."

The Neprian seemed fine with that explanation.

Ishiro'shea was feverishly tapping the controls. The *Deus Ex Machina* was beeping and blinking as if it was preparing to go to war. And Duke knew that if he didn't nail his plan with precision, they would be.

"Yep, I see 'em, Ish," Duke shouted from his captain's chair. "They're coasting. They don't suspect us at all."

"Which is good, right?" asked Po'l.

"Yes, very. See that massive ship?"

"Yes."

"That's the Armada Titan that the Four I's sent to Kelt. It sits at the very back of the squad. It's basically indestructible. I'm guessing this battle cruiser is going to deposit our good friends LePaco and Mazilda and that Shield right into the Titan's nurturing bosom."

"Which isn't good?"

"It's not going to happen. Because right before they reach the Titan, we're going to blast them out of space. Done. Dead. Gone."

"What about the Titan and the rest of the armada?" asked Po'l.

"The Titan will take a month to turn around—not worried about that. We just have to outrun the other guys. I have a feeling that the fleet will leave once they know LePaco is finished."

"Why's that?"

"Because he's paying them," Duke said bluntly.

"Good call."

"And so we might have to lay low for a while, at least until the news of LePaco's death reaches those cruisers and scout ships that are chasing us. Small price to pay to destroy the Shield and LePaco."

"And Mazilda."

"Yes, and Mazilda," Duke sighed. "Thanks for reminding me, Po'l."

Why couldn't I have left him on Neprius, Duke pondered.

The *Deus* began its final charge to close the gap between itself and the Four I's battle cruiser carrying Admiral LePaco, Mazilda Cloax, and the mystical Psitakki Shield that Queen Joe was so adamant about keeping out of criminal hands.

"Every weapon that we have... Good to go?" asked Duke.

Ever reliable, Ishiro'shea returned a thumbs-up.

"I know this is your first space battle, Po'l," said Duke. "Let's hope that it's not your last."

"Cheers to that," responded Po'l.

He has spent a lot of time at Cyborg Joe's.

The ship was now within striking distance.

"Let loose!" commanded Duke.

The *Deus* fired off a barrage of weaponry that set the celestial backdrop ablaze. The already damaged battle cruiser couldn't get off a single return salvo—it was apparent that the systems had begun to fail. Ishiro'shea guided the *Deus* closer and sent forth a piercing plasma parade that sliced and diced the hull of the Four I's vessel. The lacerations soon became gaping wounds and segments of the ship began to detach amidst a spectacle of explosions. The violent, fiery outburst continued until much of the ship was incinerated beyond recognition. Within mere moments, the battle cruiser was cosmic flotsam.

A handful of rear scout ships peeled off and circled to engage the *Deus*. The Armada Titan sat motionless.

"Coming at us, Ishiro. Looks like four. No, five."

The ninja greeted their new adversaries with some well-placed lasers, clipping two of the ships and sending them spiraling out of control and out of the theater of battle. The other three rattled the *Deus* with concentrated blasts, but the ship's auto-response reciprocated the attack with even more powerful counterattacks. The pulses split two of the ships in half. A lone scout came in for one last approach but was disintegrated by the *Deus* before it could mount any attack.

The battle cruisers that flanked the Armada Titan and some of the accompanying scouts began to shift their focus to the *Deus*. They pulled away from the fleet methodically and moved into intercept courses.

"Time for us to go," ordered Duke.

"Do we try and portal back?" asked Po'l.

"Not sure Maxx gave us that much cash," replied Duke.

"I think we just have to outrun 'em for a bit. I'm thinking we circle back around Kelt and head that way. That puts an entire planet between us and the fleet."

The speed of Ishiro'shea's command inputs increased. Duke hopped over the rail and placed his hand on Ishiro's shoulder.

"I'll drive," he said.

Ishiro'shea quickly vacated his seat. Duke could tell that he was smiling under his mask. The bounty hunter excelled at many things, especially in his own mind, but his piloting skills could never be challenged. Their best bet, no doubt, was to have Duke LaGrange steer the *Deus Ex Machina*.

The Nova Texan took a deep breath. "Hold on."

The ship dipped smoothly, all the while picking up speed, and cut towards the planet. The battle cruiser that was leaving the left flank of the Armada Titan fired an errant shot, missing badly. The scouts pursued closely, the battle cruisers in the rear. Duke began to pull away, out of reach of the scouts' weapons. But not the battle cruisers'.

One of the long-range cannons connected with a glancing blow to the back of the *Deus*. It wobbled but stayed true to its course. Another hit. The *Deus* wavered a bit more, but the impact achieved little more than slowing down the ship momentarily.

"We need to pick it up," Duke muttered to himself, jaws clenched.

Another explosion. But the detonation was a few ships' lengths behind them.

We're putting some space between us now, thought Duke.

"Oh shit."

He gazed up at the view screen. Staring at the *Deus* was the battle cruiser from the other side of the Armada Titan, surrounded by three scout ships.

"What are we going to do?" screamed a panicked Po'l.

The *Deus* jerked again and dove towards the planet's atmosphere. Both battle cruisers and the legion of scout ships continued their pursuit. Duke sped over the uninhabited landmasses of Kelt at low altitude, approaching the more densely populated areas on Kelt's major province, Oldish Kelt. It was older than the seaside metropolis of New Kelt but much younger than the sprawling wastelands on the other side of the planet, dubbed Old Kelt. It was oldish. It was also the home to Cyborg Joe's Grill N' Go & The Why Not Saloon.

"We need to avoid any extended engagements until we're beyond Oldish Kelt," ordered Duke. "We don't need any more casualties."

The *Deus* whizzed over the bar and the surrounding townships that had built up around it.

"We're clear. When those scouts and cruisers are away from the cities, let's see if we can start picking 'em off one at a time."

Ishiro'shea worked furiously next to Duke, organizing a calculated precision attack.

The bridge shook. Po'l lost his balance and hit the floor. Another crash.

"What was that, Ish? Damage report?"

The ninja ran his fingers over the panel. He glanced back at Duke and shrugged.

"What do you mean 'no damage'?"

Another slightly louder noise.

"Check the scanners."

It was clear that Ishiro'shea's excitement was growing. He motioned for Duke to turn the *Deus* around and face their attackers head-on.

"Are you crazy?"

Ishiro'shea's posture straightened.

"Calm down. I trust you."

On the view screen Duke could see that the remaining Four I's ships in pursuit were in various states of destruction. Some were plummeting uncontrollably to the hard Keltian ground. Others were engulfed in some exotic electrical field that seemed to be ravaging the ships' outer hull like termites. It was obvious that the *Deus Ex Machina* was not their primary focus. One of the battle cruisers was relatively unharmed and was now pivoting to engage the ground force that had halted its pursuit of the *Deus*.

"I didn't know the Keltians had that good of a defense," muttered Duke to Ishiro'shea.

Ishiro'shea shook his head in surprise.

"Duke, that's no Keltian army," Po'l remarked.

Ishiro enlarged the view screen.

"She's alive," Duke said. "Son of a bitch, she's alive. And pissed off."

CHAPTER 34

THE BATTLE OF OLDISH KELT

"I REALLY NEED TO ASK the Queen about those electric bolt thingies."

"You didn't know she could do that?" inquired Po'l.

"No idea. First I saw of it was back on Psitakki. Crazy stuff. Did you know that she could do that?"

"Nope."

"Any luck hailing Joe's, Ish? Surely Earl or someone will pick up."

The view screen whizzed and blinked.

"Duke, nice to see you."

It was Queen Joe, *sans* black gaseous crowns, glowing eyes, or lightning flowing out of her hands.

"I think it's nicer to see *you*, Queen," Duke replied.

She smiled back. Duke hoped his comment came across as genuine as he intended.

"How did you survive that implosion? We saw you get sucked into that mess."

"What? From that tiny parking garage falling on me? Not even a scratch," she joked. "I'm just glad Earl and Lilly stayed back to help me out of that pile of rubble."

"I know you have a few secrets and I was fine with

having to use a little imagination, but these recent events might require some explaining."

"Maybe one day, Duke. Right now, we need to figure out what to do about that Armada Titan and those remaining Four I's ships."

"I'm not worried about them."

"Why is that?"

"We blew up LePaco," Duke paused. "They'll leave now that their funds are gone."

The Queen frowned. It was a melancholy frown, not one of vitriol.

"I'm sorry, Duke. I know you and Mazilda had a history. Even complicated histories are meaningful."

"Can't believe those Four I's ships are still here, to be honest," Duke said, ignoring the urge to dwell on the emotionally-charged moment. "I thought they'd be gone now, especially since we have some ground cover as well."

A ringing sound pierced the bridge of the *Deus*.

"Never mind, Queen. I have a hunch this could be them now. I'll keep you patched in so we can take this surrender together."

The ringing continued.

"Ish, patch them in."

The Queen's image shrank on the screen to allow for a third participant.

"Are you kidding me?" shouted Duke.

"Nice to see you again, too," smirked Admiral LePaco. Mazilda lingered behind him, her gaze fixed on the floor.

"How did you? I saw you..." Duke stammered. "You went... boom."

Not my most articulate line of questioning, thought Duke.

"What? The battle cruiser exploding? We couldn't have survived that. No one could have. Are you crazy? We transferred ships before we portaled back, just in case you gave up on the Queen and tried to chase us down. Sorry about killing her, by the way. This is truly a dark day for drunkards and wastes of space everywhere."

It was Duke's turn to smirk. He nodded in Ishiro'shea's direction. He plugged away on the control panel.

"Hey, Admiral," Joe chirped.

"It can't be. You were crushed!" LePaco shouted as Ishiro patched in the Queen to the conversation. "I saw it collapse on you!"

"I have a few tricks as well," the Queen responded.

"That seems to be true," huffed LePaco. "Oh well."

"Oh well?" repeated Duke.

"Yes, oh well. I guess this just means that I'll have to destroy the *Deus* and Cyborg Joe's today, then," he sighed. "More work, but I'd have to do it someday regardless. Might as well be now."

LePaco cut his communication.

"Stay in the atmosphere," Joe commanded. "Make him come to us. I can help from the bar. Do whatever you can to render that Titan inoperable."

"Any ideas on what that is? I've never had to do anything to an Armada Titan, let alone try and render it inoperable."

"I have no idea. I'm sorry. I'll have Earl and Lilly start evacuating the area. We probably don't have enough time, but whatever we can do will be better than nothing. I can try and portal some of them to other places but I need as much energy as possible to fight LePaco's ships."

"Understood. We'll figure something out."

Duke, Ishiro'shea, and Po'l didn't say a word as they waited for LePaco's legions to break into the Keltian atmosphere. They knew the massive casualties that Kelt was going to suffer, but this was likely unknown to almost every single being on the planet. Duke's stomach turned, tied itself into a knot, untied itself, finished a complex gymnastics routine, and then turned some more.

This was a fight that they couldn't win. The bounty hunter kept peeking around corners to see if a giant red button suddenly appeared. Maybe even the *Deus* gave up on this one.

About twenty Four I's scout ships entered into view. They halted and hovered in the Keltian sky. Three battle cruisers followed suit, and stationed themselves to the left of the squad. Another ship that Duke didn't recognize positioned itself on the right flank. It had an impressive display of weaponry but its model type didn't scream 'Four I's.'

Probably one of LePaco's thugs, thought Duke.

After the other ships had made their way into the skies above Cyborg Joe's, the Armada Titan slowly lowered its bulky country-sized frame into the atmosphere.

The scouts closed in aggressively. Their plan was clear: overwhelm the *Deus* and let the Armada Titan deal with Cyborg Joe's and any ground cover. A single scout, even if it had an hour of free fire on the *Deus*, could accomplish little more than some nasty scarring. However, twenty scouts firing at the same time could cause some major problems.

"You ready, Ish?"

The ninja began to belt out blasts at the approaching Four I's scouts. Duke was still manning the aviation, but even the most skilled pilot would have had a hard time avoiding twenty ships firing from every angle. Po'l stood next to the guardrail, clinging to it for dear life.

Not a good spaceship battle for a newbie.

Ishiro'shea managed to sting a few of the ships, sending

them to an early grave in the Keltian countryside. But their offense was relentless.

"A little help, Queen," Duke yelled aloud.

Ishiro'shea tapped him on the shoulder and pointed at the front view screen. A Four I's ship was landing near to Cyborg Joe's. It wasn't firing.

A troop transport.

"Not good, guys—they're sending in a ground force," muttered Duke, as he steered the *Deus* out of the way of enemy fire, as much as he could.

He remained focused on the scene. The Queen was standing at the vanguard of what appeared to be a gathering of the patrons of Cyborg Joe's.

At least some of them have backbones, thought Duke.

The patrons made a circle around the enigmatic bar owner and started to attack the ship transport with a long-range artillery assault. As the troops poured out of the trans-port carrier, many were dropped by the Cyborg Joe's makeshift militia. However, the Queen's focus was the sky. She hurled electric bolts towards the behemoth Armada Titan. Even from this distance, Duke could see the frustra-tion in the Queen's eyes. The Titan sat motionless and showed no ill effects from the Queen's concentrated assault.

She shifted her stance and set loose a few strikes at the scout ships, dropping two. She shifted again and volleyed more bolts at the transport ship. Even so, the invaders had a clear numbers advantage. The troops pushed on, despite losing numbers to the Queen and Cyborg Joe's makeshift squadron of regulars. They would be on top of Joe's in a matter of moments.

"We have to help them!" screamed Po'l.

"We can't," replied Duke emotionlessly.

"Why? They'll all die," shouted the Neprian.

"If we help them out, these scouts will follow us.

They'll pick off the Queen and the entire lot of them without as much as a thought. They have a much better chance against the Four I's soldiers."

Po'l didn't seem satisfied with this answer, but Duke had no time for a thorough debate with the novice spaceman. He continued his elaborate maneuvering, which was designed to give Ishiro'shea as many opportunities as possible to thin out the scout herd.

"Look," shouted Po'l.

Duke fully expected to see the carnage that he hoped he would never have to witness—the destruction of Cyborg Joe's. But it wasn't. Not even close.

The troops were gone. Every last one of them. The transport ship was still docked. The road was littered with a few dead Four I's soldiers, courtesy of the Queen and the bar patrons that had defended their favorite watering hole. But where were the hundreds that had been exiting the transport only moments ago? The entire legion that had been marching towards the bar was no more.

"What happened down there, Po'l?"

"She, uh, sent them somewhere," he stuttered.

"She portaled 'em?" Duke asked.

"Yeah."

"Holy hedgehogs, that's amazing," Duke shouted, finishing on an indistinguishable sound, somewhere between a "woo-hoo" and "yippie."

Duke grinned and slid the *Deus* to one side. Ishiro'shea sprayed an array of lasers that took down four scout ships.

"The tide be a-turnin', little buddy," said Duke.

Queen Joe took out another scout with a bolt of electric death. The *Deus Ex Machina* cleaned up the remainder of the swarm, then Duke turned his attention to the Armada Titan.

"Now what do we do?" Duke asked his team. "I guess we can try to get close and then figure something out?"

Ishiro'shea returned a not-as-enthusiastic-as-it-should-be thumbs-up.

But the *Deus* was rocked unexpectedly. It rolled with such violence that all three aboard were flung across the bridge. As he tumbled and smashed into the walls, Duke noticed the floor was on fire. Thunderous claps echoed throughout the ship. It felt as if the sound waves would crush the ship like a Mega-Troll clutching a commemorative snow globe. Another boom and the ship rolled again. The vessel was out of control—the only way it would stop its current course was either an undesired handshake with the Keltian surface or for someone to get to the control panel.

"We need to stop this!" Duke screamed.

The bounty hunter regained his footing and dove at the panel. He missed entirely and crashed stomach-first into the flooring, which was now located where the wall should have been. Ishiro'shea nimbly made his way to the panel and flew through the air like a Brontortian acrobat. However, he did not account for the ship's roll and he landed on Duke's lap.

At least we'll be buried near Cyborg Joe's, thought Duke.

"Hey guys, I got it."

Duke looked up. Po'l was hanging on to the control panel.

"What do I do now?" he screamed.

"First, you need to push the eleventh lever from the right upwards, then press the silver button next to the teal one... Screw it, just start banging stuff."

Po'l punched the control panel repeatedly. He elbowed it. He even headbutted it. It fizzled and sparked.

The *Deus Ex Machina* came to a grinding halt.

Duke, Ishiro'shea, and Po'l looked at the view screen. Duke had never seen anything this horrific. This one-sided. The Armada Titan was unleashing a wave of unprecedented firepower across Oldish Kelt.

The Queen and the defenders of Joe's were nowhere to be seen.

CHAPTER 35

NEW LEPACO CITY

"**D**UKE, ARE YOU THERE?"

"QUICK, Ish, put her on the view screen," commanded Duke.

An image of Queen Joe appeared, then disappeared, then partially appeared. Static waves distorted the view screen continually.

"You're breaking up, Queen. Are y'all alive?"

"We're back at the bar. But we don't have much... That ship..."

The communication trailed off.

"...we have to take it down," she finished.

"We can't. Did you see it? I don't know what we can do," Duke replied. "I just don't know. It's too powerful."

Duke was a confident being. He knew he was a confident being. During the course of his life, he had been placed in some difficult situations and always found a way to come out of them relatively unscathed, both physically and emotionally. He also knew that many of those situations included invaluable aid from his life-long companion, Ishiro'shea, or his reality-bending ship, the *Deus Ex Machina*. Both of them were with him now—but even so, he was at a loss, a true loss. The devastation below him around the city centers and neighborhoods of Oldish Kelt was more than he could comprehend. He knew he had played some sort of role in the deaths of the faceless and nameless below him. But the enemy that he faced, the one that he would have to eliminate to save those lucky enough to have survived the Titan's onslaught, was unbeatable.

"Duke, are you there?"

The bounty hunter snapped out of his daze. "I don't know what to do," Duke replied, his voice dripping with a sadness that shocked even him. "I'm sorry."

The *Deus'* view screen started to pulse.

"Answer it, Ish. Sorry, Queen, I have a feeling LePaco's about to ask for a surrender."

"Hold. Don't answer it, Duke. Whatever you do, don't surrender. We can't give up, even if it kills us."

"What do you want me to do? I'm already responsible for the deaths that he caused. I have to end this."

"You aren't responsible for that. LePaco is. The Four I's are. Mazilda Cloax is. Not you. You pulled no trigger that struck down an innocent. They did."

"We have no way to win this. I'm sorry, Queen."

Duke's eyes met Ishiro'shea's. "Patch him in."

"Duke LaGrange, how are you?" squealed Admiral LePaco jovially. "It seems that we can't stop talking to each other as of late."

"I'm elated, of course."

"I won't waste your time. I'm sure you want to try and save some of those poor plebeians down on Kelt that are burning to death. So, please surrender, fly down to help or fly away, I don't really care. I'm going to level Cyborg Joe's now and kill that inter-dimensional bitch."

"And if I say no?" Duke asked.

"Admittedly, you will slow me down. It will take me a

bit longer to accomplish what I need to accomplish here but, don't misunderstand me, I will accomplish it. I'm giving you a chance to survive. Or help a few poor folks down below to survive. Like I said, I couldn't care less."

"Why? Why is the honorable Admiral LePaco being so charitable?"

"Let's say it's a favor to a mutual friend."

Duke felt a pain in his chest. It migrated to his stomach. His mouth grew dry. It hurt to swallow. Mazilda's betrayal was as painful to him as the horrors being unleashed upon Oldish Kelt.

Po'l ran over to Duke and whispered in his ear.

"Yes? Your answer, Duke?" the admiral persisted.

Duke looked at the Neprian.

"Are you sure, Po'l?"

He nodded in response.

"Tell Ishiro."

Po'l whispered to the ninja, whose eyes widened immediately, then he glanced towards Duke. A single nod followed.

"Sorry, Admiral. Technical difficulties. We accept your offer. I hope the Queen forgives us."

"She won't be around to hold it against you, LaGrange."

"But we would like to leave now."

"Not going to save the precious citizens of Kelt?"

"We're too insignificant to help. We just want to leave this squabble over some stupid antiques between you and the Queen. No one else needs to die, especially not me. I still have things to do in this universe."

"You're smarter than I thought," replied LePaco.

"Thanks. Good luck. You win."

"I always win," smirked LePaco.

Ishiro'shea cut the view screen.

"There are worse ways to die, I guess."

Duke fidgeted with the controls.

"Next stop, crashing into the Armada Titan."

———

"They need to name a wing at Cyborg Joe's after us if this works," Duke proclaimed.

Ishiro'shea smiled under his mask. Po'l did not respond but stood before the view screen with his chest puffed out.

He's always loved that honor stuff, thought Duke.

The ringing began again.

"Has to be LePaco again, right?" asked Po'l. "Do we answer?"

"Yes, I think so," replied Duke.

"Are you sure?"

"If we don't, he'll really think something is up. I don't think we can afford to have him question our motives as we try and kamikaze his ship into oblivion."

Ishiro'shea patched in the ruthless fugitive.

"Hello again, Duke. Can I ask you a question?"

"Sure, shoot."

"Why exactly are you heading directly at us? You aren't planning some heroic suicide mission, are you? You aren't a Valkyrie."

"C'mon, Admiral," Duke chuckled, "you know me better than that."

"He loves himself too much," Po'l chimed in.

The admiral smiled apprehensively but seemed to agree with that notion.

"It's true," Mazilda added from behind LePaco. "Duke LaGrange is no hero. He's too vain to be a hero."

"See, Admiral."

"Then why are you coming right at us?"

"I'll peel away right now. We were having some navigational issues. Our system is shot from the damage that we sustained. You had us reeling."

"That I did. Fine, then. Please course correct and exit this sector as quickly as possible before I change my mind."

"Thank you, oh merciful one," Duke said with a slight bow.

LePaco's image vanished. The *Deus* veered away from its direct course into the face of the Armada Titan.

"What are you doing, Duke?"

"Once we're out of his direct vision, we'll approach from the side. As long as we avoid that artillery ship, we'll have a direct shot at him. One ship crashing into the Titan won't do much damage... but flying right into the bridge will take out LePaco and everyone else of consequence."

"Are you sure?"

"Not in the least," replied Duke. "I'm open to suggestions. Even ones that don't involve us dying."

The ship was out of the periphery of the Armada Titan, then the *Deus* about-faced.

"Guys, here we go. Last chance to back out," Duke said. Silence.

"No takers. Okay then. Maybe we'll get a statue."

The *Deus Ex Machina* sped towards the Armada Titan's forward-facing segment.

"I also hope that this is the right part of the ship. We could have used some schematics to confirm. No wait, I think I can see LePaco's beady eyes from here."

The *Deus* whizzed by the artillery craft and approached the Titan. Then the ship stopped. The abrupt deceleration sent all three men hurtling to the ground.

"That's twice in one day," remarked Duke. "I don't like it. Why'd we stop? What happened?"

The view screen buzzed again.

"Hit it, Ish."

Admiral LePaco appeared again.

"Not cool, LaGrange. Not cool at all. I thought we were becoming friends. Guess not. You had to go and do something stupid like that. I'm lucky that Mazilda clued me in. It helps having someone that knows the complicated mind of Duke LaGrange so intimately."

Duke did not return any response.

"So, if you haven't guessed, you're trapped in one of our close-range tractor beams. We use it to slow down, suspend, and disarm any warheads with the potential of blowing us up. This also includes ships piloted by idiots with death wishes."

"You're a bastard, LePaco," Duke snarled.

"Maybe. But I'm a bastard that has you in a tractor beam. Now I'm going to make you and your friends watch me level Cyborg Joe's, the Queen, and then the rest of Kelt. The Four I's will have fun building up the planet from scratch for me. I think I'll name it New LePaco City."

"But it's a planet. Not a city."

"Whatever, LaGrange."

"And is there an Old LePaco City?"

"Shut up."

"I'm sure the Four I's are going to ask you these questions, Admiral. Just a hunch."

"Regardless, say goodbye to your precious bar and that thick-headed interloper that runs it," LePaco said maniacally.

Ishiro'shea cut off the communication again.

"Thanks, little buddy. I don't want the last thing I ever see to be that guy."

"We failed," said Po'l. "Everyone's going to die because of us."

"Don't forget we're going to die, too," added Duke.

Every single one of the Armada Titan's guns refocused on Cyborg Joe's and the area surrounding the bar.

This is it, thought Duke.

"I'm sorry, Queen," the bounty hunter whispered softly.

On the long-range scanner, Duke could see Joe standing outside of the bar again. She was throwing every bit of lightning she had at the Titan. The damage caused was somewhere between harmless sparks and slightly less harmless sparks.

The Nova Texan left his seat and made his way to the captain's chair. He sunk into its warm embrace. His face dropped into his hands. For the first time, his mind was blank.

This is the end.

Then the entire *Deus Ex Machina* was engulfed in a blinding light. But it didn't shake. It didn't rumble. However, the light was unyielding.

"Is this the afterlife?" asked Po'l.

"If it is, I think it's pretty weak that I'm still in these clothes. I envisioned the afterlife having freshly-washed clothing." Duke murmured.

The ship started to shift slightly.

"Wait, Ish, are we... Hit it!"

The *Deus* broke free of the tractor beam.

"Get us out of here!"

Another wave of illumination permeated the bridge of the ship. But it pressed on. The light dimmed. As they moved away from the light, the explosions became audible. There were so many that it was hard to tell if it was a single, elongated blast or a symphony of detonations. As the *Deus* cleared the chaos, it pivoted to ingest what was happening outside.

Hundreds of ships, all different in size and design, surrounded the Armada Titan. The only thing more varied than the ships was the cacophony of armaments that were pelting the gargantuan vessel. The majority of the attack concentrated on the heavy artillery situated at the front and lower half of the Titan. It didn't get off another shot.

"Who are these guys?" asked Po'l. "I'm guessing they hate the Four I's more than us."

"And they're smarter and chose to bring more than a single ship and a crazy lady with electric fingers," said the bounty hunter.

Ishiro'shea looked back at Duke. They exchanged nods, then the *Deus* readied its guns.

"Let's see if they'll let us join this party!"

The ring of mysterious marauders continued to shell the Four I's flagship. It was clearly injured.

"It's trying to get away!" screamed Duke.

As the Titan slowly exited the Keltian atmosphere and entered space, the attackers moved with it. The constant barrage never ceased. The Titan was not going to escape.

Seems like they've done this before, thought Duke.

The artillery ship and the few ancillary craft that supported the Armada Titan had already been destroyed or had fled at the sight of this new military force. The Titan would not be afforded that luxury. As it approached deeper space, it started to implode. It was dying; the ships picked up their assault. The hull was compromised; a chasm opened up across the underbelly. The Titan started to fold up in a "V" shape. There would be no survivors on board. Escape pods were jettisoned, but the ones that weren't picked off by lasers would likely end up on Kelt, where they would not receive a warm welcome from the locals. The attacking fleet started to back away from the dying vessel so as to not get caught up in the floating fragments that could crush most other ships.

From the fiery wreckage darted a ship like a phoenix. It headed away at unfathomable velocity.

"Damn it!" shouted Duke.

"What?" inquired Po'l. "No one could have survived that, not even LePaco."

"I agree with you. But see that ship, that's him. I know it. It shot out of the Titan."

"You don't know that," snapped Po'l. "That could have been some low-level crew member, a random soldier, or someone inconsequential. It could be one of these new guys."

"Nope, it was the admiral. Probably Mazilda, too."

"What makes you so sure?"

"I doubt a random crew member flies a salmon-colored ship with a license plate that reads 'Mister Macho.'"

"It looked pink," added Po'l.

CHAPTER 36

THE FLYING ROT

"LET'S ASSUME THESE GUYS ARE hostile," said the bounty hunter cautiously.

"These guys that just brought down the Armada Titan that was about to blow up Kelt, kill the Queen, and dissolve us into goop?" Po'l said. "I think we should be naming our firstborn children after them, rather than assuming they're hostile."

"Po'l, sometimes the enemy of your enemy is your friend," began Duke, "but then your shared enemy dies and they cease being your friend and become your enemy again."

The Neprian shook his head.

"You have *that* many enemies? How do you piss off an entire fleet?"

"I'm not saying they *are* my enemies... but you can never be too sure," said Duke, correcting Po'l. "Anyways, we're about to find out. Ish, I might regret this, but patch them in."

The ninja followed the orders. An elderly lady appeared on the screen. All three of her eyes blinked rapidly, each one focused on a different member of the *Deus*

Ex Machina. Her four arms were folded defiantly but her face sported a welcoming grin.

A three-eyed Zylantian female pirate. Only one of those that I'm aware of, concluded Duke.

"I don't think we've had the pleasure of ever meeting face-to-face," Duke began diplomatically, "but your reputation proceeds you, Mama Fong."

Not only did her very noticeable mutation separate her from her kin back home, but she also was the only Zylantian that did not use her given name. For as long as Duke had known, she was simply "Mama Fong."

"As does yours, Duke LaGrange," she replied in a high-pitched whisper. If a voice could be pointy, Mama Fong's would pierce titanium. "I'm happy that you sent me a message. LePaco cannot be taken lightly."

"Excuse me, Mama, but I didn't send you a message."

"You didn't?"

"Nope," replied Duke.

"You didn't send a transmission requesting assistance to save the Kelt and Cyborg Joe's from Admiral LePaco?"

"I did, most definitely, but not to you," Duke clarified.

"That's quite interesting then, Duke," Mama Fong pondered. "I know you're a member in good standing..."

"Hold up, Mama. A member?"

"Yes."

"In good standing?"

"Yes. A member in good standing of the Bounty Hunters Union."

Duke leapt from his chair and hopped over the guardrail. He hugged Ishiro'shea and ran over to Po'l and embraced him.

"Yes! I knew it! I knew it!"

"Excuse me, Duke," Mama Fong chirped. "What's going on? What did you know?"

"Oh, never mind. Let's just say that some folks doubted your existence. Said y'all were a scam!"

"Probably LePaco, huh?"

"Yes, for one."

"He hasn't paid any dues in years. That's one of the reasons that we didn't mind blasting him from the sky. That, and the thousands of lives that his treachery has ended," said the BHU representative. "Also, the Union has a firm stance against this Four I's organization and their attempt to outlaw bounty hunting. The fact that they're working in tandem with the admiral is a pleasant coincidence. It made the trip from Daedeaus Purple even more worthwhile."

Daedeaus Purple. I knew it. That's where they are, rejoiced Duke internally.

"We can't thank you enough," said Duke gleefully. "Despite LePaco getting away."

"We noticed that as well. It's hard *not* to notice a ship with the admiral's unique... style. Quite unfortunate, but we have some tracers on his trail. We will know where he is going in short order and, more importantly, why."

"I know where he's going," said Duke. This proclamation shocked both Ishiro'shea and Po'l.

"You do?" said a perplexed Mama Fong.

"Not specifically. But I know he's looking for the third component of an ancient super weapon."

"What is this 'super weapon'?"

"I have no idea. But it has Queen Joe in a tizzy. She put countless Keltians in danger to stop him and get this Shield back, so it has to be something like we've never seen before."

"LePaco cannot be permitted to possess any super weapon," Mama Fong replied.

"There is no denying that statement, my good Mama. I'm sure the Queen can fill you in. We have more questions for her as well."

"I trust the good Queen. If she's worried then we are worried. And I know she sides with us on the issue of the Four I's. We will pursue the admiral and see if we can slow down his plan. I hope to see you again, Duke LaGrange."

"And I hope it's at LePaco's funeral."

The aged bondswoman and senior official of the Bounty Hunters Union curtsied, then the screen went black.

The interior of Cyborg Joe's Grill N' Go & The Why Not Saloon was decidedly different than the last time Duke had graced the famous watering hole. It was clear that droves of customers had rushed out due to the looming invasion. Barstools were overturned, tables were littered with half-consumed glasses of alcohol, even the band had decided to leave their instruments strewn about the stage. The fiery barrage of the Armada Titan never quite reached the bar, so it was structurally intact. However, the nearby wounded had started to flood the bar's parking lot and front lawn. The Queen was waving them inside for medical attention. She portaled many of them directly to hospitals in the most advanced part of the cosmos, others she took care of herself. She was no medic, but even a powerful being like the Queen wasn't above slapping on a few bandages on some injured citizens.

One constant was Earl. He stood behind the bar. The image of the Glyptodian standing behind the bar at Cyborg Joe's warmed Duke's heart.

Maybe everything will be okay, he thought.

At the bar sat Lilly, the anthropomorphic musk ox from one of the moons of Gartosh. Po'l walked up to her and gave her a hug. There were a few other patrons that Duke recognized but didn't know. He made the rounds and shook each of their hands. There were a lot of questions, but not nearly enough answers.

After the group swapped play-by-play accounts of what had happened, Queen Joe made her way over. Her face was sunken with fatigue and her attire was ripped, shredded, and covered in dirt and blood, likely hers and those of the wounded that were still filing in. She leaned against the bar. All eyes, including Duke's, were on her. She positioned herself directly in front of the Nova Texan.

She said nothing.

"He got away," said Duke, breaking the silence. "His ship was in the Armada Titan. When it was going down, he escaped."

"That's not ideal," she remarked stoically.

"But..."

"Yes, Duke?" asked the Queen.

"The Bounty Hunters Union is following him. They were the ones that brought down the Titan."

The Queen looked at Ishiro'shea. He nodded, corroborating Duke's claim.

"I guess I owe you an apology for not believing," said the Queen.

Duke smiled, but continued the more serious part of the discussion.

"Mama Fong is tracking LePaco. They have a vested interest, with the Four I's trying to outlaw bounty hunting and all."

"That makes sense," the Queen said, again with little emotion.

"So what do we do now?" asked Lilly.

"We have to stop them from getting the Amplification Key," the Queen answered briskly. "They have the Shield, and its power is impressive, even by itself. Much like the Orb, it can cause much damage in the wrong hands. But, if he found a way to get all three, I'm not sure that we'll be able to stop him."

"Could he really take over the universe?" asked one of the patrons, a Sabromm outlaw named Klucky.

"Yes. I have no doubts."

"Luckily, we know that one of the artifacts is safe here," chimed in Po'l.

"For now. If he gets the Key, together with the Shield, he could wield a power that would be too much for me, even with the Orb in my control. Finding the Key is essential."

Duke slammed his fist on the bar. He could feel the dozens of pairs of eyes focusing on him.

I've had enough of this, he thought.

"Do you have something to say, Duke?" asked the Queen.

"I know that these weapons are powerful. I've seen the Orb. I've almost been turned into a burning pile of goo by that damn rock so I have no hesitation in believing that these items can rip apart the very fabric of the universe. But what..." Duke paused. "...what exactly are they?"

"A shield. An orb. A key," Po'l answered.

"I think, my Neprian friend, that Duke wants to know more details about their origins, why they are here..." began the Queen.

"And why I'm always being sucked into portals and landing on strange planets where these doomsday antiques are lying around," interjected Duke.

"I'm not sure that I have a good answer to that question, Duke. I wish that I did."

"How about let's start with what you *can* answer?"

The Queen walked behind the bar and started setting up a round of drinks. She doused the glasses in Erontian whisky.

"Are you familiar with the story of Grozzel?" she asked.

"The Psitakki Shield guy?"

"Yes, the Psitakki that discovered the stockpile of Shields that saved his planet by forcing out the mysterious shadowy invaders," she confirmed.

"I think I remember something about that," Duke acknowledged.

"Those demon creatures are from another dimension; they're not of this universe. I'm not sure that I could properly communicate their names, but it roughly translates into 'The Flying Rot.'"

"Sounds fitting," Duke added.

"The Rot weren't there to attack the Psitakki," she explained. "In all honesty, they probably didn't even pay them any attention until they started to assemble and impede their chief mission."

"And that was?"

"To find the Shields," the Queen replied bluntly.

"I don't understand," added Po'l.

"As you may have guessed, I'm not from this dimension either," remarked the Queen.

"Yeah, I had a hunch," Duke smirked.

"The Rot are a race that have destroyed more worlds and galaxies than I can count. Their original home, even their original dimension, is unknown. Even to me. After countless ages of constant warfare across my entire universe, my race was able to finally destroy them. We designed weapons that could actually kill the Rot, and kill them we did. We believed that they were entirely eliminated, every last Rot demon."

She set up another round of drinks. Those surrounding the bar were so engrossed in her tale that they almost didn't even notice the free Erontian whisky slid in front of them. Almost. They all downed the liquid and reimmersed themselves in their engaging narrator's yarn.

"As you know from the story of Grozzel, we were wrong. But before we knew of their encroachment into your dimension, our worlds experienced a sustained period of peace. Of course, not every world did—as you know, a universe is a pretty big place—but with my race acting as an overseeing security council, no major conflicts occurred to put our existence in jeopardy. We ruled that the weapons that destroyed the Flying Rot were the only things that could disrupt our universe. If combined in the correct manner with the Amplification Key, these weapons could warp dimensional reality, tear seams in the space-time continuum, and wipe out planets, systems, galaxies, even universes."

"Why didn't *you* destroy them?" asked Po'l.

"We couldn't. They were indestructible," she sighed. "We did the next best thing: disassemble them and stash them away across as many universes as we could go to. Of course, that meant that my race, the only beings that could travel inter-dimensionally, had to leave our home and be scattered for eternity, never to return. I came here with all of the remaining Shields and buried them on a primitive world. That world became Psitakki."

"Man, you're really old," blurted out Po'l. "Millions of years old."

"A million more than that," added the Queen with a slight smile.

"So the Rot showed back up again and Grozzel found the Shields before you could get there and save them?" asked Duke.

"Yes. And as the Shaman designated the Shields as trophies for winners of a tournament, I knew it would make my job even more difficult because I would have to keep track of a hundred of these Shields. But I have."

"How?" asked Lilly.

"Indirectly, of course."

"Your portals," said Duke. "You've had patrons bring back key intel without even knowing it."

"Yes. I never put them into danger, just offered a sale on a certain world or accidentally mixed up a portal location. It worked."

"And Ishiro'shea and I were your buffoons for this tournament, huh?"

Queen Joe peered deep into the bounty hunter's eyes. "I chose you to provide updates on this Shield. I had no idea what was going to happen. Had I any indication that LePaco knew of the Shield or the Orb or the Key, I would have gone myself."

Duke crossed his arms and raised an eyebrow.

"Queen Joe," a voice said.

"Yes, Lilly?"

"I still don't quite understand how the other two artifacts made it here," the musk ox said.

"My only guess is that the Rot brought them here when they pursued the Shields."

"And how did they get across the universe?" Lilly continued.

"I don't know."

"The Orb does what it wants," remarked Po'l.

"Very true," Joe began, "and since we don't know where the Key is, it's hard to hypothesize how it got where it is."

Duke rose from the barstool.

"So what you're saying is that if LePaco gets the Amplification Key, he is an Orb away from consuming planets and altering the very foundation of our universe?"

"Yes, I'm afraid so," answered the Queen.

"And this Key, what does it look like?"

The Queen approached a crusty regular sitting at the bar. She extended her hand and he placed his knife hilt-first into it, as if she couldn't have meant anything else by her advance. She stabbed the point of the dagger into the bar, cracking the wood and leaving a sizable divot. She dragged the blade until it formed the outline of an unusual oblong.

"This is what it looks like, though somewhat smaller."

Ishiro'shea dropped his katana on the floor. The high-pitched clank caused the entire room to turn and stare at the ninja.

"What is it little buddy?" asked Duke.

The ninja walked over and picked up the dagger from the bar. He added a circle extending from one end of the drawing of the Key to the other.

A necklace.

Then he began scratching again.

Etched into the bar was a crude rendering of a necklace and the words: *My Father's.*

CHAPTER 37

A STARTING PLACE

THE *DEUS EX MACHINA* DISTANCED itself from Keltian space. Duke LaGrange was firmly planted in his captain's chair. Ishiro'shea worked at the control panel.

"I don't know about you, Ish, but my head hurts thinking about it all. Magic orbs and priests lobbing javelins at us was bad enough, but now we have magic shields and keys. And don't forget about monsters from other dimensions, the Queen being able to shoot lighting from her fingers, LePaco being related to Orbius, and Mazilda, of all people, joining him. Oh, not to mention your parents could have the final piece that determines whether we'll save our universe or doom every known being in it. And we don't have any clue where they are." Duke huffed. "I think that about sums it up."

Ishiro'shea turned around and gave his bounty-hunting companion a friendly thumbs-up.

"Patch me in."

"Hey Duke," said Queen Joe. "Can you hear me fine? I haven't used one of these comm devices outside of the bar in some time."

"Loud and clear."

"Before we do this, I do hope that, in time, you understand my decision to send you to Psitakki."

"We're ready," Duke replied.

"Of course," said Queen Joe. "I want to get out as far from the bar as I can."

"Just in case you're a bit rusty?"

"Something like that."

The crackle of static permeated throughout the ship.

She must've left the device on, thought Duke.

The Queen's voice could be heard, albeit faintly, through the crackles and buzzes. "Take them to the Father."

The bounty hunters waited in silence, their eyes fixed on the view screen. The stars twinkled against a backdrop of black. It started as flashing sparks, then seemed to double with every blink of an eye. Before a moment had passed, there was a portal looking back at them, an unstable astral anomaly blazing a tantalizing crimson.

"I thought we were done with this damn thing," said Duke.

The *Deus Ex Machina* inched ahead until it breached the threshold of the portal.

"You never get used to that," Duke said as he tried to reorient himself post-portal travel.

He rubbed his eyes and shook his head. "Now where oh where are we, little buddy? Where did this bastard drop us off this time? If we're back near Neprius, I don't know what I'll do."

Ishiro'shea plugged away at the panel. The results populated on the screen immediately. The ninja swung around in his chair and locked eyes with Duke. His glassy stare was consumed with worry.

"T'ckuvu Prime."

Duke collected himself. "Hey, it's a starting place," he remarked optimistically. "Look, I know it's not a particularly great one, considering T'ckuvu Prime's reputation, but the Key was... is... our best bet. I'm sure your parents are fine."

The ninja gave Duke a half-hearted thumbs-up, then turned around to the control panel.

Yeah, he's not buying that. Come to think of it, neither am I.

THE END

THANK YOU

I hope that you enjoyed *How to Win at Pit Fighting with a Drunk Space Ninja*. If so, I'd love for you to join my newsletter at Duke LaGrange.com.

Don't forget that the adventures of Duke and Ishiro'shea continue in Book III…

How to Save the Universe with a Drunk Space Ninja!

AVAILABLE IN PRINT AND E-BOOK.

ABOUT THE AUTHOR

©JAY KEY 2018

JAY KEY knew at a young age that he wanted to be the world's first professional wrestler turned fraternity president turned digital media executive turned Society of Vertebrate Paleontology-approved blog writer turned science-fiction comedy author. At various points, Key called Dallas, San Francisco, and Los Angeles home—but it wasn't until a move to Chicago that writing professionally became a reality. Authoring a serialized version of *The Adventures of Duke LaGrange* and a popular blog on the paleobiological accuracy of dinosaurs in pop culture, Key used that momentum to complete *How to Pick Up Women with a Drunk Space Ninja* in 2017. It debuted with Star Wheel Books in 2018.

Jay now lives in a suburb of Dallas-Fort Worth with his wife, Shelley, their daughter, Finley, and their French bulldog, Olive.

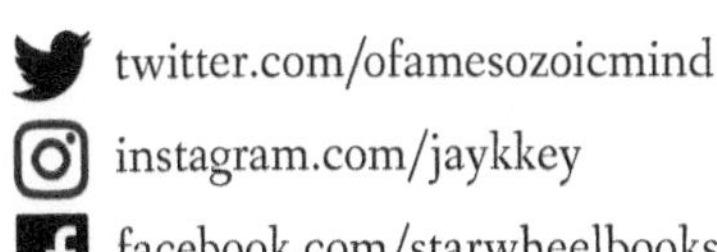

twitter.com/ofamesozoicmind

instagram.com/jaykkey

facebook.com/starwheelbooks